CERTAMEN

MICHAEL ADDERLEY

Cover design by the author with lettering by Elliott Waehner

This is a work of fiction. Names, characters, businesses, places,
events and incidents are either the products of the author's
imagination or used in a fictitious manner. Any resemblance to actual
persons, living or dead, or actual events is purely coincidental.

michaeladderley.com
certamen-the-novel.tumblr.com
facebook.com/madderleybooks

ISBN: 1987427246
ISBN-13: 978-1987427240

Dedicated to all Latin students, past, present, and future.

CHAPTER 1: JANUARY 12ᵀᴴ   CASS WASHINGTON

Jason married and ditched a lot of women.

To be clear: I'm talking about Jason the mythical leader of the Argonauts. Not Jason Ackerman from my Econ class. Jason Ackerman does happen to have a troubling past with women, but other than that he doesn't have much in common with the Greek hero.

See, everyone knows about Jason and Medea. Jason loved Medea, had a bunch of kids with her, left her for a younger more beautiful princess. Medea killed all of her and Jason's children for revenge.

Does everyone know about that? It's basic stuff for any Mythology nerd. I was raised on this. It's like my version of Mother Goose. Goodnight Moon, Goodnight Room, Goodnight Man-Slaying Axe.

What I *didn't* know was that Jason already had a habit before he even met Medea. There was an earlier woman, Hypsipyle, that Jason also married, had twins with, and ghosted on.

Even better: Hypsipyle (note to self: look up how to pronounce that name) was queen of the island of Lemnos, and right before Jason got there the whole island had committed "androcide:" They had killed every man on the island, leaving only the women behind.

I mean, we've all been there.

"Oh, and listen to this," Spencer interrupted my reading. I half-closed my book with my finger on my page. "He told me he only *pretended* to like it when I baked him things. He said I was lousy at it."

Spencer was stage-whispering. It sounded like a whisper, except that everyone in the room could hear him.

"You're not very good," I said honestly. I remembered him baking platters of cookies for Latin Club meetings, to entice freshmen to show up. They were always as hard as crackers.

Spencer glared. "I know that. But you don't say that to your boyfriend."

"Well you're not his boyfriend anymore."

Spencer gave me a look like a kicked puppy. I sighed and put my book down on my desk.

"I'm trying to be supportive," I told him. "But you need to stop obsessing. This is your queer fairy godmother telling you it's time to move on."

"I'm talking through my feelings," Spencer said defensively. "It's helpful."

"It's distracting. I like to use the time before Certamen practice to get Mythology reading done. You've been 'talking through your feelings' at me for a month, and now it's time to let me read."

"Yeah," cut in our Latin teacher and Certamen sponsor, Mr. Stanton, "Let her read, Spencer."

Spencer rolled his eyes and took another sip of his canned doubleshot. His third of the day, at least. I often wondered what Spencer would be like if he didn't consume half his body weight in caffeine every day. Would we even recognize him? He slumped into the desk next to mine and put his phone back in front of his face.

Mine was in my bag. I'd heard it buzz a few times, but I was ignoring it. I tried to get back to my copy of Ovid's *Heroides*.

It was a pretty good book. Poems from the perspectives of mythological women, tearing apart the idiot heroes who had abandoned them. Some of them even made for pretty decent feminism, although there was plenty of problematic stuff mixed in too. (Ovid kinda specialized in problematic.)

As I read, I was adding idly to my notebook. I filled each page with jumbled messes of mythology notes, pop culture references, Tumblr post ideas, and bad puns, all threaded through with doodles of sea monsters, chimaeras, Greek hoplite soldiers. The mess made sense to me. I knew where to find everything.

Tumblr was on my mind today. Usually I posted my drawings, a mixture of themes from mythology but especially same-sex couples. But occasionally I made dumb Classical memes too, and my *Heroides*-inspired post the previous night—quotes from Penelope's savage dragging of Odysseus, placed over images from Beyoncé's *Lemonade*—had gotten me a bunch of likes and reblogs. The Latin nerds on Tumblr were serious about their fandom, and I was starting to gain some traction in that rarified group. Thoodleoo had even reblogged me once. I had to keep it going.

In the desk next to me, but also in his own universe, was our Certamen team's History specialist, Brian. He was engrossed in a volume of Tacitus's *Annals*, his beat-up oversized headphones over his ears. He read faster and more voluminously than anybody else I knew. And unlike me, he never took any notes. He just remembered everything. His brain was like a computer. His personality too.

Spencer didn't like Brian very much, because Brian was the reason that Spencer was only our Certamen alternate this year. Spencer had been our team's History expert for three years. Not anymore.

At the end of last year, Spencer had set everything up for his perfect senior year: the presidency of Latin Club; State medals in History, Dramatic Interpretation, and Certamen; and the perfect boyfriend. Since then, he had lost both his spot on Certamen and his boyfriend. He *was* still Latin Club president, for all the good that was doing him.

It wasn't his fault. (Certamen, that is. The breakup was about 50/50.) The Advanced Certamen team was a tricky beast. There were four levels of Latin at our school, but only three levels of Certamen: 1, 2, and "Advanced," which combined 3 and 4. No matter how good you were in your junior year, you could always get booted out of your spot in your senior year if one of the upcoming Latin 3 students could beat you. And no one at West Oak High could beat Brian at History.

Mr. Stanton had given Spencer the alternate spot, which was clearly a pity move. Normally, the alternate was somebody who could step up and do any category on the team in the event of an absence. But Spencer could really only do History, making him a pretty poor alternate. Magister just didn't want his President upset.

I took a look around the room. The fourth member of our team wasn't there yet. On the other side of Brian was Jeff, our Grammar specialist and another Latin 3 junior. He sat with his back as straight as Trajan's column. You could see a whole future laid out for him as one of those white guys obsessed with their lawns and the cleanliness of their tile grout. Jeff was flipping through flashcards for his AP US History class. I never saw him study Latin. He must have studied sometimes, to be as good as he was. Jeff was intense, but in a different way than Brian was. Brian's brain seemed to be an accident of personality, while Jeff's was a product of his determination to be the best at everything. All he talked about was getting into the right honors program at the right college with the right scholarships. And how, if everything worked out right, he could come from behind to earn valedictorian next year.

Rounding out the room were two non-Certamen players: a sophomore named Allie and some freshman making up a test.

Allie was spinning herself in Magister Stanton's cushioned chair while he was doing something on the white board on the other side of the room. Everyone in Latin

Club knew Allie. She was in the Latin room after school almost every day, because she was in love with Mr. Stanton.

I'd never met the freshman. Which probably meant that he was in a Latin class, but didn't do Club. He didn't look happy to be there.

It was a small, quiet group. A full Latin Club meeting could see anything up to forty kids packed in the room, all talking at the same time. But Certamen teams only had four players each (plus one alternate), so our meetings were a lot more chill.

"But listen," Spencer said, breaking into my peace of mind yet again, "He's already really buddy-buddy with Liza in Calculus."

I sighed. "What's your point?" I asked.

"What if," he said, "He only left me because he wants to be with a girl? You know, he's bi, but he's only ever dated guys. Maybe he wants to experience the other side before he settles down."

"So you want him to hurry up and date a girl, so he can get it out of his system and get back with you?" I said dryly.

"Well, once he realizes what he's missing..."

"Spencer," I replaced my bookmark, put my book all the way down, and leaned toward him in my desk. "You are offending me right now."

"Oh, because you know how every single bi person feels."

"I know better than you," I countered. "We don't just go through moods. 'Oh, I think I feel more like girls today, but who knows what next week will be like.'"

"That's not what I'm saying," he said softly.

—

6

"We fall in love with people, not genders. Danny didn't break up with you because he wanted to chase girls."

Spencer did his wounded animal look again. "I didn't mean to offend you, Cass."

"And don't go making me feel sorry, either," I continued without missing a beat. "You're always doing that. I ain't tryin' to get mad at you, because you're distraught. But I am getting tired of the puppydog routine."

It was good I had stopped myself, because I had been about five seconds away from telling Spencer *exactly* what I thought about Danny and his gaggle of shallow, idiotic, no-count friends.

Before our disastrous conversation could go any further, Katie, our Roman Life specialist and the last member of our team, came through the door. Katie was Vietnamese, with an adorable heart-shaped face and black hair cut in a bob. She was shorter than everyone but Allie, and as thin as the advertising industry wanted me to think I should be.

I, by the way, am pear-shaped, but don't waste your pity on me. I love the way I look. I maintain a glorious halo of corkscrew curls surrounding my head, and I prefer a less stereotypically feminine wardrobe. On the day in question, I was wearing ripped black pants and a loose t-shirt with *Adventure Time* characters on it. My nails and lips were painted a fluorescent blue.

"Katie!" I called out. "You promised you'd show me your pictures from the Saturnalia party!"

"Oh, yeah," she smiled. She rooted briefly in her bag before producing a digital camera about the size of a deck of cards. Katie, in addition to her Certamen duties, was the Latin Club Historian. It was her job to compile a scrapbook of our activities at the end of the year. But the pictures never seemed to make it to Instagram or anything, so you had to corner her if you wanted to see them.

While Katie pulled up the pictures on her camera, Magister Stanton walked close to Brian and peered over his book. Brian moved one ear cup of his headphones to the side.

"What's the music today?" our teacher asked.

"Replacements," Brian said with a smile. I assumed it was a band.

"Ooooh," Magister made a low, approving noise.

This was something of a ritual between them. Mr. Stanton didn't have much to teach Brian anymore about Roman History, but they always loved to talk about music that none of the rest of us had ever heard of.

"*Let It Be?*" Mr. Stanton asked.

"Nah, *Hootenanny. Let It Be* is my favorite by them, though."

"Well, of course."

"Isn't that a Beatles album?" asked Katie innocently.

Brian and Mr. Stanton fixed her with identical looks of snobby pity. She returned to her camera.

I don't know why she bothered. No one else was allowed into their music talks.

Though Allie, for one, always tried her best. As soon as they started, she whipped out her phone (a hand-me-down iPhone three generations behind) and hopped off of Mr. Stanton's chair to stand near him and Brian as they continued to rattle off related bands and songs. She scrambled to type notes on everything they mentioned, so she could look it all up on YouTube later.

Katie handed me her camera, the first party picture on the screen. "You can scroll through that way," she said, and went to her own desk to pull out her worn but well-cared-for laptop.

Spencer kneeled down next to my desk while I paged through picture after picture of people eating, talking, and mugging for the camera at the Saturnalia party—the Latin nerd version of a Christmas party. It had been a particularly good party, with gift exchanges and Latin kids belting out Christmas carols off-key. Someone had found a Latin translation of "Rudolph the Red-Nosed Reindeer." There was a six-person lightsaber battle. Togas were worn.

Most of the rest of West Oak High School didn't really know that Latin Club (Junior Classical League, officially) existed. They didn't know what they were missing. There were forty or fifty of us, in our student body of over five thousand. We were never going to rival Drama or Football for numbers. But for those of us with enough sense to join, it was a way of life.

"Oh god, there's me and Danny," Spencer said. He looked away from the camera, covering his eyes theatrically with the back of his hand. "Tell me when we're not in them anymore." But then he turned his head back around and looked at them all with me anyway, letting out tiny distressed noises at every new photo.

"You guys are all over each other in those," Katie shook her head, looking at some homework thing on her computer screen instead of us. "I can't use any of them."

"Why not?" he teased. "Add a little romance to your scrapbook, courtesy of the most attractive former couple in school."

"You never know who's going to be judging the scrapbooks in the State contest," she said defensively. "We live in Texas. I'm not letting some conservative judge's prejudice stand between me and a medal."

"I never pegged you as an enemy to progress," I teased. Katie turned red, so I pivoted the conversation away from her. "You two really are gross though," I told Spencer. "Magister kept having to tell y'all to get your hands off each other."

"I know," Spencer sighed, leaning backward. "We faced such discrimination."

"Hey," Magister Stanton interjected, "It's not like that. No PDA allowed. I would have told a straight couple the same thing."

"Sure, sure," Spencer rolled his eyes. But he knew it was true. Mr. Stanton was always supportive of his LGBT+ students, unlike so many teachers in Texas. Probably one of the reasons so many of us stuck around in Latin.

Soon Magister left to make a few copies, promising to be back soon to start practice. Spencer had taken the camera now and was paging back through the pictures of him with his ex. Healthy.

"God," he said, as if to himself but projecting his voice to everybody in the room, "How am I going to win him back?"

"I don't think you're going to," Brian said blankly. His

headphones were around his neck now, putting him back in the real world. "I heard he's talking to Tanner Rosen."

"*What?*" Spencer snapped.

"Really? I saw him in Andy Hernandez's car the other day," added Allie.

Spencer groaned and threw himself onto his back on the floor beside my desk. His blond curls, normally falling carelessly over his ears and forehead, formed into a lion's mane on the carpet around his head.

"What am I going to do?" he moaned. "There's like no other gay guys at this school."

"Are you out of your mind?" Allie laughed.

"I can think of like twenty right now," Brian said.

Spencer sat back up, his face drawn. "No *attractive* gay guys."

"I can hardly think of anybody who isn't something," Allie continued. "You're gay. Cass and I are bi."

"And Brian's gotta be aro," I added.

"What what," Brian said, and made a ridiculous peace sign at his chin.

"Well *I'm* straight," Jeff said, looking up from his flashcards for the first time in the afternoon.

"Oh, we *know*," I groaned. "You and Miss Mackenzie, the perfect hetero couple."

Allie looked toward Jeff. "You have a girlfriend?"

The rest of the room erupted in groans.

"Do *not* get him started on her!" Spencer commanded. "He's sickening."

Jeff smiled at the recognition. He and Mackenzie had been dating for over a year, which was an eternity in high school. And even though they were way too Christmas-portraits-at-Sears perfect for my tastes, I had to admit that he really did seem to love her.

"Why haven't I met her?" Allie asked.

"She takes French," Spencer replied.

"*Sacre bleu!*" Brian joked. Katie chuckled politely when no one else laughed.

My phone buzzed again in my satchel. Spencer shot me a look.

"Still avoiding it?" he asked.

"Not today, Satan," I said softly.

"What are you avoiding?" asked Brian. He didn't know what he was stepping into.

"Verbal abuse," I said shortly.

"She turned down Greg Krakowski yesterday," Spencer said.

I really didn't intend to air my dirty laundry in the Latin room waiting for a Certamen practice, but Spencer couldn't resist a good story.

"Greg has decided," I said before Spencer could go on, "That my lack of interest in him must be indicative of some deep personality flaws of my own. He is now enumerating those very flaws onto my Tumblr and Instagram, via both direct message and public post."

"Block him," Katie said flatly, meeting my eyes.

"I decided to give it a day, to see if he would wind down on his own. I figured blocking him might encourage him to bring the fight into real life, which I'm not trying to start."

Spencer gave me a skeptical look. I knew he thought I

should be doing something. Reporting him, or better yet, publicly shaming him, holding him up for judgment. I didn't have the emotional energy.

"I really think it'll be over by tomorrow," I said. "He got his little man feelings hurt, and society has given him no outlet for those feelings other than anger."

I guess I got into a whole thing here. Once I got started, the discourse just kept coming out. I was on a roll.

"It is the way of our patriarchal world," I continued, talking like I was typing into a Tumblr text post instead of talking to my Certamen team. "The people who are conditioned to deny that they even experience any emotions are the ones who use their emotions to inflict the most harm."

"You're intellectualizing, instead of being constructive," Spencer said.

"Should I be 'talking through my feelings' more?" I asked mockingly.

"You could be a little nicer," Jeff muttered.

"I *what?*" I snapped.

Jeff raised his eyebrows, but continued anyway. "Most guys aren't like that. If you'd be less... direct, I'm sure fewer of them would react so strongly when you tell them you aren't interested."

I had a really good retort, but no one heard it. Katie, Spencer, and Allie all told him how off-base he was at the same time, so all anyone heard was yelling. Jeff muttered something indistinct and went back to his flashcards with great zeal.

Mr. Stanton walked in, and we all hid the traces of the

conversation off our faces. That freshman had finished his test, and walked slowly up to hand it to Mr. Stanton. He gave us all weird looks as he did. Whatever, kid.

Once the freshman finally left the room, Mr. Stanton pulled up a chair to face us.

"Shall we get this Certamen practice started?"

"I move," said Allie, with mock formality, "That we begin this practice with the pledge of allegiance to Magister Stanton's beard."

"Can we not—?" Mr. Stanton began, but everybody was already on their feet, hands over hearts. He covered his face with one hand, then went to his desk to grab his mug of tea as we recited:

"I pledge allegiance

To the beard

Of my Latin teacher Mr. Stanton

And to the majesty

Of its fluff and heft

Red and tangled

Full of crumbs

Perfect in the eyes of God and man."

This was just A Thing in our Latin Club now. Spencer had written the first draft of the pledge of allegiance the previous year, and it had caught on. Mr. Stanton generally avoided eye contact and let it happen. He knew from experience that the louder he protested, the more persistent we would become.

Mr. Stanton retook his seat as we finished, now gripping his favorite mug: dark blue with a bust of Cato the Elder saying *"Carthago delenda est."* ("Carthage must be destroyed," a war cry against an enemy of the Roman Republic.) Mr. Stanton kept it full of a constant stream of chai tea—a new cupful every class period, and another after school. It meant that his room was always lightly and pleasantly cinnamon-scented.

"Okay," he sighed, "Allie, can you start getting the machine set up?"

Allie hopped-to immediately, pulling down the box from a cabinet and starting to untangle the spaghetti-monster of the Certamen machine's buzzer cords.

Certamen (that's "kehr-TOM-in") was a quiz bowl for Latin. Hours of incredibly rigorous questions about everything Roman, using antiquated buzzer systems that hadn't changed since the 80's.

We, the devoted few, spent our high school careers studying like madmen, madwomen, and madnonbinary individuals to master our Certamen categories. People lived and died by these buzzers.

"Any reports on your assignments over winter break? Brian, you're working through your primary sources?"

Brian held up his Tacitus book. "'They make a wasteland and call it peace,'" he quoted. "I'm gonna hit Josephus's texts on the Jewish War next."

"Nice. Jeff, you've been working on your deponent verbs?"

"Yes," Jeff said with a groan.

The Junior Classical League loved to torture Advanced Grammar specialists with deponent verbs, those nasty irregular buggers. Last year's team captain, a Latin 4 Grammar kid, had fumbled the championship round at JCL

Area because of a deponent imperative. We had been one question away from State. He had complained about it for the rest of the year.

"*Utere vi, Luci*," was the sentence he'd been asked to produce. "Use the force, Lucius." Sometimes the question writers had a sense of humor while they were wrecking students' lives.

"Cass," Mr. Stanton asked me next. "You're keeping up with your literary devices?"

I winced. "Doing my best." I used to be Mythology-only, because that's what I'm good at. But I had gotten saddled with an extra job this year, because I was the only Latin 4 on the team, and none of the Latin 3 babies knew what a god-damned hyperbaton was. Mr. Stanton didn't cover literary, poetic, and rhetorical devices until year 4.

"And Katie's working on Roman authors," Mr. Stanton concluded. Katie turned her laptop around to show the online flashcards she had just been studying.

Katie was amazing to me. I complained about my literary terms because I had to add them to the only thing I'd been studying for the last three years. But at least my Mythology was still the bulk of my role. She hadn't made a peep, even though her job had completely changed.

See, Levels 1 and 2 of Certamen had lots of questions about Roman Life, and that had been her specialty for the past two years. But in Advanced Certamen they dropped the Life questions down to like one per round, and replaced the rest with questions about Roman Authors.

So all of a sudden, Katie had a completely new subject to master. And she was still all smiles. She was just *doing* it.

At least, she was trying. She wasn't Brian. It took time.

"Good," Mr. Stanton concluded. Allie had placed a buzzer in front of each of us. I picked mine up. The beautiful cylinder of beige plastic with the tiny blue button on the top. The familiar tug of the thick gray wire. I had loved it the first time I held it, and that feeling had never gone away. A little surge of excitement, the potential for greatness.

I loved Certamen. I hated that this was my last year of it. I could have kept going forever.

***

Mr. Stanton hit us with thirty questions in about an hour and a half that day. It was supposed to be an hour-long practice, but he couldn't stop himself from getting off on tangents about things he was interested in. Like when Brian narrowly missed a question on Sejanus, aide to the emperor Tiberius, and Magister wound up storytelling his way through all the times Tiberius retreated from public life to various islands, because of how much Tiberius hated other people. My kind of guy. The impromptu lecture was frequently interrupted by Brian and Spencer throwing in their favorite supplemental history facts, so it took even longer.

Allie worked the machine, as usual, calling us by our buzzer numbers when we rang in first.

"Toss-up twenty-eight," said Mr. Stanton ominously, and we leaned forward with our buzzers. "Which writer made a prediction that later Christians interpreted as a prophecy about the birth of Christ, leading the medieval poet Dante —"

Beep.

"B3," Allie chirped.

"Vergil," Katie replied confidently.

"Correct," Mr. Stanton said. "The conclusion to the question: 'Leading the medieval poet Dante to depict him as his guide through the *Inferno*.' Very good, Katie."

Spencer and I both nodded enthusiastically at her. It was actually a pretty easy question as far as authors went. But she had missed the two harder author questions earlier in the round—Lucretius and Ennius—so she needed the encouragement.

She got one of the two bonuses correct on her own, but would have missed the second if I hadn't known that Vergil's patron was Maecenas, same as Horace's. Certamen rules allowed team members to talk to each other on the two bonus questions that came with each toss-up, even though the toss-ups were strictly independent.

Truth be told, I could have probably gotten that Vergil toss-up quicker than Katie did too. I knew my mythological authors—only a fraction of all the authors Katie had to know, but an important fraction. In past practices I could easily have buzzed in on ones about Vergil, Ovid, Dionysius... But I couldn't do that. Katie was working too hard for me to go sniping her questions.

It's kind of a jerk move, outbuzzing your own teammate on their specialty. Like you think you know better than they do. And if you were wrong, that would be even worse, because they can't buzz in if a member of their own team has already answered.

"Toss-up twenty-nine," Mr. Stanton continued, and we

centered over our buzzers again. "Which literary device appears in the following line of the *Aeneid*: "*O socii—neque enim ignari sumus—*"

Beep.

"A1," Allie said.

"Litotes," Spencer said with pride. (He always took buzzer A1. Even this year, when he was only an alternate.)

"Correct," said Mr. Stanton.

"Damn it, Spencer," I seethed. A literary device question—the thing I was struggling with. Like I said: a jerk move, outbuzzing your teammate on their specialty.

"Did you know it?" Magister Stanton asked me.

"I would have gotten it," I assured him. Litotes was pretty easy: denying a negative. Like if I said that PuellaStellarum, my current Tumblr crush, was *not* an unattractive girl.

Emphatically *not* an untrue statement, by the way.

"Too slow," Spencer said in his smarmiest voice. He had been doing this to me all year. He was the only other Latin 4 in the room, and he was faster at the buzzer than I was. So he showed me up at every opportunity. He didn't mean any real harm. If anything, he was proving he was still good at something after getting beaten by Brian.

Still, he was pissing me off.

"I'm not used to listening for this crap!" I fumed. "I've always just done Mythology! Why can't Jeff learn the literary devices? They're not that bad!"

"Jeff's got enough on his plate," Mr. Stanton said as Jeff's eyes went wide. I shouldn't have suggested it. Jeff was working overtime to get his extra grammar down. Latin 3's were at a severe disadvantage in Advanced Certamen. Usually the Advanced team's Grammar specialist was a 4. But our 4 class just wasn't very strong—there were only nine of us total, and several of that nine didn't even do JCL competition—so the 3's had to pick up the slack.

"You gotta outbuzz me if you want to outbuzz the competition!" Spencer said in an overly jocular tone. I think he had noticed he was getting to me and was trying to compensate.

"Toss-up thirty," announced Mr. Stanton. "This son of Glaucus and Eurynome—"

Beep.

"B2."

"Bellerophon," I said.

"Correct," said Magister Stanton with a smile. "The full question..."

"Don't worry about it," I said. "Next it mentions him killing the chimaera or trying to fly to Olympus or some crap, then it finally says that he also tamed Pegasus, in case anyone was dumb enough to need to listen that far."

Mr. Stanton laughed and shook his head. "Right you are. It was the chimaera, for the record."

We all made it a point of pride to buzz in to every question as soon as humanly possible. In a real competition you had to. Any question that the moderator actually *finishes asking* is one that no one knows the answer to. So that's how we practiced. And the earlier we got the answer, the prouder we were of ourselves.

I dispatched with the two bonus questions easily, and that brought our practice questions to an end.

"Not bad, team," said Mr. Stanton as Allie carefully rolled up the cords and packed the Certamen machine back into its box. He brought his tea mug to his lips, but seemed to think better of drinking the cold dregs left in it and lowered it again. "Not bad at all."

"We've got to be a lot better if we're going to make State this year," I warned the Latin 3's. Only one team from every Area advanced to JCL State, and we had some tough competition.

"Don't get your hopes too high, Cass," Mr. Stanton cautioned. He then directed his attention to the Latin 3's. "Course selection is close. You three are all signing up for Latin 4, right?"

They nodded. He had asked them at least a dozen times since the school year started.

"Good," he said. "I lost a hell of a Life and Literature expert when Adair decided to go be a library aide instead of taking 4."

Katie sank almost imperceptibly. I could see that Mr. Stanton regretted saying it. Implying that he could have had better than her this year.

He opened his mouth, but it looked like he couldn't think of any way to backtrack well. He lifted his mug, but caught himself again.

"Don't go pinning all your hopes on next year, Magister," I said, rescuing the conversation from his faux pas. "I don't have a next year."

"It's an uphill battle with a team of mostly 3's," Magister said carefully. "We're going up against full teams of fourth years, sometimes fifth and sixth and seventh years in the private schools. The 3's we've got are great, but those extra years of study make a big difference."

"We were hella close last year," I countered. "Second place in finals, ten points away from first. Spencer and Adair and I were all 3's. We can do that too. And more."

The 3's glanced nervously at me. Was I being too intense? Maybe I was, but I really did want this. They would be a great team next year when these 3's were all 4's, that was true. But I was graduating, so they'd be a great team with someone else on Mythology. I wanted my own spot in State Certamen.

"I'd love for you to be right," Mr. Stanton said diplomatically. "That's a wrap. Keep studying, folks, and I'll see you in two weeks."

"You'll see us tomorrow, in class," Allie pointed out, shutting the Certamen machine in its cabinet.

"Yes. Well," he grunted, and left the room to wash out his mug in the teacher's lounge.

"Ready, Allie?" Katie asked as she slipped her laptop into her perfectly organized backpack.

"Ready when you are," said Allie, grabbing her catastrophe of a bag. Katie always gave Allie a ride home.

"Bye, Jeff!" Spencer shouted toward the door.

"Later," said Jeff's back, already out the door and in the hall. That kid was always in a hurry. He probably had a line of disadvantaged children waiting for him to tutor them so that he could write about the experience in his college essays. *Just seeing their shining faces when they realized that they, too, could succeed...*

Brian passed my desk on his way out, after spending a

few wordless minutes picking his music on his iPod (a decision of great import, to judge by the serious expression on his face) and situating his headphones on his ears. Katie and Allie followed him out.

That left Spencer and me. Spencer was totally absorbed in his phone. I took mine out for the first time in over an hour, but put it away as soon as I saw the mile-long ribbon of notifications.

"You ever gonna stop showing me up on these poetic devices?" I asked to get Spencer's attention.

"You ever gonna get the easy ones right?" he shot right back without looking up.

"Unfair! I'd be faster without you here, but you psych me out."

"I'm going to Jamba Juice, you coming?" he said, still calmly focused on his phone.

"No, I hate you," I replied.

He waited.

I thought about what my night would look like at home. No distraction from the textual harassment, for one thing. But almost worse than that, a bunch of essays to write for scholarships. My least favorite part of my life right now. I needed the scholarships, of course, and that put a lot of pressure on the essays. I was a pretty decent writer, but these had me stumped. How do you convince someone to finance your education when you have no idea what you want to do with it? What you want to do with your life in general?

It was a major stumbling block. (Not just in writing essays, mind you. Also in sleeping well, and in maintaining a peaceful relationship with my parents.)

I envied Jeff his medical school dreams, and Spencer his law school plans. Everybody in the school seemed to have their adult lives mapped out. But not Cass Washington. With the wide world in front of her, she was paralyzed in the door frame.

"Okay," I finally said, "But you're buying."

"I know not to invite you anywhere if I can't buy, you cheap bitch," Spencer said. Then he held the door open for me like a proper gentleman.

CHAPTER 2: JANUARY 13ᵀᴴ   BRIAN GANZ

I'm not aromantic.

I Googled that word that Cass used in practice. "Aro." I didn't know what it meant, but I didn't want everyone else to know that, so I played along. Then when I was alone, it took me a few tries to figure out how to spell it. "A-row?" The fact that it was in a conversation about sexuality helped for context.

"Context" comes from two Latin roots, the verb *texere*, which means "to weave," and the prefix *con-*, "together." So context is what weaves things together so they make sense.

Sorry, I do that sometimes. I really like word roots.

"Aro" is, in fact, short for aromantic, a word I had never seen before today. It derives from the Greek *a-* prefix, meaning "not," and the English word *romantic*, a Latin-rooted word with its own interesting history of change: it originally meant Roman-ness, then got repurposed to describe the family of languages derived from Latin, then narrowed to refer specifically to the French language, then narrowed further to describe verse narratives popular in France which often featured love themes, before ballooning out to its current connotation of love and desire.

This is what I love about etymology, the history of words. Words have biographies that are almost as interesting as people's. And I love to make connections. I like to see that "aromantic" is as related to "asymmetrical" and "amoral" as it is to "Romanize" and "romaine" lettuce. My lexicon (Greek root, "word book") is like a web of interrelation (Latin root) in my mind, with no word standing on its own. Except "flabbergast," which has no known etymology.

My love of connections is why I love History. There's the old cliché, "Those who do not learn from History are doomed to repeat it." As if we study History in order to predict the future. And that's not it at all. It's that tracing all the connections between people and cultures and events is the only way to actually understand the *present*.

Cliché is a French onomatopoeia for the sound made by a printing press.

I'm sorry, I wandered way away from my point. That's the thing about my love of connections: I'll chase them down strange alleyways and end up frustrating whoever is trying to talk to me. I'll try to stick to the topic at hand, and use footnotes for all those times my mind goes off into the weeds.

Anyway, I was talking about aromanticism. A term for when people experience little to no emotional need for romantic relationships. Not to be confused (warns the website from which I learned all this) with being asexual or "ace:" no desire for sex with anybody. Same "a-" prefix, but with "sexual"[1] to contrast with "romantic," because the concepts of love and sex (says the website), no matter how heavily linked they are in our culture, are not really the same thing. Aromantic people can want sex, and asexual people can want romance.

But I am neither aromantic nor asexual. I like girls. I am heteroromantic (another term I learned today) and heterosexual.

So why do my teammates all readily assume that I'm aro? No, I've never dated anybody. But neither has Katie that I know of, and they know she's straight.

I always thought of relationships as something that would just happen in high school. My dad told me about his teenage dating life back when I was young and impressionable,[2] and it all boiled down to the phrase "Girlfriends come and go."[3] Like it was effortless. Why hasn't that happened for me? Why are some of my closest friends ready to think I'm not even interested in relationships?

Are they my closest friends? I decide to make an effort to figure it out.

The next day before first period Latin, Katie sits down

---

[1] "Sex" has its roots in the split between male and female, and didn't get used to mean sexual intercourse until the 1700's. The word itself is related to the Latin *sectare*, "to cut," and is thus related to "section" and "intersect." A word that means "to separate" is at the root of a very important type of coming together.

[2] "Impression" comes from a Latin root referring to a literal pressing-in, as in a mold to a piece of clay or a signet ring to a wax seal. I like to think of that when people talk about "first impressions:" literally pressing yourself on the person's memory.

[3] Wives, too, as it turns out. He's moved on since.

in the seat next to me, like she does every day. Usually I've still got my headphones on at this point, but today I made a point of removing them as soon as I sat down. I say hi. She looks a little taken aback. But she says hi back, then takes out her laptop and busies herself with something. I want to say something else to her, but what do people even say? How do people start conversations?[4] My palms start to sweat. I stare at my desk, mind racing. I wind up studying every tiny line on the cheap grey chipboard surface.

I don't know what music or movies Katie likes. I don't know what classes she has other than Latin and AP US History, our third period. I don't have any inkling of what she might have done last night, or what she might be doing this weekend.

Those are the sorts of things friends talk about, because those are the sorts of things friends already know about each other. They are, most certainly, not things that friends ask each other in the two minutes left before Latin starts, especially when they have ostensibly[5] already been friends for the last three years.

So that's the first blow today. Katie and I are not, in fact, friends. I sit there soaking that up for the full two minutes remaining before class starts.

I keep my headphones off for the rest of the day. I try talking to all the people I consider friends. Sometimes the conversation goes just like it did with Katie; sometimes it

---

[4] *Con-*, Latin prefix meaning "together;" *versus*, Latin root meaning "turn," rendering "conversation" something like a turning-together. And the fact that I'm focusing on word roots right now *might be part of the problem*.

[5] Latin *ostendo*, "to show or present." As in, *presenting* like something, but not that in reality.

---

lasts a little longer before petering out. Every time, my heart starts to thud in my chest and I can feel sweat prickling on my brow and under my fingers. One thing becomes abundantly[6] clear: all of the people that I think of as friends think of me as an acquaintance.

On my way out after the last bell, I pass Cass and Spencer. Cass grins politely at me; Spencer gives a barely disguised scowl.[7] I don't stop—I've had enough humiliation today—but without my headphones, I can hear what they're saying as I pass.

"...see Katie *roasting* Jeff on the Certamen group chat yesterday?" Spencer laughs.

"She is so pure, so you know it's good when..." Cass replies before she goes out of earshot.

Certamen group chat? I put my hand on my own phone, sitting inert in my pocket. My phone that never makes a peep.

There's a group chat for a team that I am on, and I didn't even know.

I put my headphones back on once I'm safely on the bus. I pull up the second Meat Puppets album. Cris Kirkwood's bass riff in "Split Myself in Two" is usually sufficient to drive any other, potentially troublesome thoughts out of my mind. It makes me feel a little bit better.

At home, I log on to Reddit and start browsing the History fora.[8] Reddit has some areas I never go near

---

[6] Latin: *Ab-* "away from;" *unda* "wave." Wave after wave of uncomfortable realizations hitting me all at once.

[7] One of many words that came into English from the Norse invasions of the 9th century CE, along with other friendly words like "anger," "slaughter," "berserk," and "mistake."

because of all the trolls and creeps, but the people on the History boards are generally great. I start to browse in World War II.

It all started with one remark before Certamen practice. Cass calls me aro, and that's one little thread. I start to pull the thread, and it unravels my entire social life. Or, rather, exposes the already-true fact that I have no social life, at least not at school.

World War II doesn't distract me enough. I get on to the Byzantine Empire. That doesn't work either. I give up and finally text my friend—my confirmed, actual, definite friend—Nora.

Nora doesn't go to our school. She's the only friend I keep up with from Michigan. My mom and I moved here to Texas when I was in sixth grade, when she and my dad got divorced.

I didn't know that Nora was a girl when we were friends in Michigan. She was a boy named Devin then. Or, rather, the world thought she was a boy named Devin. She came out as trans two years ago. It's been tricky. She has taught me a lot about it. It took me a long time to consistently[9] call her by her new name, and even longer to stop accidentally letting "he" slip in my own head. It must be easier for her newer friends, who don't have all these memories of swimming together in summer and being awful at little league together in the fall.

---

[8] The correct plural of "forum," much as "data" is the plural of "datum." Likewise, the correct plural of "stadium" is "stadia." Just in case you want to sound really pretentious at your next football game.

[9] *consistere*, Latin for "to stand one's ground."

Nora had to move schools after she transitioned. She doesn't like to talk about it.

I need to talk to girls, I tell her.

Ok, she sends back. *Context?*

My friends think I'm aromantic, I type. I have settled on this as the problem at hand. Nora has been my social life's protector since elementary school. She has always been better at people than I am, so she used to help me to make friends back in Michigan. That changed when I moved here. She's always kept tabs on me—she worries—and I've always assured her that I was doing fine. I can't bring myself to tell her that I've been wrong all along. That her worries about me have all come true. That I'm a complete social isolate.[10]

What's wrong with being aromantic? Nora replies.

Nothing, but I'm not, I type. *People think I'm aromantic, and probably asexual too. I'll never get a girlfriend like that.*

Don't get aro and ace confused, she writes. *You can be one without being the other.*

I know, I read about that, but that's not the issue. How do you talk to girls? I ask. Nora is a lesbian.[11] Back when she transitioned, she had to tell me the difference between being trans and being gay, and what it means to be both.

You do it like you talk to anybody, she replies.

I know that, I type. Really helpful advice, if you don't know how to talk to anybody.

---

[10] From the Latin *insula*, "island." As in John Donne's famous maxim, "No man is an island." Mr. Donne, I present you Brian Ganz, an island.

[11] A term named after the Greek isle of Lesbos, home of the great ancient poet Sappho. As a citizen of Lesbos and a woman who loved other women, Sappho was both a Lesbian and a lesbian.

You talk to me, don't you? she says.

That's different.

Different how? she asks. I can hear her prickling even over text. She's got a hair trigger for transphobia, both intentional and unintentional. And I've been guilty of the unintentional kind plenty. But this is not one of those times.

Because I've known you my whole life. And because you don't like guys anyway.

Okay.

So, how do you talk to girls you want to date? I press her.

It's harder, she admits. I wait a minute, but she doesn't type anything else.

Not helpful, I send back.

Well, it's hard to talk in generalities, she replies. *Who do you want to ask out?*

It's my turn to pause. *I'm not sure.*

You don't have anyone in mind?

No, I say.

And you're sure you're straight?

Yes!! God, I type.

Ok, ok, she replies. *Well then, that's your assignment. Pick a specific girl you like, and if you still can't figure out how to talk to her, you can tell me all about her and I can help.*

Ok, I type. *A girl I like. I'll find one.*

You are a weirdo, Nora says, with a heart emoji to assure me she's joking. *I have five girls I like bouncing around in my head right now. And you have to rack your brains to think of one.*

Let's play the name game, I say, to change the subject. *You take Justin.*

Okay, she says, *Maurice.*

We've been doing this since ninth grade. We give each other men's names, then each of us Google Image Search the name. The first person to find a guy with a beard and send the link wins.

It's stupid. But it's funny, and it works no matter how far away you are.

A moment later she sends a link. I stop my search to open it. It's a dorky looking guy in giant 80's glasses with a patchy, terrible beard.

You call that a beard? I reply.

He does, Nora says, *and that's what counts.*

I laugh out loud. It feels good. I think about how I don't have anything like this with anybody I see face-to-face, and a pang of sadness hits. I wish I still lived in the same town as my best friend.

But I'm taking a step. A girlfriend, I reason, can be my gateway to a social life. I won't just be Brian. I'll be _____'s boyfriend. I'll meet new people. I'll have something to talk about.

I spend another hour or so with Nora before turning to my homework. I attack my History notes with vigor, but I can't work up the same depth of energy for my Calculus.[12] I promised myself last month that I would do all the homework for that class, because my mom was starting to get vocal about all the tests I was failing. My pledge has

---

[12] A *calx* in Latin is a stone. They often used small stones for *calc*ulations: the -*ul-* infix is used to mean "little." Thus, *calculus* means "little stone," and is related to the word "calcium." "History," on the other hand, derives from the Greek word for "story." You tell me what's more interesting: stories, or little rocks.

relaxed lately to settle for doing about a quarter of most assignments, maybe only the first problem if it's a bad night. This might be a bad night.

In my head, the thoughts are spinning like wheels in a slot machine. There are plenty of girls. Some I'm on speaking terms with, some I'm not yet.

But which one do I like?

CHAPTER 3: JANUARY 16TH   SPENCER OLSON

I don't know the guy's name, but he's not cute.

Danny couldn't possibly be dating him. Danny is too superficial to date someone who looks like that. No offense to either party, you understand. But still.

Who is this guy? I thought I knew every gay guy in school.

Or is he straight? He could just be some straight guy, because they're not dating.

Why the Instagram selfie then?

Those are not the eyebrows of a straight boy.

Danny doesn't even leave likes on my selfies anymore. I've been using his favorite filters. He's ignoring me.

That's Alfred Trevino, Cass responds to my text after what feels like forever.

I check the time. Actually it only took her a minute after I asked to respond.

He is gay, yes, she continues. *They might be dating. I haven't heard anything.*

You really haven't? I reply. *You're not just trying to spare my feelings?*

For real, she types back. *I'll keep my ear to the ground for you.*

We need to go do more fun things, I say. *So I can take more pictures and make him miss our good times.*

I will do fun things with you when you want to hang out with me. Not when you just need a friend-mannequin to make your ex jealous. I told you, I'm done nursing your obsession.

Cass had laid that little dictum at my feet the last time we'd hung out. I maintain that I am perfectly capable of having a great time with my friend *and* making my boyfriend jealous on Instagram at the same time. But Cass says she feels "used."

Boo, I type back. My phone suggests the ghost emoji, which I add, along with a couple of sad and angry faces, and a dagger being plunged into my heart.

Yeah, just let me know when you're ready to talk about literally anything else.

K, hate you, bai.

I love you too Spence. She knows I hate it when she calls me that.

Mrs. Chernov, the theater teacher, has been talking for a while, so I figure I should tune in. She's been going through the blocking for the scene we're about to run. I think I'm in it. But I always wing my blocking, and she usually likes what I do better anyway.

It will help that, in this year's musical, I'm playing a part I was practically born for.

A few minutes later, I'm waltzing across the stage, my head bobbing forward, my hands in my pockets—Mrs. Chernov promised that I'd be in a zoot suit, so I'm already picturing it—as I describe my plot to kill little orphan Annie and run off with the prize money. My voice is full Humphrey Bogart. I can almost see the pencil-thin mustache I'll be drawing on. At one point I run up to Jenny, who plays my sister, and do that thing where I put one hand on her shoulder and sweep my other arm out in front of us. Pure stage chintz. It would look stupid in a good play, but in *Annie*, it hits all the right marks. Mrs. Chernov is pleased.

I'm also the only one off-book already. Everyone else is walking around holding their scripts, but I've already got mine memorized. I have a quick memory. That's why I was so good at Certamen History—until I got compared to Brian, that is.

"Should I have a toothpick in my mouth?" I ask Mrs. Chernov when we're about to wrap.

"It might mess with your enunciation..." she says hesitantly.

"He's already talking out of one side of his mouth anyway," Jenny points out.

"And when I say 'Chump,' I can flick it derisively away," I add, miming the motion.

Mrs. Chernov cringes. "How will somebody find that to strike it?" One of her biggest pet peeves is anything at all being left on the stage. Two years ago, when they were doing *Of Mice and Men* for One Act, George Milton's handkerchief fell out of his pocket during his first meeting with the farmhands and it stayed on the stage for ten full minutes before anyone picked it up. It was all Mrs. Chernov could talk about for the next year.

Part of me does enjoy imagining her face in the audience when it was going on. I can picture exactly how she was chewing the inside of her cheeks.

After practice, grabbing our backpacks out of the drama room, I catch Jenny's attention.

"You're reciting for me tomorrow after school, right?" I ask her.

"Yup," she says, grabbing her backpack from the edge of the wooden mini-stage set up along the far wall of the room. "I've got it all memorized, I just need some pronunciation tips."

In addition to being Certamen alternate and a bang-up History specialist, I'm also captain of Latin Club's Dramatic Interpretation team. A perfect role for a crack memorizer, and one that's helped me fine-tune my Latin pronunciation and scansion. This year I'll be reciting in Latin a speech of King Priam of Troy, the one just before he is brutally murdered by the Greek warrior Pyrrhus. Jenny will be portraying Queen Tanaquil choosing the next king of Rome.

"Joey!" I say, as if I had just noticed that Joseph Zamora was standing there. In fact, I had brought up Dramatic Interpretation exactly because he was there. "Still not too late to join the team, you know." Joey is a Latin 2, and I don't have a boy in the Latin 2 slot.

"Man, I got enough to memorize for *Annie*," he says, not making direct eye contact. "I don't need to add a whole Latin speech."

"Oh don't be a wuss," I say. "Besides, it's an intense speech. You'd be Verginius sacrificing his own daughter for the greater good. Fraught with emotion. Way fun."

Joey leaves muttering something about thinking about it. I know he won't.

"Like he even has that many lines in this stupid play," I roll my eyes to Jenny. She laughs.

Joseph is playing Punjab, the mysterious Indian bodyguard of Daddy Warbucks. I know—problematic, right? It's not the only questionable thing in this show, but I doubt Mrs. Chernov realizes it. Baby boomers don't know anything.

I unwrap a power bar and take a big bite as I walk out with Jenny. I'm giving her a ride today.

"Do you know Alfred Trevino?" I ask her, my mouth still full.

"Yeah," she says, looking warily at me.

I swallow my bite. "What?" I ask of her expression.

"Because I know he's dating Danny, and I don't want to go there with you again."

"Then he *is* dating Danny!" I erupt.

"Spencer, it's been a month."

"What do you know?" I shout, overdramatically. "You're just a sophomore, you know nothing of life!"

We get to the car. "Do you even know where your fake, overblown drama stops and the real stuff starts?" she asks me.

"I try to keep a handle on it." I shut my door and start the engine. Florence and the Machine starts to play, but I shut them off. "You want to go do something fun?" I ask Jenny.

"I have homework," she answers.

"I'll pay."

Jenny shakes her head. I sigh and pull out of the parking lot, taking another big bite of my power bar as I do. Alfred Trevino. What a rat bastard name.

CHAPTER 4: JANUARY 28TH   KATIE NGUYEN

Tibullus: two books of elegiac poetry. Two more attributed, but probably not genuine.

Catullus: one book of lyric poetry. Most famous for love poems to a woman he called Lesbia, theorized to have been an alias for Clodia Metelli.

Propertius: four books of elegiac poetry. His literary lover was Cynthia.

Suetonius: series of twelve biographies commonly called...

"Relax, Katie," Cass spoke up at my side.

"Was I talking out loud?" I asked.

"Whispering," Cass said. "You know, research shows that last-minute cramming doesn't help you nearly as much as the stress of it hurts you. You're better off chilling. It gets you centered and ready for the coming trial."

"Then why are you on your laptop?" I countered.

Cass turned her screen around. She was cleaning up a drawing of two Greek warriors gazing lovingly into each other's eyes. Probably either Achilles and Patroclus or

Odysseus and Diomedes, if the rest of her Tumblr was any guide. The drawing looked gorgeous, as always. Cass is really talented, and she never runs out of interesting source material with all the reading she does for Certamen. She really knows a lot about Mythology.

A lot more than I know about Roman Authors.

Lucretius: poet and philosopher, *De Rerum Natura*. Describes everything in the world in terms of Epicurean philosophy, in epic poetic meter. Also among the first to describe an atom.

Cass, Brian, and I were sitting on the floor in the cafeteria of a strange high school across town. The posters on the walls were all red and gold instead of our green and black. There were butcher-paper spirit posters up for their basketball team, just like at our school, but all the slogans were unfamiliar. Everything the same, but different.

It was a Saturday, and we were here for an invitational Certamen meet. It wouldn't count toward our standing or influence who made State. It was just practice. Mainly, it was a chance to size up our competition.

But I didn't care that this meet didn't really matter. I was studying because I needed to show that I could compete seriously at Advanced Certamen. My team had counted on me to learn my authors this year, and I was *not* about to make them regret trusting me. At every practice, Mr. Stanton had been going out of his way to be kind to me about it. He would tell me how well I was doing, even though I knew it wasn't true.

Katie Nguyen does *not* need a teacher's charity.

The three of us were all sitting against the same brick

wall. Spencer had wanted to come for moral support, even though we didn't really need an alternate, but there was an *Annie* rehearsal today that he wasn't supposed to miss. Jeff was in another room, doing the official draw for our position on the bracket. He was our team captain. Not because he was the best leader or anything (that would be Cass), but because he was the Grammar person. The Grammar person is always team captain. They get the most questions.

Further out in the cafeteria, three of the four Latin 1's of the Novice team were playing Mafia with another school's Novice team. They had no idea what they were in for today. They thought Latin was easy. They would spend their rounds today getting destroyed by private school kids who had been eating, drinking, and sleeping their Certamen categories for the past year.

I could see the private school Latin 1's now, on the other side of the cafeteria, poring over copies of Wheelock's and Morford & Lenardon. They were mostly seventh graders. I remembered what it was like to go against them. Tiny, vicious, relentless question-answering machines. Buzzing in before I'd even started to *think* of an answer. Now I went against the upperclassman behemoths that these tiny demons would grow into.

I watched our innocent Latin 1's for a moment. The experience would be good for them. They would come away from the day knowing how much more seriously they had to take this if they wanted to win, and they'd spend the month between today and the JCL Area competition cramming. The same thing happened to my team two years ago. We too had been dumb, carefree freshmen at this competition, had gotten our butts kicked, and had gotten serious afterward. Except our Grammar guy. He had quit the team, and Jeff had joined up in his place. Jeff had *always* been serious.

The Latin 2 Intermediate team was huddled a few yards away from us. *They* knew what they were up against today. Allie was sitting in the center of the group, reading them questions that Mr. Stanton had brought. She wasn't on Certamen, but she was a Latin 2, so those were her friends. She had no business here, exactly, but she couldn't stand to miss a Latin Club event. Mr. Stanton had let her come on the flimsy excuse that, since the Historian (me) would be in Advanced Certamen rounds all day, we needed someone here taking pictures of everything. I had loaned Allie my camera.

I spotted Jeff moving toward us at a trot. Cass closed her laptop. Brian paused his iPod and removed his headphones. This was it.

"First round in fifteen minutes," Jeff said when he was close enough. "Room 206." He picked up his backpack from the floor next to Brian and swung it over his shoulder. The rest of us began to pack, and Jeff rocked nervously on his heels.

"Who are we up against?" asked Brian casually.

"Channel Heights and Our Lady of the Seven Sorrows," Jeff said gravely.

"Our Lady of the Seven Sorrows," Cass groaned. "Those kids buzz in before the moderator even *starts* talking."

"The next round will be better," Jeff promised. "Anderson and St. Ignatius."

St. Ignatius was another private school, this one good but not unbeatable. Anderson was no competition.

We were the first team in to room 206. Regular Certamen rounds happened in normal classrooms, with the walls covered in math charts or US History timelines or, in this case, some assignment where students had traced their bodies to create grotesque character maps for everyone in *Romeo and Juliet*. The final round with the top three teams would be played in the auditorium with *everybody* watching, but most of the preliminary rounds had no audience. Sometimes you'd have a couple of friends cheering you on, or somebody's parents. The desks being used for the round would all be circled at the front in three groups of four, and the rest of the desks, the "audience" section, would always be wherever the teacher had happened to leave them.

We claimed the middle desk grouping with the B buzzers. It was an old superstition of ours when we had our choice: B is better than C, but not overconfident like picking A.

"We've got this, guys," Jeff said nervously, "Don't let Our Lady of the Seven Sorrows get in your heads. We know our stuff too. Just because they're hideously fast and know every question..."

"Would you relax?" Cass interrupted.

"Your 'pep talk' is making me *more* nervous," I agreed.

"Cass, whatever happened to this being the year we have to make it to State?" Jeff leaned over to ask her. He was B1 and she was B4, so Brian and I were both between them.

"This meet doesn't count for anything," Cass replied.

"Because I *have* to make it to State this year," Jeff barreled on without listening to Cass. "Especially after AcaDec screwed up last weekend."

Brian laughed hollowly. He was on the Academic Decathlon team too.

"AcaDec didn't make State?" Cass asked, eyebrows raised. Our AcaDec team *always* made State.

"Missed it by two slots," Brian reported. Cass whistled.

I already knew. Their sponsor was my AP English teacher, Mrs. Gomez, and she had been down in the dumps the whole week because of it.

"I can't believe I wasted my time on AcaDec," Jeff rested his forehead against his hands. "I knew I should have stuck with Debate instead."

"It's not really our fault," Brian countered. "We're used to having two coaches, but they only gave us one for some reason. Gomez did the best she could, but we were at a disadvantage."

"Excuses get me nowhere," Jeff waved him off, "If I'm going to get into—"

"The pre-med program at Johns Hopkins," Cass and Brian recited together.

"Then I need," Jeff said, louder and more insistently, "A good résumé. Multiple State-level finishes. My HOSA State won't be enough. I need Certamen this year."

"You've got another year," Cass pointed out, "Unlike me."

"No, I don't," Jeff replied. "Next year will be too late.

By the time State happens, they'll already have sent the acceptance letters."

"Translate 'they will have already sent' into Latin," said Mr. Stanton, breezing into the room and picking up on the last thing Jeff had said.

Jeff knitted his brow. "*Iam miserint*," he said after a few seconds' concentration. Certamen moderators gave you five seconds, exactly, after buzzing in to answer. Jeff's answer was surgically within that limit. Training.

"Excellent," Mr. Stanton said casually. "Bonus 1: Differentiate in form between '*miserint*' and its corresponding perfect subjunctive."

"Easy," Jeff said, "There is no difference in form."

"Good," Magister said. "Bonus 2: Calm the hell down and let your friends enjoy themselves."

Jeff rolled his eyes.

"Are *you* proctoring this round?" I asked Mr. Stanton apprehensively.

"Nah, they've got me across the hall," Mr. Stanton said. "I think they've managed to arrange it so we don't proctor to our own teams at this one."

"Aw man," Brian said. He *liked* getting Mr. Stanton at real competitions. I hated it. It was more pressure.

"Anyway, just checking in," he continued. "You've all got paper and pencil?"

We showed him our supplies, lying at the ready on our desks.

"Of course," he smiled. "Flag me down if you need me. I'm going to go wrangle the Latin 1's."

"See if they have one piece of paper to rip up and split

between them?" Brian said.

Magister rolled his eyes to the ceiling. "I brought extras this year. Freshmen. Always the same." He turned to leave the room.

"Wait!" Cass called. "Can we touch your beard for luck?"

Mr. Stanton continued toward the door like he hadn't heard her.

"Mr. Stanton!" Cass pressed. "If we lost this tournament today, could you really live with yourself knowing that you could have helped?"

Mr. Stanton stopped, then turned slowly back. "Fine," he sighed, and leaned over our desks. We laughed as we each gingerly touched the edge of his beard. Even Jeff did it.

"You are the worst. Good luck," Magister said on his way out the door.

A moment later, the team from Our Lady of the Seven Sorrows filed in. You could tell it was them because of the matching school sweaters, and the two parent holders-on who followed them in holding laptops. The parents would watch the round on the edges of their seats, take copious notes on every question their team got wrong, and later use their notes to file official complaints with the people running the competition. Every competition. Even the invitational ones that didn't count for anything. And crazy protests too. The moderator paused too long, or not long enough, or pronounced a long vowel short.

I guess they had to practice every aspect of their strategy today, just like we did.

A teacher blew in right after them, wearing a tweed blazer with elbow patches (standard issue for all male Latin teachers), carrying a binder that every eye in the room went straight to. He was obviously our moderator, and those were our questions.

"Okay," he said, straightening his glasses as he looked at a single piece of printer paper on top of his binder. "Do we have the delegations from West Oak, Channel Heights, and Our Lady of the Seven Sorrows?"

"No Channel Heights yet," Jeff told him.

"You are?" asked the moderator.

"We're West Oak," Jeff said.

The moderator made a note on his sheet. "Then you're Our Lady of the Seven Sorrows?"

"Correct," said the Our Lady of the Seven Sorrows captain confidently. He looked like he had been carved out of wax instead of born. Like a portrait of a football player from Yale in the 20's. Like he had learned to steer a yacht before he had learned how to drive a car.

Our Lady of the Seven Sorrows had sat themselves at the A buzzers, of course. In their case, that wasn't even hubris. It was just self-awareness.

The team from Channel Heights showed up shortly after, and we commenced with the reading of the rules and the Aurelia passage. The latter was a short bit of Latin text meant to get us used to the moderator's Latin reading voice, and it was the same at every competition. We all had it memorized by now.

"*Aurelia, cui urbs placebat, erat in Aegypto cum familia sua ingenti et equo suo. Tredecim ludos magnos Iovis in amphitheatro*

Alexandriae spectabat. Tandem, equus iratus domum recurrere coepit. Eheu!"

The OLotSS parents were already clacking on their keyboards. The moderator said his v's and c's the Italian way, and his vowel quality was awful. I felt for Jeff and Cass, who had to listen up for more Latin than I did. We tested our buzzers and were ready to go.

The round lasted about thirty minutes. Our Lady of the Seven Sorrows outbuzzed me on every Author question, including the ones I actually knew, which was only about half. But I got the jump on them for the sole Roman Life question of the round. It was one about the unlucky days to have weddings, because the doors to the Underworld were supposed to be open. The Our Lady expert looked upset to have missed it. I was proud of that.

Brian grabbed over half of the History questions. He was quite fast on the buzzer, probably because while the rest of us sweated under the pressure, he always seemed completely unaware of it. It wasn't that he was any stronger than us. It was more like he didn't even *notice*.

But Cass and Jeff felt the same pressure I did. They got outbuzzed on every one of their questions. Jeff's eyes got darker and his shoulders more hunched as we went. By question nineteen he was pressing down on the desk so hard with his pencil I thought he'd punch a hole through it.

At the end of the twenty questions, we had 65 points to Our Lady of the Seven Sorrows's 250.

250. Anything over 100 was really good. 200 was just showing off.

Channel Heights didn't manage to score at all. They

didn't seem to care much. They were already laughing at private jokes at their desks while the scores were being read out.

The OLotSS team came robotically over to shake our hands after the round was over, as they always did. I acted polite. Cass made a face. Jeff looked shell-shocked. Brian was placid.

When the rest of the Our Lady crossed the room to shake hands with Channel Heights, one of them stayed behind at our table. He was their History person, the most relaxed looking of them, a tall boy with feathery black hair and piercing eyes. He directed these toward Cass.

"You're BlackAthena17, aren't you?" he asked with a bemused grin.

Cass nodded, her eyes narrowing. BlackAthena17 was her Tumblr handle.

"I recognized you from your selfies," he said with a warm smile. "I love your blog."

"Oh, uh, thank you," she said.

"Your art is gorgeous. And I show the rest of my class your Roman memes all the time. Actually, you remember that question on the emperor Vitellius being found hiding in his dirty laundry by the soldiers who came to kill him? I only remembered that because of your 'It's laundry day' post."

"I loved that one!" Brian chimed in.

"'Vitellius, hide and seek champion, AD 15-December 69,'" the other boy quoted. He and Brian laughed, and I could see Cass start to seethe.

"I can't believe I gave that bastard an answer!" she

hissed to us after he walked away.

"I told you," Jeff said. "Nothing good comes of Tumblr."

"The untold dangers of garbage-posting," Cass groaned.

"Lighten up," Brian chided. "I thought he was cool."

"He is not cool," Jeff spit. "He is our sworn enemy."

"He is Carthage," Cass agreed. "He must be destroyed."

***

Our next two rounds went better. Most of the way through Round 2 we were pretty neck-in-neck with St. Ignatius, though they managed to edge us out on the last question. We won Round 3, but not by a lot. Certamen meets consisted of three rounds plus finals, and only the teams with the top combined scores for the first three rounds made finals. We were in fourth place after Round 3. We wouldn't be in finals, and only by one spot.

But that was alright with me. I had managed to get some Author questions in Rounds 2 and 3, and that increased my confidence. The meet itself didn't count for anything, so I was actually relieved not to have to play in finals.

Jeff didn't feel the same way. He walked stiffly toward the cafeteria away from the score board, like a snake coiling and rearing to strike. We walked a step behind him. No one spoke to him, knowing that the next words to come out of his mouth would be shouted, no matter if the recipient deserved it or not.

Cass's reaction was closer to mine. She had gotten

some of her Mythology questions, and a couple of Literary Device ones too. I would have bet that Spencer's competition in practice had helped her. Though I was sure she would not have admitted that.

Brian already had his headphones on.

As soon as the four of us entered the cafeteria, we were met with a flash in our eyes. Jeff fumed and sputtered. Allie peeked out from behind my camera.

"Didn't go well?" she asked sympathetically.

"We're fourth," Cass answered, and Jeff stalked off into the crowd in search of lunch.

"Bummer," Allie said.

"How'd our other teams fare?" I asked her.

"Latin 2 is going to finals," she said with a grin. "They're third, so they're underdogs, but anything can happen in finals."

That was true. Unlike in the previous rounds, your scores were wiped clean going into finals. Whoever scored highest in the final round won first overall, even if they'd been behind in points earlier.

"Latin 1 got creamed," she continued, her smile widening. "They're licking their wounds over at that table."

"I'll go talk to them," I said. Club officers considered it part of our duty to guide the freshmen in the right direction. "I can take over the camera now, Allie, since I'm not playing anymore."

Allie gave me back the camera with a look of disappointment. I could tell she had enjoyed feeling useful. As I walked toward the freshmen, I paged through a few of the pictures she had taken. Most of them pretty good. A few out of focus, including the one she had just taken of us.

I found the freshmen sulking over their lunches. Hot dogs and greasy piles of French fries on flimsy paper plates. I took a seat at their table.

"Hey Katie," said Roger, the Roman Life person who knew me because he was in the study group I ran.

"Hey guys," I addressed the group. "How are you doing?"

They grunted in reply. This team was all boys. Boys tended to be sorer losers than girls. I mean, Brian notwithstanding.

"Rough rounds?" I asked.

"What do they feed those Catholic kids?" spat a boy with a shock of curly brown hair.

"Yeah," agreed a tall and lanky kid in a hoodie, "They look like they're eight years old, they buzz in when the moderator's said two words, and they know every. Single. Answer."

I nodded appreciatively. "I know they seem crazy," I said. "I remember being here *my* freshmen year. They seemed like they had superpowers. But you know, they just study. A lot."

"We can't catch up with them," said the one with the glasses.

"Did you get *any* questions?" I asked.

They nodded.

"Did the other teams not know them, or did you outbuzz them?"

The boys looked at each other for a second.

"Mixture of the two, I guess," said the one with the

glasses.

"That's good!" I said honestly. "My freshman year here, I think my team only managed to get one or two questions total. And that was all Brian. By Area, we managed third place. We buckled down in the month between, and we figured out how to *do* this."

"You beat some of the Catholics at Area?" asked the lanky one.

"Yup," I confirmed. "But only Our Lady of the Seven Sorrows is Catholic. All the 'Saint' schools are Episcopal or Anglican."

"Close enough," said Roger.

I laughed. "Yeah. Close enough. Anyway, you'll get 'em next time. If you practice."

"She's a smart kid," said a voice from behind me. "You should listen to her." I turned toward Mr. Stanton.

"You listening in on my pep talk?" I chided him.

"Just a little," he said, grinning. "Go get yourself some lunch before they close down the lines."

Lunchtime was almost over, and then finals would start. We would cheer on our Intermediate team when their turn came, and cheer on anyone who challenged Our Lady of the Seven Sorrows when the Advanced round came. It's what we always did.

I hurried into the far shorter of the two lunch lines: the vegetarian option. I had become a vegetarian two years earlier for ethical reasons, after we had studied the effects of factory farming during our Human Geography class. It had the side effect of making me extremely conscious about what I ate, so I ate healthier than anyone else I knew.

Except on competition days. Most Latin competitions' vegetarian options were an afterthought. Usually a salad, and not even an entree salad. A *side* salad. One time it even came without dressing, and we had no option to add any. But this time, it looked like I was lucking out. Black bean burgers. And a table of options for condiments. This school knew what was up.

The person in front of me in line turned around. "Hey, Katie Nguyen," he said.

I was taken aback. Then I recognized him. It was the History guy from Our Lady of the Seven Sorrows, the one who had recognized Cass. He must have remembered my name from when we all had to say ours before the round started.

"Hi," I said awkwardly. "You're a vegetarian?"

"Yeah," he said. "It's mostly a moral thing, but it also pisses off my red meat-loving stepfather, so that's a plus too."

I laughed. Why was I laughing? It was a pretty sad thing to say. But he said it with this easy, lopsided smile. He had on his school's uniform wine-red sweater and yellow button up shirt, with the sleeves of both rolled most of the way up his forearms because it was really much too warm inside for a sweater. I noticed a pin on his collar, a crossed pair of percussion mallets.

"Are you a percussionist?" I asked.

He tweaked the pin. "Oh yeah, I do pit."

"I play marimba in the pit," I told him.

"Marimba is so cool," he said. "How do you like it?"

"Oh, I love it. Pit is the best because we don't have to

56

march."

"We don't march at all at Our Lady," he said.

"Lucky!" I laughed.

"We're too small. There are only two of us in the pit, so I play a lot of instruments."

"There's *sixteen* of us in our pit," I told him.

"Whoa," he marveled.

"I don't always do marimba," I elaborated. "I started on piano when I was a kid, so I play that some for the band. Don't say it, I know. An Asian who plays piano. Stereotype alert."

"I think you break the stereotype enough by playing marimba," he chuckled.

We had our food, but we were still standing just out of line.

"But, yeah, I also do synthesizers for Winter Drumline, and some piano for the jazz band."

"Oh man, you guys have a jazz band?" he groaned. "You are so lucky. I'd kill for a school jazz band."

I shrugged. "It's not really my kind of music."

"No way," he said.

"I like the Romantic composers," I explained. "Tchaikovsky, Prokofiev, Debussy, Chopin..."

"I respect that," he nodded. "What are you playing in jazz band?"

"Duke Ellington, Louis Armstrong, Artie Shaw, something more modern by Herbie Hancock..."

"Have you heard Thelonious Monk?" he asked.

"Not really," I admitted. I had heard the name.

"A piano player not knowing Monk, now that's a

crime," he said.

"Is that so?"

"Try out 'Liza, All the Clouds Will Roll Away,' and go from there," he told me.

I laughed at his confidence.

"Attention," came a voice over the loudspeaker, "Finals will begin in the auditorium in five minutes. Finals in five minutes. Novice teams, please report to the auditorium immediately."

"Oh man," I muttered. I hadn't even *started* eating.

"See you around, Katie Nguyen," said the boy from Our Lady of the Seven Sorrows, with another of his easy smiles. He wheeled back through the crowd toward his team. I stood frozen for a long moment. He *was* cute, wasn't he?

I slapped that thought away like it was a mosquito buzzing by my ear, and headed for the West Oak table.

*** *** ***

A hastily gulped burger later, I was filing into the auditorium between Cass and Brian. Cass was running down her favorite scene in the most recent *Outlander* episode, which I had watched, though I had been doing homework through it so I was hazy on the details.

"Katie!" came a voice from the row next to me. I looked up and saw the cute boy from the Our Lady of the Seven Sorrows team. He gestured to an empty seat next to him. I shook my head.

"I'm sitting with my team," I whispered. He nodded, and smiled at me as I passed anyway.

Cass was still talking. She hadn't noticed a thing. I

agreed with whatever she had said last, and she, Brian, Jeff and I took seats near the front. The seats were pretty comfy, plush with dark red fabric. Cass put her feet up on the seat in front of her as soon as she sat down, crossing her arms on top of her knees. Brian took out a book. Jeff pulled out a study guide for some class.

I thought I could feel his eyes boring into the back of my head. The boy from Our Lady of the Seven Sorrows, that is. But when I looked around, he was always either watching the stage or looking at his phone, like everyone else. Maybe I had it the wrong way around. Maybe I was starting to stare at him. I decided to stop.

The Novice round was won by the prepubescent Our Lady of the Seven Sorrows Team, of course. Our Intermediate team came in third of the three teams on the stage, but we cheered for them as if they'd won the whole thing. Just being *up* there was fantastic.

Between the Intermediate round and the Advanced, Brian got up to use the bathroom. Cass put down her feet and turned to me.

"Okay Katie," she said, her voice hushed and serious. "*Scandal.*"

I felt my cheeks turn red. She must have noticed me talking to that boy, or looking around at him. *Now* I was going to hear it.

But Cass was reaching into her bag. She handed me a paper CD sleeve. Inside was a silver writable disk, labeled in Sharpie. "BRIAN'S MIX FOR CASS."

I gaped. "You don't think..."

"Of course I think."

"He has *feelings*?" I said incredulously.

"And apparently they're for me," Cass said. "That poor misguided straight boy."

"You like both though," I clarified.

"That doesn't make him my type," she said flatly. I wondered if I had said something rude.

"What did he *say*?" I asked.

"He left it at my place at the lunch table when I got up to use the bathroom. When I noticed and looked at him, he was just reading his book."

I handed her back the CD. "You've texted Spencer?"

She shook her head. "Normally he'd be the first I'd tell. But you don't necessarily tell him something you want to keep secret. And I don't think Brian deserves everybody knowing this."

"Then I'm honored to be let in on the secret."

"Had to tell someone," she said. "Now I gotta let another white boy down without hurting his precious feelings..." She shook her head. "I gotta think about something else. What do you want to bet on?"

I considered. "How many points will Our Lady of the Seven Sorrows win by?"

"Not bad," Cass said. "Stakes?"

I rummaged through my bag. "I've got strawberry sour punch."

"I've got a sleeve of thin mints."

"What's our over/under? Fifty points?"

"You kidding? Seventy."

I laughed. "I'll take over."

"Alright, I'll take under then."

We placed our wagers on the armrest between us. We'd started this game when we were in PreCal together the previous year. Our teacher said the word "okay" the way some people *breathe*. "So you take the variable, okay, and you divide out, okay, to get it on this side, okay..." Cass and I started to bet on how many times he would say it in the class period, using whatever snacks we happened to have in our bags as stakes. Ever since, we'd found ways to replicate the game whenever we were together.

As the round got underway, it also gave me an excuse for the interest with which I watched the Our Lady of the Seven Sorrows team that day. I could pretend it was the bet, instead of the boy.

Before, their team had seemed like a personality-less monolith, but now that I sort of knew one of them, they all seemed more human. All ungodly quick and accurate at Certamen, of course, but with individual personalities now. The girl on Grammar got this twinge in her eye every time she composed Latin off the top of her head. The guy on Mythology held his hand up every time he needed to think, as if telling the world to wait a minute. And of course their History guy was as calm as can be. He kept his buzzer low and casual, but rang in as fast as any of them. You could tell how sure he was in his answer by how much of his lopsided smile he showed.

At every score check, Cass cheered for St. Ignatius and hissed when Our Lady of the Seven Sorrows's was read. I clapped pointedly, despite Cass's sneers. I had a stake in their success, after all.

In the end, they won by ninety points. I applauded

them with the rest, and took my winnings from the armrest.

St. Ignatius came in second. They usually did. I thought it must have been hard, always coming close, but always losing the match to the team whose position in State Certamen was virtually a guarantee.

The OLotSS team briefly looked out to accept the audience's accolades. I could have sworn he looked straight into my eyes. I clapped harder.

What was I *thinking*? An Our Lady of the Seven Sorrows *Certamen* player? I was betraying my team. I couldn't *possibly* like him. He was the Soviet Union to our NATO. He was everything I'd hated since ninth grade. He was nothing to me.

He was really cute.

It was only as we were getting on the bus to go home that I realized.

I had no idea what his name was.

How could I be so stupid?

CHAPTER 5: JANUARY 28TH-FEBRUARY 2ND
CASS WASHINGTON

I was pretty freaked out about the mix CD thing. When we got home from the competition Saturday evening, I left it sitting in my bag untouched. But keeping it out of sight didn't help. It throbbed on the edge of my consciousness like the Tell-Tale Heart.

Of course it meant he liked me. Which had never been on my radar.

And of course I wasn't interested.

Normally when I'm not interested, I say it. I'm open with my feelings. I think that's how people should be. Sometimes it gets a little ugly (looking at you, Greg effing Krakowski (or not, because I finally blocked you, like you deserved)), but it's still better than lying and pretending.

But Brian was different. We spent a lot of time together. We were on a team. Plus, Brian was hard to read, which made him dangerous. I really didn't think I had ever heard him express an emotion of any kind. Making me a mix CD was the closest thing to a feeling I had ever seen

63

him have.

I worried that he was one of the "nice guys finish last" types. The quiet boy who thinks of himself as sensitive and kind, and takes rejection way too personally. I didn't need him getting his privileged ass bent out of shape, deciding that my lack of romantic attraction to him reflected poorly on my character. I wasn't looking to have the words "friend-zoned" anywhere near this conversation.

Not when we needed to stay united as a team.

Not when we needed to beat Our Lady of the Seven Sorrows.

Brian wasn't in my phone contacts. I thought I had numbers for everyone on the team. Maybe that was just last year's team. He wasn't on the Certamen group text, which I had never realized. I decided to text Spencer. But I still didn't want to tell him everything.

Do you have Brian's number? I asked Spencer.

Why would I have Brian's number? he answered immediately.

Uh. Because we're on a Certamen team with him?

Then why don't you have his number? he asked.

I thought I did, I typed.

I thought I did too.

You don't have it? I replied. Did anyone have this kid's number?

No, I totally do.

????? You said you didn't?

No, I said I thought I did. I was right.

Spencer, I swear by all of the gods...

HO MAN and you know a lot of those.

He sent me the number. I added it to my contacts.

The door flew open, and my little sister came bouncing in. She was seven. Cute as a button, and so annoying sometimes I could smack her.

"Mom says time for dinner," she said.

"What have I told you about barging in?" I growled.

"Mom said to come get you!"

"You still knock, Phoebe!"

"Are you coming?" she said in a needling voice.

"Tell Mom I'll be there in a few."

"Okay," she said, and didn't move.

"Go now!" I thundered like Craggy-Browed Zeus on the peak of Mt. Olympus, and Phoebe dashed out, leaving the door open.

I looked back at my phone. *What do you need it for?* Spencer had asked, as I knew he would.

Nothing, I typed back, convincing nobody.

Is there some Certamen team drama brewing? Spencer replied quickly. I could almost see the glint in his eye as he typed that.

Some other time, Spencer.

If only the team had a backup History expert waiting in the wings after you crush his poor heart...

You are the worst.

Shuffleboard tomorrow? he asked.

Shuffleboard? *The hell are you, 80 years old?*

You just wait, he typed. *It's catching on.*

Some other time, Spence. He hated when I called him that.

***

At dinner that night, my mom gave me some more crap

about colleges.

Over Christmas, she had taken me on a full tour of the colleges in Texas within striking distance for someone with my GPA. And under extreme duress, I had finally picked the University of Texas at San Antonio as my first choice, though I had applications in at three others.

But to meet my mother's standard, I also needed to win a huge pile of scholarships.

"An intelligent Black woman like you should be getting so many scholarships, they'll be paying *you* to go to college," she was saying for the thousandth time.

Maybe that's how it worked in your generation, I was thinking, *but it sure as hell hasn't been my experience so far.* "I'm having trouble writing the essays for them," I said instead.

"Because you don't have a major," my mom said angrily. And correctly.

"You should go for Engineering," my dad chimed in. This one I had heard *ten* thousand times.

"She doesn't have the Math and Science grades," my mom sighed.

"I wouldn't *like* Engineering," I said. "I don't have the grades because it ain't what I care about."

"Well there's no money in Roman history or Greek fairy tales," Mom said dismissively. "And don't use 'ain't' in this house, it makes you sound uneducated."

Black, Mom. It makes me sound Black. I thought, but did not say.

Phoebe was staring directly at the potatoes she was eating, as if she wasn't taking in any of this. But I could see the malicious joy dancing just behind her eyes. She didn't understand everything we were talking about, but she could certainly get the gist. And she loved to see me in trouble.

"She could be a writer," my dad pointed out. "Journalism, or creative stuff. Plenty of money in that."

"It's unstable," my mom countered. "She could be making six figures one year and not have a pot to piss in the next. Do you think she can save wisely enough for that? It's even worse than trying to make a living off her art."

I ate my lamb chop silently. It was best to let them argue about my future without my input.

Say what you will about personal drama about the boy on your Certamen team who has the hots for you, at least it's a simpler problem than trying to plan your entire future.

Progress reports would come out soon, and I was still sitting on C's in Physics and Economics. The dread cycle was about to start up again. Every progress report since the 7th grade, my parents would ground me for two weeks for every grade below an 80. Since I had a lot of those, and progress reports came out every three weeks, I'd spent much of my high school career on a semi-permanent semi-grounding. When each report came out, my parents would get all serious again, lecture me about my prospects, and redouble their grounding efforts. Then over the next few days, they'd forget their resolve and let me wiggle through my restrictions little by little. The result was that, though I was technically almost always grounded, I was never very hampered by it. A quasi-freedom.

I told myself that I would spend that Saturday evening bringing up those two C's, but when I got down to it, I couldn't think of anything that would actually help. So I spent the night doing the inking, then the Photoshop coloring, for a piece I'd done of the Cumaean Sibyl wasting away in her jar, having been granted long life but not eternal youth. I also threw together my next care package for Amber. I packed up a bunch of sour apple Jolly Ranchers, a roll of animal stickers, and the copy of Ovid's *Heroides* I had recently finished, addressing the package to Beaumont, Texas.

Amber was part of a group of high school Mythology nerds on Tumblr who went to Junior Classical League competitions. We only got to meet face-to-face once a year, at JCL State. But we communicated online and in a big group text, through Classics memes on Tumblr and through care packages in the mail. The packages were mainly for sharing Mythology study books, but we included other items of personal significance. I'd gotten *Heroides* from fellow-nerd Warren, and was duly passing it on to the next person who wanted to read it.

It was nice, both sending the packages off and getting them in the mail.

There were only a few months left before I'd see them at State and be able to thank them all in person. If I wasn't too busy playing Certamen, that is.

***

I didn't end up texting Brian that Saturday night. Or Sunday. I kept typing things, but I deleted all of them.

I'd rejected people before.

They'd reacted badly before.

I'd been called names, threatened.

It left me unsettled, put me on my guard. But I'd

gotten over it each time. And so had they.

This thing with Brian felt different. With the other assholes, I had at least known they were assholes before they'd even started, so I could prepare myself. Brian was a blank slate. I could fill that nothingness with all sorts of positive attributes, but that sort of optimism could get you hurt, or worse. I had no choice but to fill the void with the worst kinds of personality traits I could think of.

Before long, the Brian of my imagination had migrated from robot to fragile male ego to abusive manipulative monster. This wasn't healthy. This was why I usually cleared the air sooner.

I saw him a few times in the hallways once the school week started. He walked as he always did: headphones on, eyes straight up to make up for the fact that he couldn't hear anything. He reacted to me as he always had: a smile, a nod. He seemed unaffected.

I finally put the CD into my computer on Wednesday night.

I knew Brian liked punk, so some of the music conformed to expectation. There was loud, angry, distorted music performed by adolescents (or thirty-year-olds stuck in adolescence—hard to tell the difference). There was a My Chemical Romance song on there. That one might have just been him pandering to me. I still wore an MCR shirt from time to time. A vestige of my more sentimental youth, a whole three years in my past.

But most of the disc was way weirder. No choruses on a lot of the songs. A kind of brood that refused to lift into anything, misery without catharsis. A lot of feedback and noise. Shouting. Muttering. A blues recording that sounded like it was from the 20's. The weirdest was a song by Nick Cave that sounded like being lost in a smoky room with no entrances or exits.

When the disc ended, I was more confused than when it started. These were not love songs. There was a lot of morbidity, death, existentialism. It felt more like a cry for help than a love letter.

Maybe I had misread this whole thing? Maybe Brian didn't really have feelings for me? Maybe I had jumped to the wrong conclusion?

Didn't seem likely.

I wished I knew how to read this kid.

Thursday was Certamen practice. Five days since the CD. Five days of spinning out the worst possible scenarios. Before practice started, though, everything seemed normal. Brian was reading with headphones on. Katie was studying her authors. Jeff was taking notes for another class. AP US History. I remembered the textbook well. That was my least favorite year of Social Studies until I got to Economics this year. Had the gods ever created anything as hideously boring as Economics?

And Spencer was talking my ear off. At least he was starting to move on from Danny. Though I couldn't say I loved his new conversational track.

"How's the college planning going?" he asked me after he had run out of dirt to report on people I knew.

"It's, y'know," I mumbled, "Going."

"Still thinking UTSA?"

"Yeah," I replied. Then, because I knew I was

supposed to: "How about you?"

"I'm waiting to hear from UCLA and George Washington University," he said casually, swirling the mostly empty Red Bull can in his hand. "Those are my two favorites, fabulous atmospheres with good PolySci programs but still enough of the Arts that I can indulge myself. And UT, of course. I haven't heard from them, but it'd be weird if I didn't get in."

I sighed, unnoticed by Spencer. The University of Texas at Austin was his safety school. My grades were so far off from their acceptance points that it would be a waste of energy for me to apply. And Spencer was a shoe-in.

I was happy for him, with his dreams of Los Angeles and Washington DC, but it also made me feel like an idiot. Like a waste of life. I never used to care about grades before this. Neither did Spencer, actually, which made his astonishing academic record that much more irritating.

Spencer became distracted by something on his phone, and I didn't try to reclaim his attention.

"What's the music today?" Mr. Stanton asked Brian. I noticed Allie hovering just behind his shoulder.

"The new Nick Cave," Brian responded, moving aside one headphone.

"I haven't heard that yet. Any good?"

"Only if you like having your heart destroyed. In a good way."

I recognized the name this time. I was doodling absentmindedly in my notebook. There were the usual mythological references, Poseidon and a bunch of dryads, but as I considered Brian some punk rock themes were taking root as well. I worked in an impression of what I thought Nick Cave must look like: a brooding caveman with a cruel expression. Maybe the worst of what I was imagining Brian might be?

I was oddly relieved that there were so many people around. I could pretend that that was why I wasn't talking to Brian. Instead of the truth, which was that I was a coward.

Practice started. We did a post mortem on our performance at the invitational meet. We planned how we would do better at Area. Jeff was way too intense on that point. I wanted to go to State and all, but he was determined to get there if it killed us all.

We did some practice questions. Spencer outbuzzed me on some Literary Devices, because I was distracted. I barely even got my Mythology questions.

Mr. Stanton said something blandly encouraging. We packed up. Katie took off with Allie as usual. Spencer ran away to be late to his *Annie* rehearsal. Jeff left to do more homework. Mr. Stanton went to wash his mug.

It was just Brian and me. I had no excuse left.

"Brian," I said.

"Yeah?" he said like nothing was up.

"That mix," I started.

"Did you like it?" he asked with a smile. It threw me off.

"I," I froze a moment, then I clenched my resolve and barreled forward. "Am I wrong, or did you do that because you like me?"

"Yeah," he said, a little sheepishly. How old was this

kid?

"It's sweet of you," I said, "But I'm not interested."

"That's okay," he said immediately. "I didn't make you uncomfortable, did I?"

That threw me too. "Uh, no," I said. "Well, yes, actually." He had turned me into a bumbling idiot.

"I didn't want to make you uncomfortable," he said simply. "That's why I waited for you to bring it up, instead of asking you about it."

I nodded. "Well, thank you for that."

Brian threw his backpack over his shoulder. This kid had never shown the slightest sign of liking anybody. Was I the first girl he had ever flirted with? I wouldn't doubt it.

I had to say something else. Not like it was my job or anything, but I guess I didn't want him to retreat back inside himself.

"It's just," I said. "I'm crushing on this one girl I know from Tumblr."

"Is that right?" he said.

"She lives in Dallas," I told him. "She'll be at State."

"There's some more incentive to make it to State."

I laughed. "So," I said awkwardly. "I thought you were aro?"

"No," he said. "I didn't actually know what it meant when you said it."

"And that's what made you want to ask me out?"

"Yeah," he said.

"Was it just to prove it to me?"

"Oh no, no," Brian looked flustered. (Brian, the flattest, most expressionless person I had ever met, was flustered.) "You made me wonder. About how people even start relationships. And I realized, if I didn't try to start one, I'd never have one. So I was trying to think of who I even like, and you happened to be the one I decided I did."

"You decided."

He nodded. "Did I do alright?"

"You mean, with liking me?" He nodded. I shrugged. "It was... okay. But not really how you should go about it. It's like, you threw something at my window from the street, instead of starting a conversation."

"What do you mean?"

He wasn't being mean or anything. He was curious, like a kid or a puppy.

Mr. Stanton came back in. He nodded to acknowledge us and went to his computer.

I couldn't unpack all this with Brian. Not standing in the Latin classroom after Certamen practice.

"I've got to go," I told him. "I'll talk to you later."

"I made you uncomfortable again," Brian said sadly, "I'm sorry."

"You're fine," I told him on my way out. "I'll talk to you later, okay?"

And I was out the door, tail between my legs.

***

I was going to get caught up on Econ, maybe pull a low B for that progress report. But Brian was too present on my mind when I got into my room after school. I pulled up Tumblr on my laptop and found PuellaStellarum already online. The fellow Latin kid from Dallas. My crush. I started a chat.

74

Hey beautiful, she replied, and I blushed. We had reblogged each other's Classical content a few times, but it was a selfie of mine that had made her finally contact me personally.

Pitter patter went my heart.

I broke down the Brian situation for her. She was sympathetic.

I feel this, like, obligation to help him, I wound up. *But is that some weird cultural-expectation head-zap? Is that problematic? Am I supposed to be this savior figure that takes him under my wing? Why should I owe him that?*

I guess it depends on WHY you feel you should do it, PuellaStellarum typed back. *Is it because you feel bad about turning him down and want to make it up to him? Or is it because you actually want to be his friend?*

I hovered over the keys for a moment. It was a good question. This girl.

I think more the latter. I don't know him too well, but today he was good. He was a good person trying to do his best and not knowing how. It made me think I'd like to know him better.

There you have it, then, she said. *Help him. Not because you have to, because you want to.*

It'll probably be better for the world, too. If I don't give him advice, someone else will. And who knows what kind of jacked-up crap they might tell him.

PuellaStellarum and I spent another hour or so plotting the future and shooting the breeze before dinner. I still didn't know her real name yet. We were saving our real names until we met in person for the first time at State.

Her handle, incidentally, meant "Girl of the Stars."

Accurate, as far as I could tell from her selfies.

At dinner that night, my mom asked a million things about my grades and scholarships. I told her some plausible-sounding fictions. Not lies, exactly, just my most optimistic intentions for the future.

Not for that night, though. A new sketch of Perseus with the severed head of Medusa took a lot of my attention, and a text chat with Spencer took the rest. I had plenty of future left.

CHAPTER 6: FEBRUARY 2ND   SPENCER OLSON

I am not getting over Danny.

I am pretending, for the sake of the people around me.

I'm calling it a fast. At first I was trying to abstain from thinking about Danny, but that was doomed from the start. So now it's a fast from talking about Danny to anybody else.

It's nice. At least, I think it's nice for them. It's really terrible for me.

Now I'm telling Cass all about what's going on in Theatre before Certamen practice. Drama drama, if you will. It's about to blow up again during rehearsal today. I just hope I don't miss the good parts.

The it-couple of Theatre, two talented seniors named Stephanie and Cameron, are on the rocks. Last night Stephanie found pictures of a certain nature (wink, nudge) from another girl on Cameron's phone. They spent all of Theatre class on opposite ends of the room. All their best friends have picked sides.

But they won't be able to stay separate at rehearsal.

Stephanie is Annie and Cameron is Daddy Warbucks.

Which, don't get me wrong, was gross to begin with. But now it's going to be nuclear.

Cass seems distracted. I mean, she's never been as into gossip as I am, but this is pretty primo stuff.

I'm talking a mile a minute but my thoughts keep drifting back to Danny.

I think I actually might be talking with neither of us listening to me. I should get some kind of achievement award.

Soon a notification from Instagram leads me back down into Danny's world. Looking in from the outside.

The thing is, Danny broke up with me because I was "too dependent." I was clingy. I only cared about him, and he wants someone with a life outside the relationship. He doesn't want to be someone's entire world. So at first, I was self-consciously posting lots of pictures of myself with my other friends, so he would see that I do have a life outside him. Now I'm trying to really live that reality. It's not enough to *look* like I have a life, I have to actually *have* one.

The fringe benefit of this plan is, when I'm out hanging out with other people, I think less. Which means I think less about Danny. Which means I'm less depressed. Which means I'll be in better mental shape when he finally takes me back.

When practice starts, Cass is definitely distracted. She barely reacts when I outbuzz her on the Chiasmus question. She doesn't even care when I get the Simile. The Simile! The easiest one!

Maybe it's the invitational meet getting to her? It

wasn't an encouraging start, and she really does want to make State this year. If that's the problem, she's having the exact opposite reaction from Jeff. He's taken his usual intensity to newer, scarier heights. He's leaning over his buzzer as if his facial proximity to Mr. Stanton will grant him an advantage. I guess because of the speed of sound. He's pounding the desk when he gets answers wrong. From my slightly recessed position as alternate, I can see him sneaking Aspirins when no one is looking. Dude's so stressed he'll pop a blood vessel.

I do know how they feel though. If I were properly on Certamen, I'd want to make State just as badly.

I mean, we will all make State individually. Even if we didn't, we'd all go anyway. Certamen is the only event at State with a real bar of entry. When it comes to the individual tests, as far as the Junior Classical League is concerned, anybody who registers for State can compete. But the school district pays for your trip if you make it in the top five at JCL Area. If you don't, you pay for your own trip. Worth it for the experience, but if you're not top five in Area, you don't have much of a chance at an award at State.

We're all consistently top five in our categories at Area, so we'll all get that free ride. Individual prizes are a lot easier to win than Certamen, since there are five places up for grabs instead of just one spot. Sometimes we even scrape some individual prizes at State.

But to get up on the stage at State Certamen finals. That's the dream.

The dream. There I am, on the big stage at State. Brian

has had some sort of dire emergency. Intestinal distress, death of a family member—well, let's not get into that, because it spoils the fantasy. Just the important thing: he's not there, and I'm the History player. It all comes down to the last question. The score is tied. It's an easy History one, something about Nero. I clean it up, and the two bonuses. We're first place in State, making Club history. The team is mobbing me in a group hug. Hoisting me on their backs. Cass hugs me. I guess I'm not on their backs anymore. Brian is flabbergasted. Or wait, I guess he's not there. But he will be flabbergasted, when he finds out. It'll wipe that smug smile right off his face. (He doesn't really have a smug smile, more of a mouth-breather-neutral expression most of the time, but it works in my fantasy.)

Finally, through the crowd, here comes Danny. He's as beautiful as he was on our first date, wearing my favorite jeans. He's rushing toward me. He's so overcome with emotion, we kiss before I even know what's happening. But then he is so soft, he tastes so sweet. We're the only ones in the room.

As I said. I can't stop myself from thinking about him.

It's a pretty bad Certamen practice. No one is really on their game. But I've got no time to sit around and discuss it. As soon as we finish our question set, I'm off to *Annie*. Jeff is out the door right beside me.

"What are you hurrying for?" I ask as we powerwalk together down the hallway.

"Wetlands restoration project," he answers.

"For your résumé?" I tease.

"Of course."

"What do you ever do for fun?" I ask.

"This is going to be fun," he bristles.

"I mean, *just* for fun," I say.

"Time with Mackenzie," he answers, with a soft note in his voice.

"Oh, barf," I say. "I'm sorry I asked."

"I've got half an hour on the phone with her tonight."

I raise an eyebrow. "She's on your schedule?"

"Everything is," he says with a shrug. "It has to be, if I want to fit everything in."

"Does Mackenzie have to call your secretary to get scheduled in?"

"Ha ha," he says in a mocking tone. "I *wish* I had a secretary."

"You saying that makes my skin crawl. It sounds too much like you mean it."

"I've only got one shot at high school," Jeff says, his path toward the parking lot starting to diverge away from mine toward the auditorium. "I've got to make it perfect if I want a perfect future."

I shake my head. "Go fix your perfect wetlands," I tell him. "Schedule in an extra minute to stop and smell a single rose, would you?"

Practice is in full swing when I step into the auditorium.

"Spencer!" Mrs. Chernov whirls around in her third-row seat, the only person in the audience other than a techie in the seat next to her. "Where have you been?"

"Latin Club?" I say hesitantly.

"We open in a week!" she yells. Rehearsal has stopped

dead.

"I'm the President," I say, trying to keep my voice respectful. "When I asked you earlier, you said you didn't need Rooster until halfway through practice anyway."

She glares at me a second longer, then turns back around. "I guess we didn't, did we? Go get your voice warmed up in the hall," she says, not facing me, "We'll need you soon."

I duck back into the hallway. I'm glad for the out, because I was about to lose it at her. What does she want to call me out in front of the entire cast for?

Rounding a corner, I see Daddy Warbucks making out with his secretary. Cameron does move along quickly. Danny flashes back into my mind. I go further down the hall until they're out of sight. I don't actually warm up.

I usually love to ham it up as Rooster. I'm not feeling very funny today.

After practice, I convince a couple people to go get shakes at Jack in the Box with me. I knew Stephanie could be convinced, what with all the Cameron drama. It's a pretty lively crowd, and we have a good time. It's almost eleven by the time I'm meandering home.

It's when I pull into my driveway that the feeling settles in again.

Even when I'm surrounded by other people, I feel so alone.

I won't sleep if I'm thinking like this. Maybe a movie will do the trick. At least it will while away the hours until morning.

CHAPTER 7: FEBRUARY 2ND   JEFF MILLER

I get home just before sunset, in a pink haze. As soon as I'm parked in the driveway I pull my mud-soaked work boots out of the trunk. On the back patio I hit them with the hose and leave them to drip dry. The light doesn't fail me as I'm doing this, which is all I had hoped for.

Once inside, I see a pile of disorganized mail on the kitchen table. I sort through, recycle the junk, and tuck the bills in my back pocket.

I stop by my father's study. He is hidden up to his eyes in stacks of medical books.

"Any new grades today?" he asks me in a cursory fashion.

"A couple of daily grade 100's and a 94 on a test in Physics," I answer readily, having anticipated his usual question.

"A 94?"

"They're hard tests, sir," I explain. "The teacher lets us make up the credit with extra practice, so I'll be doing that as soon as she lets us next week."

"Good, good." And his attention is off me again.

I move to the kitchen. I pull out a packet of instant oatmeal. In the few seconds the water takes in the microwave, I open the bills and lay them on the table. I pour in the oatmeal, stir, and open the online banking app on my phone. Log in with my dad's credentials.

Electricity has to be paid on time because they shut us off right away—on the app I set the payment to send two days before the due date. Internet gives a grace period, so I set it to pay next month. The water people don't even seem to notice if you don't pay for a while, so I ignore that one. No gas bill yet this month.

I have to keep track of these things. When Dad was in charge, he would put the bills in a stack to deal with later, and we'd end up getting our power shut off. Mom took care of the money before.

Dad doesn't seem to realize how little money we have. How far we fell back when he stopped practicing to take that professorship. I don't think he even knows that I canceled the cable and the Netflix. The TV in the living room hasn't been on in months anyway.

Maybe I should get a job. I've been thinking about that a lot. Jobs look okay on résumés. Just not as good as the volunteer stuff I do now. What I'd give up wouldn't be worth the extra money. We get by. Almost. I know I'll get scholarships, anyway.

I check the oatmeal. Perfect temperature now. Warm, but not too hot to eat, even if you forget to blow on it.

I recycle the bills on my way to the stairs. A moment later I'm gingerly opening the door to my grandma's room.

"Grandma?" I say quietly.

She's sitting upright and awake with her lamp on, watching the local news on the little antenna TV by the foot of her bed. I come inside even though she doesn't acknowledge me.

"Grandma," I say again, muting the TV, "I've got oatmeal for you."

"Grandma?" she laughs, looking at me for the first time. "I can't be your grandmother, I'm only twenty-two."

"I am your grandson, Jeff," I tell her. I offer her a spoonful of oatmeal. She doesn't fight me this time, just takes the bite.

"Have you seen my sister?" she asks me after she swallows.

"Not lately," I tell her, giving her another bite. Her sister died a decade before I was born.

My dad practically never comes up here. He's so busy. Being a professor instead of a doctor was supposed to free up his schedule, but I don't think he knows how to stop working so much. So I make sure there's time in my schedule to sit with Grandma every morning before school and every night before she goes to sleep. Tonight I read to her from the newspaper. I try to read from current affairs, but she can't keep up, so I revert to her favorite section: the obituaries.

Fed and happy, she falls asleep while I'm reading. I gather up the empty cans from the meal-replacement shakes that provide her nutrients during the day. I switch off her lamp and TV for her.

Back in the hallway, I see I've got a text from Mom.

To my traditional question asked just before I left the wetlands, *Skype call tonight?* she has given her traditional response: *Sorry kiddo, duty calls.*

I close myself in my room, and pull the Aspirin bottle out of my bag. I have at least four hours of homework tonight, so I'll need a little artificial motivation. I slide out one of the not-Aspirins into my hand.

Mackenzie hated me taking Adderall, so I stopped telling her.

They're only helping me reach my potential. I need every advantage I can get.

I can feel my heartrate accelerating as I sit on my bed for my half hour call with Mackenzie. Grandma fell asleep a little early, so I'll be able to call eight minutes ahead of schedule. After that, it will be time to get serious about that homework. I've wasted enough time tonight.

CHAPTER 8: EARLY FEBRUARY   BRIAN GANZ

Cass posted a song from my mix to her Tumblr. "Adore" by Savages. I'm glad she liked that one. I was thinking of using "Sad Person," which rocks a little harder, but I thought its best line ("I'm not gonna hurt you/'cause I'm flirting with you") hit a little too close to home.

A few days later, I get a text message on my phone. No one really texts me except Nora and my mom. I don't recognize[13] the number.

Hey Brian, I've got an idea, it says.

Who's this? I type back.

Sorry, the number says. *It's Cass. I got your number from Spencer.*

Spencer has my number?

I'm assuming, since I'm talking to you now.

Oh, no, I type. *This is José.*

Real funny Brian. You want to hear my idea or not?

Of course.

---

[13] From the Latin verb *cognoscere*, "to get to know" or "to recognize," with the prefix *re-*, "again." Making "recognize" a redundant verb: to re-recognize.

How does this sound? And she sends me a paragraph that, based on how quickly it comes, she must have typed beforehand and copied over:

Calling all history nerd followers! it says. *A friend of mine is learning to flirt with girls. He is straight, cis, 17, and really into Punk Music and History of all kinds. He is pretty cute, and a gentleman. If any of my mutuals would like to chat with him, PM me. Please, only kind and patient souls willing to help someone new at this. Do not reblog.*

I'm still 16, I say, a little flush from the "pretty cute" line. Then, *You want to post this on your Tumblr?*

I learned to flirt online, she explains. *All my first crushes were over Tumblr or FanFiction.net. You need experience, and this is a way to get it.*

Seems really sketchy, I reply. *Tumblr is full of weirdos.*

Weirdos like you.

Fair point, I say.

But that's why I want it to be my mutuals,[14] she explains, *So I know them, and know they're not terrible.*[15] *To make it as safe as possible.*

Isn't meeting up with people you met online really risky?

I don't mean you'd meet them irl, she explains. *You just practice online. They're like computer flight simulators for flirting.*

I don't know, I type.

Up to you, man, she replies. *I've been thinking I want to help you, and I'm no master matchmaker, so this is what I've come up*

---

[14] Ultimately related to the verb *mutare*, "to change." "Mutuals" is Tumblrspeak for people who follow you and you follow them back. Mutual subscribers.

[15] From the verb root *terrere*, "to scare." As in, "Meeting random Tumblr people scares the hell out of me."

with.

You don't owe me anything, I tell her. *You don't need to feel bad for me just because you don't like me like that.*

You're right, I don't owe you anything, she says. *I want to help you because I want to be your friend.*

I stare at her words on my phone screen.

Okay, I say. *Post it.*

I tell Nora that night while we're playing *Overwatch* online. She thinks I'm crazy. But, Nora pretty generally thinks I'm crazy.

I don't know, myself. Maybe this will help.

At the very least, Cass added me in to the Certamen group chat once she had my number. That's progress.[16]

Cass gets three bites pretty quickly and sets up my first chat for the next night. She gives me a pseudonym.[17] She lets me know when she sends the target my Tumblr username, and I sit tensed[18] over my keyboard for a moment trying to relax.

Hi Marcus, comes a PM from LetThemEatTruffles.

Hi, I say. *What's your name?*

Emily, she says. *I'm from Tennessee.*

Texas, I reply.

I compliment her on the Marie Antoinette twist in her username. She likes French Revolution history, and we talk a bit about Robespierre and Jean-Paul Marat. She asks me about my favorite eras, and she knows a little about the

---

[16] Latin: *pro-* means "forward" and *gressus* is a step. A baby step. That's all.

[17] That's a Greek one: *pseudes* meaning "false" and *onyma* meaning "name."

[18] From the Latin verb *tendere*, "to stretch," as in my muscles are all stretched tight. As in, when I'm tense, I think even more about word roots.

Byzantine army too, so we geek out about that for a while.

BlackAthena17 also mentioned that you like punk, she changes the subject. *What kind?*

I listen to a lot, I say. *My favorite is the post-hardcore boom of the 80's, the bridge between Black Flag and Nirvana. Minutemen, Meat Puppets, Replacements, Hüsker Dü, that sort of thing.*

Lol, the only band I knew in that list was Nirvana, she replies. *I'll have to check that out. I like Blink-182.*

Mm, too pop for me, but to each his/her own.

Pop? she types. *How are they pop?*

Catchy hooks and melodies, I explain.

I just don't think pop when I hear them. They're not Katy Perry.

I don't mean it in a negative way, I backtrack, feeling like I might have offended her. *I'm not just making this up, their subgenre is called pop punk.[19] Like Green Day or Good Charlotte.*

I like Green Day. What's wrong with Green Day?

Nothing, I say. *They're one of the greatest bands in pop punk. I just don't like pop punk much.*

Let's change the subject, she says abruptly.

But the conversation doesn't really get going again from there, and she signs off with a *goodnight.*

I promised I'd message Cass, so I do.

How did it go? she asks.

Not great, I admit.

I didn't think the first one would, she says.

You're like a swim coach throwing me into the deep end?

---

[19] The word "pop" when used for music is a shortening of "popular," from the Latin *populus*, "people." I can see where the offense comes from, I guess, since the punk ethos (Greek loan word) is all about being *un*popular. But the Beatles were pop, for Christ's sake...

I could have thrown you a lot deeper, she replies. I wonder what types of people qualify as her deep end. *Where do you think you went wrong?*

We were good at talking about history. But it went wrong when we talked about music.

Did you go all professor-mode on her?

I talked like I do about history, I say.

That's a yes, then. She got out of her depth?

I think she thinks I insulted her taste.

That's easy to do if you come off like a know-it-all, she replies.

Now I'm the one getting insulted.

Learning to talk to girls is not for the faint of heart, she admonishes me. *You have to learn from your mistakes.*

Okay. Can I be done learning for the night?

You're done when you say you are, she says.

Good. Going to listen to music and read about dead people.

Dead people don't care if you like their taste in music or not, Cass replies. *See you at school.*

***

"It's hard," I explain to Nora over our headphones and mics during a *Gears of War* game a few days later, after my third conversation with one of Cass's Tumblr girls.

"I don't know how real it is," Nora responds. "These manufactured[20] conversations with girls you'll never meet. On your left, your left!"

"No, they're definitely helping," I protest. "I've been able to figure out what turns people off from me."

"Then I switch my objection," Nora says. "I feel for

---

[20] From Latin, literally "made" (*factus*) with one's "hand" (*manus*).

91

these girls. You can't keep torturing them with your repellent personality. Like lab rats being subjected to radiation."

"Are you being tortured[21] right now?"

"By your ineptitude in dispatching these creatures, absolutely. By your personality, not so much. I'm immune through long-term exposure."

***

Before our Certamen practice the next week, Cass takes the seat directly next to mine. Jeff is there too, studying, and Allie is drawing some ridiculous stick figure mural on Mr. Stanton's board. I'm in position with book and headphones, but I reluctantly take the headphones off when Cass keeps looking at me.

"Want to tease me about how I'm doing with your Tumblr friends?" I ask.

She looks taken aback. "No, I was going to begin a light conversation because we're being friends now."

"Oh," I say. "Sorry."

"That's okay, you're still learning," she grins. "How have you been?"

I shrug. "It's weird. Putting myself out there."

"It gets easier," Cass tells me.

"Does it?"

"I assume," she laughs. "I've always been pretty social, so it wasn't that hard for me in the first place."

"Were you one of those horrible people who was popular in middle school?" I ask with a shudder.[22]

---

[21] From the Latin *torquere*, "to twist." I'll let you provide your own mental images.

"What? Hell no. We went to the same middle school, you don't remember?"

I shrug.

"Of course he doesn't," says a voice across the room. Cass turns.

"Spencer!" she says. "When did you get here?"

"I've been here," he shrugs. He's slouching so far in his chair that his Starbuck's can almost obscures his face. "I didn't want to interrupt your private conversation, lovebirds."

"It's not like that," I explain quickly, while Cass makes a face.

Spencer turns his body toward us in his chair and doubles over, pantomiming laughter. "I was *kidding*, but I see I touched a nerve. Good to know."

"Come over here, you dingus," Cass spits at him.

"What *is* going on here, anyway?" Spencer asks as he approaches. Tink, says his can as he puts it on the desk.

"I'm teaching Brian how to talk to people," Cass explains, "With the eventual aim of finding him a girlfriend."

"Aww," Spencer says, "You're *She's All That*-ing him?"

"I prefer *My Fair Lady*," Cass said quickly.

"*My Fair Lady*," interjected Mr. Stanton from behind his computer, "is based on a George Bernard Shaw play called *Pygmalion*. Name the mythological reference."

"Pygmalion and Galatea," Cass says without a moment's hesitation.[23] "Sculptor sculpts the perfect woman

---

[22] See, that's an etymology joke: *horrere*, the Latin root of "horrible," means "to shudder."

93

out of marble, falls in love with her, and prays to Aphrodite to make her real. Parallel to Professor Higgins creating a society girl out of Eliza Doolittle and falling in love with his own creation."

Spencer guffaws loudly looking directly at Cass. Her eyes narrow.

"Could everyone in this room please stop shipping me and Brian? We don't like each other like that."

"Mr. Stanton, do you just listen in on everyone's conversations?" adds Spencer.

Magister Stanton throws his hands in the air. "People sit in my classroom talking loudly, and get offended when I hear them. I have ears, you know."

"Mr. Stanton has ass's ears," Cass says.

Magister and I both laugh.

"I don't get that one," Spencer says.

"King Midas," Cass begins.

"He pissed off Apollo," I continue, "So Apollo gave him the ears of a donkey. He covered it with a hat, so only his barber knew."

"The barber can't live with the secret," Cass picks back up, "So he goes into the reeds by the river, digs a hole, whispers 'King Midas has ass's ears' into it, and buries the words."

"And then?" Mr. Stanton asks with a teacherly arch to his eyebrow.

"When the wind rushes through the reeds, they repeat the secret," she concludes.

---

[23] From a Latin verb *haesitare* that, itself, comes from *haerere*, "to stick or cling." Like you're metaphorically stuck and can't make a decision.

"Good," Magister says.

"Brian, I didn't know you knew any Mythology," Cass says.

I shrug. "I've picked some up."

"I thought Midas was the golden touch guy?" says Katie, who has just stepped into the room.

"Same guy, different story." Cass says.

"Guy had a busy life," I joke.

"How do you guys remember all this stuff?" Katie asks with a frustrated sigh, throwing herself into a desk. She pulls her laptop back up, obviously about to start her trusty Roman Authors Quizlet set again.

"I just like stories," Cass explains, "The weirder the better."

"Me too," I say. "But I also use a mind palace."

They all look at me for a moment, puzzled expressions on their faces.

"Like from *Sherlock*?" Cass asks. I'm not surprised by the reference. I know from her Tumblr that she devours[24] every show put out by the BBC.

"Yeah," I confirm. "It's a real thing. It's, like, a place in my head. Every time I learn something, I put it in a certain spot, with a tag on it so I can find it again."

They look at me again. Jeff puts down his book and turns around. Allie stops drawing.

"What the hell are you talking about?" Spencer asks.

"Okay," I say. It's not something I'm used to putting into words. "Katie, can I see your Authors?"

---

[24] The Latin verb *vorare*, "to swallow," gives us "devour," as well as "voracious" and "carnivore."

She hands me her laptop.

"My mind palace," I tell them, "Actually looks like my first house, the one I moved away from in sixth grade. It's the easiest place for me to picture, the first place my mind goes. You have to know every inch of your mind palace. So, let's see," I look at the first random card to pop up on Katie's Authors Quizlet. "Vergil.[25] I know who he is, he wrote the Aeneid. In my mind palace, he's down in the basement—part of the foundation of Rome—and he's wearing a beekeeper's suit and holding a pitchfork, because of his farming poems."

"And the dude loved bees," says Cass.

"Right," I say. "He's part of a group of poets surrounding the emperor Augustus, but Vergil is the tallest. He doesn't look happy either, because Augustus made him stop writing what he wanted and devote the rest of his life to the Aeneid. Those are all the tags that help me remember him."

I go forward by one virtual card in Katie's Quizlet.

"Here's one I don't know. Apuleius." I click to flip the card to the description. "He wrote novels, so I'll walk up the basement steps and put him in front of the third shelf in my dad's study. That's where he kept all his Stephen King and John Grisham. Apuleius was accused of practicing black magic, so I'll give him a big pointy hat. And an iPhone—the Romans would have thought that was magic—with a bunch of apps. So I can remember his

---

[25] His name is most often spelled "Virgil" in the larger world, but both spellings are correct. Latinists have a slight leaning toward the "Vergil" spelling because his name in Latin is *Vergilius*.

name, APPuleius."

"That's heinous," Spencer says of my pun, but with a smile of approval.

"Tags don't have to be good to work," I say. "Sometimes dumb things help you remember even better." I go back to the description on the screen. "His most famous novel is the *Golden Ass*, so he'll be sitting on a donkey."

"This is seriously how you remember things?" Cass asks, a blank expression on her face. Like it sounds like the stupidest thing she's ever heard.

"It's all more automatic[26] than I can describe," I explain. "I've been doing it forever. I read an article on it online two years ago, and figured out that what they were describing was a lot like what I had always done anyway. But now I do it deliberately, and it helps. You get good at it. Marcus Aurelius is in that study too, in my mind palace, writing his philosophies on a golden chair,[27] while his terrible son Commodus is sneaking out of the window and into a toilet."[28]

"Where's Cicero?" asks Mr. Stanton.

"Out on the porch, asking everyone who passes what they think about him," I say immediately. Magister and Katie laugh.

---

[26] Greek, *autos* meaning "self" and *matos* meaning "think." All the word-dissecting I do, by the way, is automatic too. It thinks for itself.

[27] Greek, *philo-* is "love" and *sophia* is "knowledge." Marcus Aurelius had a strong love for knowledge. For Greek, too, as a matter of fact. And his name, "Aurelius," derives from *aurum*, "gold."

[28] Commodus's name in Latin actually means "suitable," but the pun with "commode" is too good to pass up.

Katie takes back her laptop and begins to page through her Quizlet cards, mouthing silently to herself. Cass, Jeff, and Spencer all consider me for a moment, then take out study materials as well and begin to pore over them. Silence takes the room. I watch them for a moment, but none of them are looking at me. They're in their mind palaces.

I take up my book and headphones and go to my own.

Before I go under, I notice Mr. Stanton looking amused.

Almost an hour later I notice that people are talking, and I take my headphones off.

"I can't believe how well this is working," Katie says, paging through her Quizlet cards. "I've been trying to get these down for months, and now it's happening so fast."

"My mind palace is a temple on the top of a mountain in India," Cass says.

"Have you been to India?" asks Allie.

"No," Cass replies, "But I can picture it perfectly."

"Mine is a well-organized file cabinet," Jeff says.

"We didn't get to any practice questions," I say sheepishly.

"Oh, that's quite alright," Mr. Stanton assures me. "I'm going to consider this a successful practice. Brian, can you come talk to the lower levels next week?"

CHAPTER 9: FEBRUARY 7TH-8TH   KATIE NGUYEN

I got up early to wash my hair and spend some time in my new mind palace.

Mine was the library in my neighborhood. I kept most of the Roman authors in the stacks, but other places too. Martial was in the bathroom. Petronius was perusing the vending machine. Seneca was manning the circulation desk.

I saw the whole thing from a height of about four feet. The library had been my favorite place when I was a kid, so that's how I remember it best. All the librarians used to know me back then. It was walking distance from the apartment we used to live in before we got our house, so I would go every Saturday during the school year, and almost every day over the summer. I still went from time to time, but usually for business rather than pleasure. Nowadays I had to research science fair projects and historical biographies, not look for more chapter books with happy endings.

I tried putting a padlock on the door of my mind palace, but *he* kept getting in.

In the car on my way to school, I tried Chopin. It didn't do it for me. I tried Tchaikovsky. Nothing. I sighed. There he was again. I put on Thelonious Monk. That was the stuff.

Why could I not get this Our Lady of the Seven Sorrows guy out of my mind?

The previous week in jazz band, I had asked the director to let me improvise a solo during a run of "Sweet and Lovely." He was pleasantly surprised. There were a couple of students who were really good improvisers, and he had been trying to get me to try it ever since I had joined. But I just couldn't feel it. I had no idea what I wanted to play. That had changed. He pointed to me, and I threw down a few sweeping bars. I started by comping some strange seventh chords, just to hear where I was going. Then I plucked out a melody from them, throwing in a few looping clusters of chromatic notes outside the key, just like Thelonious Monk would have done. I could hear what I wanted to play now. It wasn't perfect that first time, but I enjoyed it. The guitar player even complimented me as we were packing up. I liked to think that Monk himself would have liked it.

Because I still didn't know his name, I was thinking of the Our Lady of the Seven Sorrows guy as "Monk." I liked that it worked two ways: he loved Thelonious Monk, and he went to a Catholic school.

I couldn't help myself. I had tried to find Monk. The best I could think of was to go to the Our Lady of the Seven Sorrows website, a hideous atrocity from a bygone era of web design. Of course they didn't just have pictures of all their students on their website, but they had a few images: team captains and club presidents and such. I scrutinized every page, but I couldn't find Monk's feathery hair and crooked smirk anywhere. I did the same with the school's Facebook page, even though I didn't have an account myself. None of the profile pictures looked like him. Of course there were lots of profile pictures that were dogs and memes and inanimate objects, and it just burned me up that Monk might be hiding in plain sight behind one of them. As a last gamble, I combed through the notes on Cass's Tumblr posts, since I knew he had seen those. This proved to be equally impenetrable. Social media was no help in finding my crush.

My crush that I didn't dare tell another soul about. What was I *thinking*? He went to *Our Lady of the Seven Sorrows*. He was on their *Certamen* team. He was our *rival*. He was *The Enemy*. I couldn't tell a single Latin kid. Even though, if he was a senior (I didn't even know that!), then Cass or Spencer had a better chance of knowing his name than anybody else. They might have been competing against him for years.

Once, sitting next to them in Certamen practice, I almost broke down and asked. I talked myself out of it. The chances of them knowing were so slim, and the risk so great. I couldn't even decide which of them would be the less dangerous option. Cass hated Our Lady of the Seven Sorrows with such vitriol, but Spencer was the biggest gossip I knew.

Lost in these thoughts, I pulled into the parking lot at school. I shut them off with the car and the music. Latin was my first period, and I swore that I would not blaspheme our sanctuary with unholy thoughts about Our Lady of the Seven Sorrows and its delightful Monk.

When I came down the hallway toward Mr. Stanton's room, I noticed a crowd at a closed door. I could make out Brian in it, so I knew it was our Latin 3 class. That was odd. There were teachers who were habitual latecomers, so you'd often see crowds of students in front of their locked doors. But it never happened at Magister Stanton's room.

When I got closer, I could see through the window in the classroom door that the light was on. Stranger still.

"He's in there talking to someone," Christine, a girl from our class, explained. "It looks serious. None of us wanted to interrupt."

Everyone was murmuring among themselves, wondering what was going on. The bell rang to start first period. A few seconds later, the door opened a crack.

"Jeff?" Mr. Stanton said softly. Jeff pushed his way through the crowd.

"I need to take care of something," I could hear Mr. Stanton tell him softly. "Could you pick some words from yesterday's reading and lead the class through parsing them?"

"Of course," Jeff said.

"Thank you Jeff," Mr. Stanton whispered. "Just a moment."

The door clicked shut, and a moment later opened again.

Allie stepped out. She was draped in Mr. Stanton's tweed blazer, which went down past her knees, and seemed to be in her pajamas underneath. Mr. Stanton walked a step behind her.

"Make a path, please," he said to the group. We did. Mr. Stanton and Allie made their way through the crowd. Allie avoided eye contact with any of us, staring only at her feet, which were in flip flops.

We all walked tentatively into the room and took our seats, buzzing about what we had seen. Mr. Stanton's cup of chai tea was on his desk undrunk. Jeff set his textbook awkwardly on Magister's podium.

"Okay guys," he said. "Whatever that was, it's none of our business, so we're gonna try some parsing."

He started with a deponent verb, then an objective genitive. It was rough.

"Maybe do some simpler stuff, for those of us who aren't you?" Brian suggested.

Mr. Stanton walked briskly back into the classroom, his tweed coat back on his shoulders.

"Thank you, Jeff," he said perfunctorily, and went straight to his tea. The class began to pepper him with questions about Allie.

"Folks, I really can't talk about it," he said. "If you could all turn to page 129, please..."

***

I was so busy thinking about Allie, I almost forgot to think about Monk all day. Almost. Jazz band was fourth period, and even though my solo was less than inspired that day, soloing at all conjured his image on top of my piano keys.

Between fourth and fifth periods, I finally spotted Allie again down a hallway. She was wearing a borrowed bright orange jacket, zipped up to the neck, and what looked like school-issue gym shorts. She saw me too, and started directly toward me. I met her halfway.

"Katie," she said loudly, then brought her voice to almost a whisper. "I need to talk to you."

She began to eye all the other students passing around us.

"Girls!" We turned and saw Mr. Stanton at his doorway a bit further down the hall. "This is my conference period. Do you need a quiet place?"

Allie nodded vigorously, and we both ducked into his empty room.

"I'm going to go check my mailbox," he said, in order to leave. "If either of you are late to fifth, just tell your teacher to email me, okay?" And he was gone.

"What's going on?" I asked Allie.

She sat down on top of a nearby desk. Her eyes were puffy. She started to talk, and stopped immediately. She was almost crying, but it was like she wouldn't let herself.

I sat down next to her and put an arm around her shoulder. She melted into me a bit, then started to tell me what was going on.

I promised Allie that I would never tell another soul exactly what she told me that day, and I think that includes you. So I'll stay general.

Allie couldn't go home. She had fled around 2 a.m. in her pajamas and walked her neighborhood until her bus had come. She had borrowed the flip flops from someone at the bus stop, because until then she had been walking barefoot. As soon as she reached campus, she had sought out Mr. Stanton. He had delivered her to the counselors, who had let her shower and loaned her clothes.

The late bell rang while she was talking, and we both ignored it.

She didn't tell me why she had wanted to talk to me. I guessed it instead.

"Do you need somewhere to stay?" I asked her.

She nodded, mute.

"*Yes,*" I blurted, "*Absolutely.* I mean, I'll talk to my parents. I know they'll be okay with it tonight, and I'm sure they'll be able to let you stay longer."

"I don't want to be a burden," she started.

"No, no," I said. "You're my friend. I want to help."

She let a few tears go then. I drew her into a hug, and she let herself relax. We stayed sitting in Mr. Stanton's empty room for a while. The rest of fifth period, in fact. I'd never skipped a class before, though I'm not exactly sure that this counts. Anyway, it was Stats, and we never did anything in there.

When the bell rang for lunch, Allie assured me she'd be okay without me. She went back to her counselor to tell her that she had a place to spend the night, and to catch a cat nap on the cot in the office. I hid in a bathroom stall and called my mom.

"No sleepovers on school nights," she said.

"It's not a *sleepover,*" I explained. "She doesn't have anywhere else to go."

"You want to bring some girl home to stay?" she lapsed into Vietnamese. "For how long?"

"I don't know," I answered honestly, still in English.

My mother made some noises into the phone. I was pretty sure it was Vietnamese she had never taught me. She wouldn't tell me the swear words.

"She really needs this?" she asked me.

"She really does."

"She won't judge our filthy house?"

"Mom," I said. "Our house is *immaculate*. You could do *surgery* in it. Assemble *microchips*."

"Not what I asked."

"No, she won't judge," I said, thinking of how the outside of Allie's house always looked when I dropped her off.

"Let me talk to your father," Mom said, "But, if your friend is in trouble, I want to help."

"Thank you so much, Mommy," I said, in Vietnamese specifically to melt her heart.

"I'll text you later," she replied in English.

She texted me the all clear when I was in Calculus. I smiled. The teacher barked at me to put my phone away. I apologized sincerely.

***

Allie was waiting for me at Mr. Stanton's door after school. They were talking in hushed tones. Both waved when they saw me.

"I'm so glad you could help," he told me.

"It's my pleasure," I responded.

"Really," Allie said on the car ride to my house. "Thank you for this."

"I'm happy to do it," I repeated.

My mom made a chicken casserole and a giant tub of

106

mashed potatoes for dinner. A fried eggplant for me, the vegetarian. I could tell she was making a white-person dinner to make Allie feel welcome. I wondered how long Allie would be here before Mom broke back out the pork cơm tấm and crab bánh canh.

My eight-year-old brother Thomas asked Allie ten thousand questions over dinner. Not about why she was there or anything, just general questions about her and her life, the way kids do. My thirteen-year-old sister Nancy was characteristically silent, watching everything, obviously wondering what was up. I wondered how much my parents would tell her. I knew that she would ask them later, instead of me, because she never talked to me anymore. Thirteen-year-old reasons.

That night, we found some of my clothes that would fit Allie for the next day of school. She sighed.

"We'll have to go back so I can grab some stuff soon," she said forlornly.

"What all do you need? Maybe we could just replace it," I suggested.

"I left my inhaler," she said. "I didn't need it today, but I can't cheat fate forever."

"Is there a time we could go when *he* wouldn't be there?"

She shook her head sadly. "He does shift work, so it isn't regular. I never know when he'll be home or not."

"We'll bring my dad," I said firmly. "Someone who could use some muscle if he tries anything."

Allie smiled. "Your dad is the nicest guy though."

"Still," I said. "It'll keep him in check."

***

The next day after school, my dad took off work early to go with us to Allie's house. He drove, because he couldn't stand to be in the car with me behind the wheel. I watched his face grow grim as we parked in front of her house. The lawn was dead in some places and overgrown in others. Two of the windows were gone and covered with cardboard.

"His car isn't here," Allie breathed. "He's probably not home."

"Good," my dad said. "Let's get in and out quick."

As Allie let us in, I felt like we were in a police drama. Moving fast and quiet, sneaking around. My dad decided to wait by the open front door, both to warn us if Allie's stepdad was coming, and to make it clear to him that we weren't burglars. Allie and I powerwalked back to her room, two duffel bags from my house in our arms.

It was terribly drafty with those broken windows. I had to step around trash, laundry, and broken household equipment in the hall. The place smelled awful. There were strange stains on the walls. I tried not to look too hard at anything, because I could feel Allie burning with embarrassment in front of me. She *never* let people into her house. I was determined not to give her any reason to regret it.

In her room, Allie dug hurriedly through her drawers, pulling out clothes and flinging them to me to stuff in the duffel bags. She grabbed her inhaler, her school things, her DS, a necklace that she put gingerly around her neck like it meant something to her.

"I think that's everything," she said.

"You sure?" I asked. I couldn't help but make a mental checklist of everything I'd want to take with me if *I* were fleeing *my* house, possibly for good. It would have been more stuff than this.

"Just need to get my shoes at the door," she said, hurrying back out into the hallway.

While Allie put on her shoes, my dad was staring at the state of the inside of the house. I caught his glance and raised my eyebrows slightly, and he directed his eyes back out at the street.

The inside of the car was silent as we left Allie's neighborhood. After a long, tense ride, we pulled into our garage. My dad shut off the engine.

"Allie?" he said softly. She looked at him.

"Stay for as long as you need, okay?" he said in almost a whisper. He headed for the house, and we followed.

CHAPTER 10: FEBRUARY 11ᵀᴴ   SPENCER OLSON

Lupercalia is my favorite Latin Club party. Most people like Halloween for the costumes, or Saturnalia (pagan Christmas) for the gift exchange. But Lupercalia, aka terrifying pagan Valentine's Day, is special to me.

I'm dressed in period-accurate costume as one of the youths of the Luperci. These beautiful young men (hem hem) would rise early on February 15th, sacrifice a ram at dawn, and make loin cloths for themselves out of its skin. They would make little whips out of the skin too, and run through the streets of Rome, naked except their loin cloths, whipping every living thing—but especially young women—to give them fertility for the coming spring. It is that wonderful bit of Roman culture that I am accurately reenacting tonight.

Okay, so I didn't sacrifice anything this morning. And Cass convinced me to wear a flesh-colored full-body-sock under my loin cloth to protect the poor innocent freshmen. And my whipping strap is harmless soft fabric, not fresh goat hide. I still get to run around whipping people.

Danny isn't here. He hasn't been coming much to Latin Club stuff this year. Something must be keeping him away. Cass says it might be something about the president being his psycho ex. But I know that I am, in fact, his on-again off-again boyfriend, and we'll be on-again soon enough.

I'm circulating through the crowd at Sandy's house. As vice president, Sandy is in charge of social events. This is her night, and I am merely a figurehead. Still, she's letting me DJ off my laptop. Watching Latin kids awkwardly attempt to dance to the latest hip hop and pop hits is a highlight of every social gathering. Right now it's "Hotline Bling." It's so sad and wonderful. All it would take is one good dancer to kill the mood and shame everybody into stopping. Luckily none ever show up.

A Latin 2 passes me with a plastic cup. I take a whiff without him noticing. Just soda. Magister Stanton isn't here. He stays out of most of the social events. Not his scene, I guess. I still make sure everything is pretty clean, because I don't need any idiots tarnishing the reputation of our erudite and respectable club.

I adjust my loin cloth and smack a freshman lightly on the shoulder with my strap. She drops her pizza bagel back onto her plate.

"Spencer!" she yells over the music.

"*Io Lupercalia!*" I grin back, and duck back into the crowd.

I spot Cass standing with Brian a few yards away. I like that we're talking to Brian now. I mean, I've tried to hate him all year because of Certamen, but it was always like trying to hate a bag of potatoes. You can't keep up much anger against something that just sits there. Turns out, he's a pretty sweet guy.

Still, it feels like she's been with him an awful lot lately. Is he stealing my best friend like he stole my Certamen seat?

Katie is talking with them too. Allie is just behind her. She spends more time with our group now than with the other Latin 2's, ever since she moved in with Katie's family under mysterious circumstances. *That* gossip has been under lock and key, and none of my usual lock picks have worked on it. I'll find out somehow.

I don't think Jeff is here. He never comes to the social functions.

"You guys doing well?" I ask my Certamen team.

"I was better before I saw that costume," Allie says.

I flip up my loin cloth derisively to show my crotch. They all instinctively recoil, even though I'm wearing a body sock. I look like a Ken doll down there.

"It's glorious," Brian says. "I wish I had your confidence."

"It's easy to be confident when you're the best," I say, flipping some imaginary hair over my shoulder.

I feel a hand on my back. It's Sandy, the mastermind of the event, a very serious and very tiny junior with giant round glasses and red hair that exists just to make her name a lie.

"Good party," I tell her.

"Thank you," she says, businesslike. "It's time."

I smile. "Leave it to me." To my friends: "Duty calls,

see you on the dance floor."

I make my way through the crowd to Sandy's parents' surround sound, which has been supplying the music for the party. I bring down the volume on Katy Perry on my laptop, which is plugged into an aux cable.

"Friends, Romans, countrymen, lend me your ears," I call out. There is jeering at the super basic reference, but most people listen up.

"It is time," I say with ceremony, "For the most important part of Lupercalia."

"Your beautiful abs!" Cass yells. General laughter. I run my fingers over the smooth pink of my bodysuit.

"No," I continue. "The lover's lottery!"

A mixed reaction. Laughter, chattering, low murmurs of concern.

"Magister Stanton said we shouldn't do this!" Allie yells.

"What Magister doesn't know won't hurt him," responds Sandy, with an uncharacteristically mischievous grin.

"For those of you who are new to this," I say, "Our resident expert on Roman Life will explain.

"During Lupercalia," Katie speaks up in a prepared speech, "The ancient Romans would put the names of every young single woman into a jar, and every young single man would draw a name. They would pretend to be lovers for that night only."

More laughter, and more noises of concern from the freshmen.

"Thank you Katie," I say. "We will now put the names

of everybody single into my magic bag of love," I hold up a paper grocery sack. "And I will draw them two at a time, irrespective of gender."

Howls of laughter at this announcement.

"We've never done it like that," says a Latin 3 near me.

"As president, I feel it important not to assume heterosexuality as a default," I say in my best moral-high-ground voice. This gets a laugh too.

"So," I conclude, "If everybody single will put their name on one of my slips of paper and drop it in the bag, we'll get this started."

I start the song I have queued up for this on my laptop: "Single Ladies" by Beyoncé, of course. People start to take the slips. I move quickly through the crowd collecting names.

At my group of friends, Allie, Katie, and Brian all jot their names on slips. I hold the bag out to Cass.

"Actually," she says with a sheepish grin, and takes the hand of a guy I hadn't noticed before. He waves awkwardly. I recognize him. He's in my English class.

"Travis Spierman?" I gasp. "Since when?"

"About a week," she shrugs.

"And this is how you tell me?" I say melodramatically.

"I thought you were into some girl from Tumblr," Brian adds.

"I can like more than one person," she says defensively, grabbing Travis's arm.

"Oh no, was that a bad thing to ask?" Brian asks quickly. "Did I make you uncomfortable?"

"You're fine," Cass laughs.

"Fine like you don't mind, or fine like that was a normal thing to ask?" Brian says.

"It was a normal, if slightly presumptuous, thing to ask," Cass explains.

"Yeah, it's just this part that isn't normal," I say.

"I love that you like girls too," Travis adds to Cass.

"Don't be a pig, Travis," Cass says shortly.

I hear the song change. It's on shuffle on my party playlist, so it just goes to Taylor Swift.

"Look what you made me do, I was supposed to be back up there before the song ended!" I scold. "Cass, I'm very happy for you two, and also I hate you."

I dart back to the laptop and pause T Swift, to general opprobrium.

"We'll go back to it," I brush off the objections. "Now if the other officers can join me for the lottery."

We take turns drawing two names at a time and reading off our temporary couples, to the accompaniment of many hoots and hollers. The fact that only a small portion of them are boy-girl makes it even more fun. I especially enjoy when I pair up a track jock with a Dungeons & Dragons-level nerd, both boys.

Katie ends up paired with Allie. I'm with Brian. Almost everyone seems to be paired with friends, in fact. The gods of Lupercalia smile on us.

"Alright, new couples and old," I announce when we finish. "It is time for our lovers' dance. You must dance to the next song with your new partner. After that you may ditch them. But who knows what sparks may fly when the music plays…"

I put on my song choice. I knew I needed the corniest possible slow dance for maximum effect, so I went with "Time After Time." The couples I've just created grab each other awkwardly by the waist at arm's length and begin to sway like at a bad middle school dance.

This is why I love Lupercalia. Pure magic.

I take Brian's hand. He looks uncomfortable, but he's smiling.

"You're coming along well with this whole social thing," I tell him as we sway.

"You think so?" he says.

"Definitely. You're still obviously a naïf, but I feel like I know you a lot better than I ever have before."

"I feel like I know *everyone* a lot better than before," he says wide-eyed. "Everyone has so much going on."

"I know, isn't it wonderful?" I agree, thinking of all the juicy stories teeming around me.

"I think I assumed before that other people were just not worth it," Brian says, looking at his feet as they do a thing that resembles, but is not, dancing. "And I'm figuring out that I was wrong."

"Oh god, you're not becoming an optimist on us, are you?" I tease. He laughs.

"No, most other people are still garbage. But I think the ratio is just better than I realized."

"Same," I say.

The song ends, and so does the obligation to be in the fake couple. I give an exaggerated bow to Brian. He curtsies back, and I laugh. Brian really is growing a personality lately.

As the couples separate, I see Katie and Allie hug. When they pull apart, both have tears in their eyes.

God, I need to pry the lid off that story.

The party starts to wind down. The younger kids start going home, and we more experienced JCLers start helping Sandy clean up. I can feel the dread start to settle in.

Where is Danny right now? Is he having more fun than I am?

I try to push the feeling down, but it rears its head every time I've got nothing else to keep me occupied. Danny laughing with his friends. Danny brushing the hair off of some guy's forehead. Danny in bed with...

"So," I say, making my way to my Certamen team, "Who's up for some after-party? There's that 24-hour pizza place down by Tex Bar."

Katie looks at Allie, then checks her phone. "My parents told us 11, so we should go."

"I'm in," Brian says to me with a grin.

Cass eyes me skeptically. I think I know what she's thinking.

"I won't take any pictures for Instagram or Snapchat," I assure her. "I just want to hang out."

"It isn't about Danny?" she presses.

"It isn't about Danny," I half-lie.

"Alright, I'm in," she says.

"Great! I'll drive," I say.

If I'm lucky, this will buy me another two hours, and I can be tired enough when I get home to fall asleep without thinking.

Am I still surrounding myself with people because I

want to get Danny back?
  Am I doing it to get over him?
  Has it just become habit by now?
  I can't tell.

Chapter 11: February 18th Brian Ganz

Annie is a pretty bad play.

I mean, just in general. Not that the Theatre[29] kids are doing a bad job with it, just that the play itself is bad. They're doing the best they can with the bad material they have.

Especially Spencer. He's hilarious.

I'm sitting next to Cass. She drove me here to support Spencer. Katie and Allie are sitting with us too, but they're mostly talking to each other.

This is the first school play I've been to since elementary school. I can see the appeal, even if it is *Annie*. It's a pretty cool way to spend a Saturday night.

Spencer is in an exaggerated zoot suit, hair straightened and puffed up in a pompadour, pencil-thin mustache painted on his upper lip. Talking like a Mafioso in an old movie. He's miming like he has a toothpick, though I don't

---

[29] "Theatre" came to English via Latin and French, but it is ultimately from a Greek root, related to the Greek word *theasthai*, "to behold." Behold! A bunch of high schoolers pretending it's the 30's!

know why he doesn't have a real one. I think most of the lines that get the biggest laughs are his own ad-libs. I know all those *Rick and Morty* and *Rocky Horror* references can't be in the script.

I like seeing him pretending to be someone he's not. Even though I'm starting to feel like that's something I do a lot now.

Cass set up a bunch more Tumblr chats before I told her I was done. I said I thought I'd gone as far as I could online, and I was going to try to go face to face now. Really, it was continuing to weigh on me how dubious[30] it was to learn to flirt with total strangers online. But mostly, I just kept breaking into sweats every time one started, because I knew how quickly it would fizzle. They all did. Cass had learned to talk to people online, but that wasn't how it was working out for me. It's making me worry that maybe I can't talk to people at all.

But Spencer and Cass really seem to like me now. It makes me self-conscious when they say things like "Wow, Brian can actually start meaningful conversations now," but all the same, they're saying what I'm feeling. I'm starting to feel less broken now. At the same time, they've known me a while. Are they just being nice because I used to be closed off? Are they just humoring me? Will I be able to generalize my new skills, and start talking to new people?

Cass and I split a bag of Red Vines at intermission.[31] That's a thing that friends do.

I've been telling her that I'm talking to girls in some of

---

[30] Latin *dubium*, "doubt." Related to "double," like being of two minds.
[31] Latin *missus*, "sent," with the prefix *inter-*, "between."

my classes. Trying to apply my flirting practice to the real world. I haven't really. I want to. There are a couple of different girls I've got my eye on. I plan it all out during class, what I'm going to say to her on our way out. But I chicken out every time. I know it would just fizzle like the Tumblr chats.

Nora is the only one I'm really honest with about my progress. She gives me encouragement. Says it's good that I'm working on friendships instead of relationships. That I can't be a good boyfriend until I learn to be a good friend, so I should start there and not worry so much about flirting.

I think about the Red Vines again. Are Cass and I flirting? She has a boyfriend that she never talks about. Is that serious at all?

People are applauding. The play is over. It's closing night, so there's a standing ovation. The stars and the teachers get flowers, and some people make speeches. Annie and Daddy Warbucks kiss each other, which gives the whole audience the willies.

We find Spencer in the lobby. He has scrubbed off the mustache, but most of the rest of his stage makeup is still intact. It looked good from far away. Up close he looks like a grown up version of one of those creepy antique dolls. Powdery skin and too-red cheeks. Thick black lines around his eyes.

Cass gives him a hug and tells him how good he was. I take her cue and do the same. He smells like the makeup. Chemical.

"Thanks for coming out," he says jovially.[32] His energy

is still really high from being on stage.

"It was a fun show," Cass says.

"Worst musical we've done yet," Spencer says with the same big smile.

"Well, yeah," Cass agrees.

"Glad it's over?" I ask.

"You bet!" he says. "Look, Brian got an emotion right!"

Like I said. Awkward, but accurate.

"You guys got any plans after this?" Spencer asks. "Up for some late-night jaunting?"

Cass checks her phone. "Too late for me," she says. "Mom has me on a schedule. I have to be up with her at 8 tomorrow, and any moment I'm not spending on scholarship essays I have to do housework."

"Yeesh," I say.

"Allie and I need to go too," Katie says. I notice she doesn't give a reason.

Spencer looks at me.

"I'm game," I say, "As long as you can drive me home afterward."

"Great!" he enthuses. "I'm gonna go back and see if I can get any Theatre kids to join us."

I text my mom to tell her I'll be a little later than I said. I hide her response. (*Brian! Are you making friends? OMG.*)

Spencer comes back a few minutes later and tells me

---

[32] "Jovial" comes from "Jove," an alternate form of Jupiter, the king of the Roman gods. A jolly fellow who liked to cheat on his sister-wife with scores of mortal women. Why does that feel so appropriate for Spencer? Except the women, of course.

it'll just be the two of us. He proposes IHOP. I propose a movie at my house. My plan wins. In his car, he hands me his phone.

"I know you're into music, but I don't like loud angry stuff," he says, with a flair for reductionism. "So you can pick whatever you like, but off my phone."

As we're leaving the parking lot, I'm scrolling through his library—pop trash and 80's oldies best left forgotten.

"I can feel the waves of judgment coming off of you from here," Spencer says as we turn onto the freeway, "So you can save it."

"Oh, it isn't judgment," I say, "It's pity. You really do need help."

"I said save it!" he says louder, but he's smiling. I decide that this is a joking situation, and I can press on without offending him. Though I keep a close eye on him.

"Where to begin," I mutter. "Well, we'll start with a big one. Bon Jovi."

"Don't you dare impute the merit of the greatest American songwriter!" Spencer protests.

"I just threw up in my mouth a little when you said that. And Meat Loaf, really. What bad junior high dance from our parents' generation did you take all this from?"

"Okay, you're talking, and no music is happening. I'll prove you wrong about Meat Loaf. Try the song 'You Took the Words Right Out of my Mouth,' and tell me it's not amazing."

I oblige, despite my serious reservations. The song has a long, strange introductory speech, which is kind of funny. Then starts this saxophone and glockenspiel thing that sounds like a bad Bruce Springsteen outtake. We're at a stoplight, so I give Spencer a significant look.

"Keep listening," he says.

I do. About halfway in, I start to hear it. It's so overblown, so operatic, but all based on silly high school fluff lyrics. Its seriousness collapses under its own weight and becomes something else. It's not exactly sarcasm or satire, because there's no winking self-awareness about it. It's just...

"Okay, I like it," I admit.

"Thank you," Spencer says, as if I owed him.

"You've got a lot of musicals on here too," I say.

"Have you met me?"

"Which ones are worth listening to?" I ask.

"Oh, fasten your seatbelt."

"I assume you mean metaphorically, because my literal seatbelt has been fastened this whole time."

"Yes," he says.

"Because I value my life," I continue.

"Yes, yes, you're very clever, shut up now."

We end up sitting in his car in my driveway going through musicals for almost half an hour before we actually get out to go in my house. We're going to see if *Chicago* or *Rent* is on Netflix. My mom is watching some crime drama in the den when we come in.

"Hey Mom!" I call. "I brought a friend!"

"Oooooh," she squeals. "Is it Cass? I've been dying to meet her!"

"Just me Spencer," Spencer says in a sad drawl like Droopy Dog.

"That's great too!" my mom says, scuttling around the couch and into the entryway to shake Spencer's hand. She obviously wanted it to be a girl, but she's still pretty excited that I've got a friend over at all. "Can I get you two anything?"

"Dom Perignon if you have any to hand," Spencer says in an affected uppity voice.

My mom laughs a little too loudly, just as Daisy scampers up to see what's going on. She sees Spencer and makes a beeline[33] for the sofa table he's standing next to. Spencer starts petting her immediately.

"Brian, I didn't know you had a cat!" Spencer says. Daisy is purring and mashing her face into Spencer's arm with vigor. "He's so nice!"

"That's Daisy. *She* loves everyone, except me," I say.

"She loves you," my mom assures me.

To prove the point, I move slowly over to Daisy and lift my hand to pet her carefully. She changes gears in an instant, rears back and threatens me with her claws. Spencer laughs.

"What did you do to her?" he asks accusingly.

"Nothing!" I protest. "She's hated me since mom brought her home when I was in the eighth grade. Loves my mom. Comes right up to guests."

"Cats do what they want," my mom says with a shrug, her standard line when we're talking about Daisy's unaccountable animus[34] toward me. She turns the

---

[33] A term with English roots, referring to the idea that bees home directly to sources of food. Vergil would have loved it.

[34] *animus* is Latin for "spirit." In Latin it refers to any kind of spirit, unlike in

conversation to Spencer again. "I, um, like your makeup."

"It's from the play he was just in," I say before Spencer can make another joke and risk fracturing my mother's perfect facade of enjoyment.

"You were in the play?" my mother asks in her whoa-so-cool parent voice. "Aren't you exhausted now?"

"Baby I could go all night," Spencer growls.

"We're just gonna go watch Netflix upstairs," I tell my mom, ushering Spencer toward the stairs. He doesn't move quickly—he's enjoying the easy audience my mom is giving him. Daisy hops from the table and follows at Spencer's ankles, purring so loudly it reverberates off the walls.

"You let me know if you'd like snacks or anything!" she calls.

"We will," I grunt. God, you'd think I'd never had friends over before.

You'd think that, because I hadn't. Not since we'd moved.

Progress. Baby steps.

English where it refers mainly to the malevolent kind.

CHAPTER 12: FEBRUARY 23ᴿᴰ-24ᵀᴴ   KATIE NGUYEN

Thursday was our last Certamen practice before Area, which was that Saturday.

We did Certamen practices every Thursday, but nothing had been feeling any different. I was slowly getting better at Authors, but not good enough. Cass and Brian were like ninjas at Mythology and History, though Cass was still pretty frustrated with the literary devices. Jeff was in a private hell with his Grammar and Vocab questions. It was looking like Area would be just like the Invitational meet. We'd do well, but not well enough to win. Our Lady of the Seven Sorrows would go to State, again. I could only hope that, during their ascension to glory, their History expert might stop to notice me.

At 3:15, everyone was there except Mr. Stanton. Cass, Spencer, and Brian were all talking in a knot. Jeff was behind me studying.

I was flipping through my Authors Quizlet set before practice, as always, when I looked up at Brian. He was laughing with Cass, his headphones around his neck instead of on his ears, but it was the book on his desk that attracted my eye.

"Suetonius?" I asked him, pointing.

"What?" he said, looking away from Cass.

"You're reading Suetonius?" I clarified.

"Re-reading," he said. "It's an Empire year, and he's one of the prime historians of the era, so since I haven't read it since freshman year—"

"I got a question on Suetonius wrong last practice," I said. I remembered it well. His books start with Julius Caesar, not Augustus. "Did you know it?"

"Well," he said, hesitantly, "Yeah."

"But you didn't buzz in."

"I didn't want to make you feel bad," Brian said, his brow furrowed.

"I wouldn't have felt bad!" I protested.

"Wouldn't you?" Cass interjected. "If someone from your team beat you at your specialty?"

"I don't think so," I muttered.

"I think I would," Jeff said from behind me. "I mean, I don't think I *should*, but I would. I'd hate it."

"Same," Cass said.

I thought about it. I had been pretty touchy about my Authors questions. It was really hard work, getting them all down. I wanted to be good at it.

But that was stupid. I was trying to memorize names off of flash cards, and here someone on my team had read the guy's book. Twice. Of course he would know that author better than I would.

"Have you known things in *competition* and held back, or just in practice?" Mr. Stanton asked, making us all jump. No one had seen him come in.

"There was a Tacitus question at the Invitational meet that I was silent on," Brian admitted.

"That could have cost us a round!" Jeff sputtered.

"Don't jump on him," Mr. Stanton said. "We're learning something important."

"And he's not the only one," Cass volunteered. "I've known some of the author questions too."

I sank. I was starting to feel like we were losing rounds because everyone was tiptoeing around me. I'd been feeling like the weak link in the chain all year, and this...

"I had no idea," Mr. Stanton said. "Specialization in Certamen is all well and good, but it's not meant to be exclusive."

"It's about ego," Cass said. "We'd all feel too bad about stepping on someone else's toes, because we know they're working as hard as we are, and we know how we'd feel."

"Well, I don't want to lose because of my ego," I declared. "Take all the Authors questions you can. I don't care who the points come from."

"This doesn't need to be just about Authors," Mr. Stanton said. "Is there anything anyone else has been holding back on?"

"Well," I said, balancing the story on my tongue. It still felt wrong to say it. Talking about our weaknesses like this, it was like seeing each other naked. "At the Invitational meet, there was a history question that had to do with the army. I had a hunch about it because the army comes up a lot in Life, but St. Ignatius beat Brian to it."

"And you would have been right?" Jeff asked. I nodded.

"The army has always been a weak spot for me," Brian conceded. "I'd be happy to have some help there."

"What else?" Mr. Stanton prodded.

"I know you've got some Mythology in that mind palace," Cass said to Brian. "I remember you digging on that Midas story with me."

Brian shook his head. "I couldn't get any of the Mythology questions at this level, they're insane. But I know word roots. I could get the Derivative questions."

"Really?" Jeff said. His voice sounded politely interested, but behind his eyes he looked wounded. "Word roots?"

"I kinda think about them all the time," Brian said sheepishly. "Like, when I said I was silent about that Tacitus question just now, that was a derivative joke. Because *tacitus* means 'silent' in Latin."

"That's stupid," Cass said as Mr. Stanton chuckled.

"I can get some of the Vocabulary questions," I volunteered. "I usually know the 'Which one doesn't belong in this list' ones."

"Oh, good, I hate those questions," Jeff said more genuinely.

"Okay, I've obviously done a pretty slapdash job coaching you," Mr. Stanton said. "You guys are really good as a group of four individuals, but you've never learned how to work as a team. We've only got two days, but let's make a go of it."

We decided not to take out the buzzers. Instead of asking his questions Certamen-style, Mr. Stanton laid the questions before us and we each discussed what we knew and didn't know about them. We figured out what each other knew. Brian and Cass went through my Quizlet set with me and I deleted out all the authors they already knew, leaving me with a manageable list of dramatists and rhetoricians to solidify in my mind palace before Saturday. Brian's etymologizing and my vocabulary retention complimented Jeff's grammatical ability nicely. We stayed late, and felt *different* when we left.

Though we hadn't had one scheduled, we had another practice on Friday. Even Jeff left looking satisfied.

Saturday wasn't going to be just another competition.

"I can't believe what a difference a couple of days have made," Allie said as we were getting ready for bed. We were going down early, planning to get lots of sleep for the next day. Latin Club only had three competitions per year, so each one of them was a big deal.

I was playing Thelonious Monk on the little speaker on my bedside table. Allie wasn't much for instrumental music, but she commented on it.

"I feel like I'm in a classy 60's movie," she said. "Like I could be swirling a martini right now."

I blushed. Of course I was playing it because tomorrow was my chance to see *him*. Monk. I was determined to at least find out his real name.

Allie didn't notice. She plopped down on the air mattress she had slept on for the past few weeks, and looked up at the ceiling, lost in thoughts of her own. I laid back on my own bed, feeling awkward being two feet above her. I had told her she could sleep up with me on the bed, but she didn't want things to feel weird. She didn't chase straight girls, she had said, and she wasn't going to make me doubt it. I had even offered to alternate nights so she could have the good bed sometimes, but she had refused that point blank.

This was looking like a semi-permanent thing now. Child Protective Services had been by. A stressed-out-looking case worker had interviewed Allie for all of five minutes, then spoken to my parents. They weren't official foster parents or anything, but the case worker said Allie should stay at our house until further notice. And that we shouldn't hold our breath for further notice. Fine by us. None of us wanted Allie to disappear into a foster home.

"You have all day to worry about tomorrow," Allie said lazily.

"Huh?" I said, thinking about Monk. Then, "Oh, yeah, uh huh." We all took academic tests in the morning, and Certamen went on for the whole afternoon. The Certamen kids were the busiest students at the competition.

"I just have to go fail a Greek History test," Allie said, "Then model my Hecuba costume in the afternoon for like half an hour."

"The costume is beautiful by the way," I told her.

"Thanks," she said proudly. "Your family was really nice to get me so many supplies."

"You look like a proper Trojan queen."

"Whose husband has like fifty concubines," she

laughed. "You think you're ready for Certamen?"

"As I'll ever be," I replied. I took another stroll through my mind-library. Waved to Marcus Aurelius, Lucretius, Lucan. I knew them all.

"Are you worried about Our Lady of the Seven Sorrows?" she asked.

"*What?*" I sat bolt upright in bed. On my speaker, Thelonious Monk launched into a new solo, seeming to betray all of my secrets.

"They're our biggest competition, right?" Allie said innocently.

"Oh. Yeah," I said, lying back down.

We lay without talking for a moment. The only sound was the jazz coming from my bedside table. My thoughts drifted again toward their favorite subject.

"You want to turn off the light?" Allie asked.

"Can you keep a secret?" I blurted.

Allie was sitting on the edge of my bed before I even noticed what was happening.

"Katie," she said solemnly. "I would take your darkest secret to the grave. I would consider it a personal failure of an extraordinary magnitude if I ever betrayed you."

I laughed a bit, but I was still nervous to say it out loud. "So, there's this guy on the Our Lady of the Seven Sorrows Certamen team..."

"Oh my *god*," Allie gasped, grabbing my knees. "You're in love with the enemy!"

"'*Love*' is a little strong," I said, feeling the blood rush to my cheeks. They must have been crimson. "But I've got a crush. He's the one who told me about Thelonious Monk, actually."

"That is so adorable," Allie grinned. "You guys are like Romeo and Juliet. Star-crossed lovers from mixed backgrounds. Could the world ever accept your love?"

"You're not making this any better," I said to my pillow.

"I'm sorry," she said sincerely, leaning closer. "I mean, it *is* actually hilarious. I think you're too close to it to realize that. But I don't think anybody on our team would actually mind if they knew."

"I don't know about that," I muttered.

"I'm pretty sure," Allie said. "But, as I said, I would not divulge your secret, even under torture. What's his name?"

I took a breath. "I don't know."

Allie laughed so hard she fell backward off the bed.

CHAPTER 13: FEBRUARY 25ᵀᴴ   CASS WASHINGTON

I was leaning over a buzzer on an uncomfortable plastic seat at a cafeteria table in another unfamiliar high school. This one had the worst of all cafeteria setups: long tables with the attached round plastic stools. The ones that squeaked every time you moved, which was constantly, because there was no such thing as a comfortable way to sit on them. I said a silent thank you to the gods that the West Oak cafeteria had real chairs instead of this crap.

At my right elbow was Brian, at my left was Jeff. The Latin 1 and Latin 2 Certamen teams were there with buzzers too. It wasn't a round. We weren't even practicing Latin questions. Lunchtime at Area was way too late to be cramming any content. We were just warming up our thumbs.

Allie was at the machine. She had invented an ingenious game for us.

"Now I'll say numbers," she announced, "And you will buzz in when you hear an odd one."

"Odd mathematically, or just out of place and socially

awkward?" asked Brian.

"Shut up," said several people at once.

His glib calmness in the face of any upcoming ordeal tended to rub people the wrong way.

Allie began. "Two. Forty-six. Eighty. Nine hundred thirty-eight. Fourteen. Six. Seven."

Beep.

"A3," she announced, and a Latin 1 celebrated. They had really gotten serious since their humbling experience at the invitational meet.

"Ninety-eight. Fifty-two. Four. Thirty-six. Fifty-nine."

Beep.

"C4," Allie said. We high-fived Katie.

"Who are we up against in our first round?" I asked Jeff again. He rolled his eyes, but he rattled off all of our rounds. He had, of course, memorized the list as soon as it had been posted. We didn't go against Our Lady of the Seven Sorrows until the third round, the last of the regular rounds before finals. (Save the worst for last.)

I thought I saw something pass over Katie's face when Jeff said Our Lady of the Seven Sorrows. She had always been the most nervous one on the team.

"I love our chances this year," I said.

"Thanks to new strategies," Brian said.

"And Brian's mind palace," Katie grinned, looking over at Brian.

"I don't use that," Jeff scowled. He was in a foul mood, as he always was before any competition. "Too slow."

"I don't use it either," I admitted. Though my

notebook, which was on the table under my right hand at that very moment, was not unlike a mind palace in its own way.

(*Not unlike.* Litotes. Literary devices.)

"Well, I could never have done without it," Katie said resolutely.

Brian shrugged. "Works for me, that's all I ever said."

"Okay," Allie announced. "Now I'll say the names of animals. You buzz in when I say a reptile."

Feeling pretty warmed up, the Advanced team moved a couple tables over. Brian took out his Roman History test from the morning and started looking over questions.

"How many do you think you got wrong?" I asked him.

"I had to make an educated guess on four of them," he responded, turning to his phone. "Googling the correct answers now."

The rest of the team shook our heads as he typed. On a seventy-five-question test designed to be partially impossible, only getting four wrong would be an almost sure bet for first place, at least at Area. I averaged ten to fifteen wrong on my Mythology tests these days, and that was damn good. No one had any doubt of Brian making State for History.

Top five in our tests. That's all any of us needed for the school to pay for us to go to State. We didn't need Certamen. That would only be icing on the cake.

Icing that Jeff was determined to taste, even if it killed him.

"I need some real résumé items," he was saying again.

"Area is an everybody-gets-a-medal bonanza. I need something really competitive to set myself apart. I need this Certamen win to get into Johns Hopkins."

I shook my head pityingly, as usual. But hearing about college applications set my brain going to bad places. In my mind's eye, my mother and father started planning out my future for me again. *Oh, what about medical school? Do you think she has what it takes? No, she probably doesn't have the patience.*

Progress reports had come out the week before, so if you asked my parents, I was "grounded." But this was a school event, so of course that was alright. So had been the Certamen practices on Thursday and Friday, and the extended "study session" Spencer had held with Brian and me at his house on Friday evening. Travis had joined us for that one. I think there was a Latin book open somewhere in the room.

I saw Mr. Stanton arrive at the team's table to collect the Certamen machine. The other students were packing it up. We drifted back in their direction.

"Getting the Certamen rooms set up?" I asked our Magister.

"Yup," he responded. Each Club loaned its machine to the host school on the day of the competition so there would be enough to run all the rounds.

"Which level are you reading?" Katie asked.

"Novice," he said. The Latin 1's looked green.

Jeff checked his phone. "Round One was supposed to start twenty minutes ago."

Mr. Stanton looked at his watch. "My god, you're right. Could we be... *running late?* Cass, have you ever known a

Latin competition to run *late?*"

"Late?" I said with a gasp, playing into his sarcasm. "A Latin competition? Never, sir."

"It's unprecedented," Brian joined in.

"Lighten up, kiddo," Mr. Stanton said to Jeff with a grin. "You'll worry yourself to death. Certamen will happen when it happens."

Spencer came into view, leading a shell-shocked looking freshman girl.

"How'd you fare?" Mr. Stanton asked him.

"Oh, mine went well," Spencer said, referring to his Dramatic Interpretation speech. "Didn't flub a single word, even over all that sticky enjambment, and my scansion was on point."

"Good job," Mr. Stanton encouraged. Then he turned his attention to the freshman. "Maisy, how was yours?"

Maisy shook her head mutely. She looked like one of Odysseus's men who had just seen his best friend get eaten by the cyclops. Spencer patted her on the arm.

"Go get some pizza," Mr. Stanton said gently. She hurried away,

"She had a long wait," Spencer told him. "Lot of novice-level girls this year. She spent the whole time psyching herself out. Got in the performance room and just panicked." He looked at her wistfully as she grabbed her lunch. "And she's so good normally, too. What a waste."

"Nerves will get you," Magister said. "You stayed with her?"

"I don't leave any of my thespians behind," Spencer said dutifully.

"Good man," Mr. Stanton grunted. "Now, I really do need to take that machine in. *Bona fortuna vobis omnibus*. I'll see you on the other side."

***

The first round got underway about fifteen minutes later, with Spencer and Allie cheering us on from the desks behind us. We were up against St. Ignatius and someone we'd never heard of. It turned out to be two guys from a school with no organized Certamen. They were just there to mess around. Which was fine, more points for us.

It was just like in practice on Friday. We knew exactly what each other knew, so we knew when to be on our guard. Katie got the first vocabulary toss-up, setting Jeff up to get the more difficult grammatical concepts on the bonuses. I grabbed a toss-up about Ovid, leaving Katie and Brian the bonuses on other authors who ran into trouble with emperors. Brian spiked a derivative question and answered the bonuses without even pausing for thought. We zig-zagged through each other's specialties like synchronized swimmers.

I saw the looks St. Ignatius started to give us around toss-up fifteen. They were the looks we usually gave Our Lady of the Seven Sorrows: Awe at what we knew. Resignation toward a hopeless cause. Toward the end, just praying to get a couple more face-saving questions. Just a little bit, so they could say they gave us a fight.

But we didn't let them have much. Brian didn't miss a single History question in the round. Katie, Brian and I managed every one of the Authors. They got some Mythology questions away from me (I never could remember the real names for the hundred-handed monsters), and some Grammar questions off of Jeff (Latin-4-level questions, so it was really quite understandable, though I could see he wasn't forgiving himself).

In the end, we dealt them a bloodbath. We took 205 points. St. Ignatius scraped 40. The others made it onto the board with 10 for a lucky guess on a toss-up that both of us had already missed.

Our team left the room walking on a cloud. I wanted to run and tell somebody, but everyone who cared had been in the room with me. We all ran over to the big board (which was really just a couple pieces of white butcher paper stuck up in the hallway) to see them write our 205 points up. Our Lady of the Seven Sorrows's round had ended too—they got 190.

We had outscored them. It was surreal.

"Dude," Spencer said, shaking his head. "You guys are incredible."

"I know!" Katie bounced. She was overjoyed.

"I wish we'd have learned to be a team years ago," Brian chuckled.

I texted Travis the good news about our first win. He shot back quickly with *Good job, babe! Knock em out!*

I guess my grunt of disgust was external, rather than merely in my head as I had meant it to be. Spencer appeared at my elbow and looked at me hungrily.

"I keep telling him," I sighed to him without introduction, "I hate when couples call each other 'babe.' It's disgusting."

"You never say anything nice about Travis," Spencer

said, laughing slightly. "Do you even like anything about him other than his Bowie-esque cheekbones?"

"He's got nice hands."

"And?" he smirked.

"Okay, when we started going out I thought he was mysterious. Dark and brooding. Turns out he just doesn't say much because he doesn't have a lot going on."

"And how long are you going to keep stringing him along?"

I glared at Spencer, then softened. He was right this time. I didn't need to be wasting either of our time.

(Besides, I took it as a pretty bad sign that dating Travis hadn't had any effect on how often I thought about PuellaStellarum. I hadn't even told her about him.)

Jeff was talking to Katie and Brian, and I slid back into the conversation. "We can't get cocky," he said. "I know it's looking good for us, but we're not to State yet. We have to stay sharp."

Though I didn't agree with Jeff's tone, I had to agree with his sentiment. We couldn't get complacent. We were still the underdogs, and we had to keep fighting.

Still, it was a lot easier to keep fighting with a number like 205 on the board.

The number 205 figured into my inter-round doodling, along with a few themes from the Iliad with Greek names I was trying to remember, and our four Certamen team members sitting on high thrones like Roman gods.

CHAPTER 14: FEBRUARY 25ᵀᴴ   **KATIE NGUYEN**

Our second round at Area went similarly to the first. The other two teams didn't even know what hit them. We were sitting now at the B buzzers, waiting for the other teams to show up for Round Three.

This was the round I had been waiting for. Not because it was the last round to get us into finals. We were virtual shoe-ins at that point. It was because soon, Our Lady of the Seven Sorrows would be filing in and taking their traditional seat at the A buzzers.

I was about to see Monk again.

I didn't have any plan about what I would do. I needed to find a way to talk to him without my team noticing. I had hoped to find him in the vegetarian line at lunch again, but I ended up getting roped into spending lunch practicing instead. I had no idea how I was going to start a conversation organically with him again.

But this much I swore. I would pay attention when the teams introduced themselves so I could at least learn his *name*.

The other school—the Andrew P. Greene Charter School for the Medical Sciences, a catchy name if I ever heard one—showed up before Our Lady of the Seven Sorrows and took the A buzzers. We chuckled about that. But of course, Our Lady of the Seven Sorrows was unflappable. Perfectly capable of demolishing us all from the C buzzers instead of the A.

Finally, the OLotSS team filed into the room. As usual they were dressed in identical wine-red school sweaters over yellow button-up shirts. They moved in lock step. Each had a sheaf of paper in an identical leather-looking folder with their school crest embossed in gold on the front. They took their seats. I gaped in horror for a moment, then looked away, self-conscious.

Monk wasn't there.

My mind raced all the way through the reminder of rules and the recitation of the Aurelia passage.

Maybe Monk couldn't make it, and his alternate was here today?

I inspected the team. They were all readying their pads with identical looks of experience.

I thought about how Monk had said he only got an important question because of one of Cass's Tumblr posts.

Monk was the alternate. Their real History guy had missed the invitational meet, but he was here today.

The horror of not seeing Monk was compounded with the thought: they had destroyed us that easily in January *without their full team*.

The round began. I tried to concentrate, but my mind kept wandering. During bonus questions, I scanned the small crowd of Our Lady spectators crowded into the back of the classroom, hoping Monk would be among them. Spencer caught my eyes once when I was doing this. He mouthed *focus*.

I got outbuzzed on almost all the Authors questions, and even the one and only Life question for the round. The rest of our team didn't fare much better. Brian was especially wrong-footed. The last time we had played Our Lady of the Seven Sorrows, he had gone up against their History alternate. Their main guy was a lot more formidable.

We got destroyed. OLotSS got 290, Greene got 145, and we got 60.

Our Lady of the Seven Sorrows came by our table for their usual handshakes. It was a show of sportsmanship, but they gave us each such superior looks that it cancelled out the magnanimous spirit.

We met Mr. Stanton at the board, waiting for the results to come in from the other rooms. At the end of Round Two, we looked almost guaranteed to go to finals. Now, with only 60 in the last round, we could be edged out with a strong showing by a team in a different room.

"Your scores have been amazing today," Mr. Stanton told us.

"That last round was inexcusable," Jeff said darkly.

"I'm proud of you," Mr. Stanton said resolutely. "Even if you don't make finals. You've had a great day, and I couldn't have asked for a better Advanced Certamen team."

"If we do make finals, we just have to face Our Lady again," Cass muttered. None of us were in love with that prospect.

Allie came running up and celebrated when she saw our scores for Rounds One and Two, which she hadn't seen yet. She had a ridiculous beard drawn on her chin in magic marker. Her costume contest had not gone according to plan. She was part of the couples' costume contest, which the Junior Classical League had set as King Priam and Queen Hecuba of Troy. She was doing it with another sophomore girl named Maddy—JCL didn't mind gender-bending, and girls are generally more eager to enter Costume than boys. But she and Maddy's wires had gotten crossed, and they had *both* shown up to Area with dresses made for Queen Hecuba. Since Allie's costume was slightly less feminine, they had slapped a beard on her and tried to pass off her dress as kingly royal robes. They were aided and abetted by an explanation from Mr. Stanton about how the Romans viewed Eastern peoples, such as the Trojans, as more effeminate because of the way they dressed. It kind of almost worked. But she still looked like a king in a dress.

The last few scores made it onto the board. Spencer gasped and jumped for joy. The rest of us were a little more reserved.

"Looks like you're in for a rematch," Mr. Stanton said.

By coincidence, the lineup for our finals would be identical to our previous round: us, that medical prep school, and Our Lady of the Seven Sorrows. We were in third place, and we had only made it into finals by twenty points. Our Lady was in first by a couple hundred.

But that didn't matter. Finals were a clean slate. Nothing counted toward your place other than your score in that one round. We still had a fighting chance for that one State spot. It was a longshot, but it was a chance.

Lower-level Certamen finals in the auditorium felt like they took *days*. There is nothing slower than other people's Certamen rounds when you're waiting for your own. My stomach felt like a black hole collapsing in on itself. Time crawled past us. I felt like if I dropped a pencil, it would take ten minutes to hit the ground.

I was reciting Authors under my breath like a mantra. I also found plenty of time to scan the crowd for Monk. But there were about two hundred people in the auditorium, and the lighting was low. I was worried he wasn't here. Could that be? Did anyone come to a Certamen invitational—basically a practice Area—and not to the real deal? If you had a conflict, maybe. Was he off playing lacrosse or something, somewhere miles away, never to think about me again?

I snapped pictures for the scrapbook. Nerves about Certamen and boys notwithstanding, I took my Historian duties seriously.

All three of our school's Certamen teams had made finals, so at least I could cheer on our lower levels. Both lower-level teams finished third out of the three teams in their own final rounds. Which was what my teams had done every year we had made finals too. Which was what my Advanced team was probably about to go do now.

Mr. Stanton got on his feet to applaud and yell for both of the lower-level teams, like he had done for my teams every year. He met them coming down the aisle, and confounded their disappointed faces by high fiving them and telling them they had done great. Which they had. Just making it to finals was hard enough.

I didn't want him to do that for us. I wanted him to congratulate us on making State.

And I wanted to find that stupid boy.

Finally, they called for the Advanced finalists to take the stage. Our Lady of the Seven Sorrows claimed the A buzzers. We took B. Greene Medical Sciences took C. We were at long tables now instead of classroom desks. A mic sat in front of the moderator, another on each of the teams' tables. Stage lights shone on us from the rafters, plunging the audience into total darkness. I could barely even tell there were people in the seats. But I couldn't forget they were there.

The moderator took his sweet time through the usual announcements, and the Aurelia passage. I looked only at my hands and the blank piece of notebook paper in front of me. I didn't want to look toward the crowd, even if I couldn't see it. I knew that out there somewhere, Allie was taking pictures of us with my camera. Mr. Stanton was leaning forward in his seat, gripping his knees out of nerves for us. Monk was sitting with his friends from Our Lady, I hoped. But I didn't want to think about any of them. This time, I was going to keep my head in the round.

The questions started, and this round couldn't have been any different from the last one. Brian got a History question right out of the gate, with both bonuses for the full 20 points. The next two toss-ups were Grammar questions, and though OLotSS got the first one, Jeff grabbed the second one with one of the bonuses, 15 points.

Number four was Vocab: OLotSS got it wrong, and I was able to use their wrong answer to get the right one. Jeff helped me get both bonuses, 20 points. The next few went to Our Lady. We weren't blowing away Our Lady of the Seven Sorrows the way we had St. Ignatius, but we were holding our own. The round progressed with our score never more than twenty points away from Our Lady's. We were evenly matched. We had found our footing against them. All four of us were not only performing the best we ever had individually, but also filling in each other's gaps. I saw something I had never seen before: worry on the faces of the OLotSS robots.

Poor Greene couldn't get a word in edgewise.

Before question twenty, the final question of the round, there was always a score check. Before question twenty in the final round, the score was Our Lady of the Seven Sorrows 145, West Oak 130, and Greene Medical Sciences nil. Or, as they always said, "has yet to score."

Our team made a very quick bit of eye contact. It was tight. We had to get the last question right, and both of its bonuses. Anything less than perfection would mean a loss to Our Lady, or perhaps a tie, with a nerve-wracking tie breaker. And the whole team had to be thinking the same thing I was.

There had only been one Author question so far this round.

This last question was coming straight at me.

I caught the gaze of the Our Lady Literature specialist. She had obviously reached the same conclusion. She was staring holes into me. I focused on the moderator instead.

"Toss up twenty. Which Roman writer," he started, and I tensed, "who was forced to suicide by the Emperor Nero—"

Beep.

My heart plunged.

"A3," the moderator said calmly.

"Petronius," spat the Our Lady of the Seven Sorrows girl.

"I'm sorry, that is incorrect," the moderator said. "I will continue the question."

Alarm bells were going off in my head. She had ruined herself. There were *multiple* authors forced to suicide by Nero. She had guessed too early. Now her team couldn't buzz in for this question at all.

That didn't mean we were in the clear. Our Lady was still up 15 points. If I got this last question wrong, we would lose. If Greene got it before me, we would lose. The whole game was balanced on my buzzer thumb.

"Which Roman writer," the moderator began again, taking his sweet time, "who was forced to suicide by the Emperor Nero, wrote a ten-book epic poem about—"

Beep.

"B2," the moderator intoned.

"Lucan," I said confidently.

"That is correct," the moderator said. "A ten-book epic poem about the war between Julius Caesar and Pompey the Great. Ten points to Team B."

Cheers erupted from our school's section of the audience. Our Lady of the Seven Sorrows looked nauseated. On either side of me, Jeff and Cass patted my hands. But my work wasn't over yet. The score was now 140 to 145. I needed to get both of these last two bonus questions to avoid a loss or a tie.

"Bonus one," the moderator began. "What author of Stoic philosophy and tragedy was the uncle of Lucan?"

Bonuses could be discussed with the team.

"Seneca the Younger," I whispered to Jeff. The third author forced to suicide by Nero. Nice guy. I high-fived the version of Seneca by the circulation desk in my mind palace.

"I defer to Katie," said Jeff automatically. All team answers had to come from the captain, unless he specifically deferred to another teammate. Jeff almost always did, because mispronunciation of a name could cost us a question.

"Seneca the Younger," I said more loudly.

"That is correct," the moderator said.

More cheers from West Oak. The score was tied, with one five-point bonus left.

"Bonus two," the moderator said. "Lucan wrote of the civil war between Caesar and Pompey. Who was the first Roman author to write about this war?"

I wasn't sure, but it seemed likely to be a historian. I looked to the end of the table, to Brian. He was already smiling.

"Suetonius?" I whispered across Cass to Brian.

"No," Brian said, laughing good-naturedly. "It was Caesar himself."

Jeff heard, and there was no need to defer on *that* answer. "Julius Caesar," he said confidently.

"That is correct."

Our section of the crowd erupted. I looked out in their direction for the first time in the round, beaming at them even though I couldn't see them. Our Lady of the Seven Sorrows crumpled in their seats. I wondered if they would have it in them to shake our hands this time.

"Your Certamen champions," announced the moderator, "And representatives for Area E at the Certamen tournament at the Texas State Junior Classical League Convention: West Oak High School."

The cheers from our Club grew into a frenzy. We shook hands with the dejected Our Lady of the Seven Sorrows team and the mildly disappointed Greene Medical, then marched down the ramp off the stage.

Allie was the first to hug me, right at the foot of the stage. A bunch of Latin 3's followed. Mr. Stanton threw an arm around my shoulders and congratulated me. Everybody in my Roman Life section hugged me. Spencer hugged me. Monk hugged me.

I almost didn't realize it.

I gaped at him for a moment when he released me. "Hi," I said.

"Hey Katie Nguyen," he said. "Congratulations."

"Thanks," I said dumbly. This may have been the worst possible time in the competition for him to talk to me. Allie was already trying to get me together with the rest of the team for a picture on the edge of the stage. I gave her a look. She realized what was happening, and started to stall for me.

"Sorry we beat your school," I told Monk.

He laughed. "No biggie. They need some humbling sometimes. Listen," he glanced at my friends, "I don't want to keep you. But I'd kick myself if I let this competition pass without talking to you again."

I looked into his eyes and felt my head swim. "Yeah?" I managed.

"Yeah," he laughed again, nervously. "Here," he handed me a scrap of paper, folded. "Text me, okay?" And he disappeared back into the crowd.

I posed for my picture and accepted a bunch more congratulations in a daze. I laugh when I look back at that team picture today. My gaze was a thousand miles away.

When we retook our seats for the full awards ceremony, I opened the scrap Monk had handed me. His phone number, and under it, his name.

Jeremy.

Beautiful Jeremy from Our Lady of the Seven Sorrows.

I glanced across the row at my friends. Nothing had changed. Yes, we had won finals and we were going to State. But that didn't mean I could date the enemy. I wasn't going to betray them.

"You were amazing," Cass told me when we'd settled into our seats for the awards ceremony.

"So were you," I said truthfully.

"Wager to make the awards ceremony go faster?" Cass suggested.

"Sure," I laughed. Awards ceremonies at Latin competitions tended to be long, tedious affairs. They had to read off first through fifth places for Latin levels one-half through five in every category, and the list of categories was as long as your arm.

"What can we bet on," Cass wondered aloud.

"If Brian gets first in History?"

"Not interesting enough," Cass replied. "Something we have to count."

"What are you talking about?" asked Allie, who was sitting on my other side.

"We bet on dumb stuff," I shrugged.

"Want in?" Cass asked her.

"Sure," Allie grinned.

"Okay," Cass continued. "Total number of awards won by our team?"

"Too calculable," I said. "We know how many people we have here."

"How many first place awards Our Lady of the Seven Sorrows gets?" Allie suggested. I hoped Cass didn't notice my face go a little red.

"That's not bad," Cass considered.

"How many names the readers are obviously garbling," I suggested.

Cass laughed. "It's pretty subjective, though."

"Count the stutters, then," Allie countered.

"That'd work," Cass said. "She's a natural. Stakes?"

I pulled out a couple of chocolate chip muffins in plastic wrap. Cass rummaged produced a bag of Twizzlers.

"I've got pocky," Allie said.

"Chocolate?" Cass asked. Allie nodded. "Good. I hate that strawberry crap. Why mess with perfection?"

Counting stutters definitely did make the awards ceremony more interesting. I got third place in Roman

Life—and they stumbled over my name. (Come on, who hasn't heard Nguyen before?) Brian got first in Roman History. The rest of the Certamen team got top five in their categories. Spencer was second in Dramatic Interpretation. Allie managed fifth in Greek History, even with all her talk about being terrible at it. Everybody got their paid-for trip to State.

At the end we counted fifty-eight stutters. Well, Cass counted fifty-nine—it did end up being pretty subjective. But either way, Allie won the wager.

The school got third overall in the Area. Mr. Stanton beamed holding up our trophy in the group picture. He had the Certamen team pose for a hundred more pictures with our medals. We still couldn't believe what we'd done.

Allie fell asleep quickly when we got home that night, but I lay awake. I kept telling myself not to do it. I wasn't going to get involved. And even if I was, tonight would be *way* too quick.

But I couldn't help myself.

"It's Katie," I texted. "Are you going to State?"

"You bet," Jeremy texted back almost immediately. "I assume you are too, Certamen champion?"

"Yep," I confirmed.

"I'll see you there then," he replied.

"Yeah, see you there," I said. "Just wanted to find out. Good night."

"Good night Katie."

I put my phone under my pillow. I could feel myself blushing, even with nobody looking.

CHAPTER 15: MARCH 1ST   SPENCER OLSON

I'm texting and walking between classes, trying to coordinate something for after school. A message buzzes from Mr. Stanton to our Latin Club officer group chat.

"EMERGENCY officer meeting after school," it says. "Don't tell people."

Emergency? That's not a word I've ever associated with Latin Club.

Naturally, Mr. Stanton's room is packed after school. You don't send a message like that without everybody hearing about it.

"I guess I brought this on myself," he mutters, running his fingers through his uncharacteristically rumpled hair. "Could the officers at least come to the front of the crowd, please?"

We move into position. He counts us. President, Vice President, Secretary, Historian, Treasurer. All here.

I'm standing next to Katie. Most people just look curious, but she looks worried. Not as worried as Jeff, of course, but that should go without saying.

"Okay," Mr. Stanton says with a breath to the whole Latin Club. "You should all hear this anyway. The district pulled our funding for State."

It's like a lightning bolt has hit the room.

Everybody is talking at once. Shock, confusion, anger.

"How can they do that?" Jeff asks when the rabble dies down a bit. "When we're so close to it?"

"Well, it turns out they did it a long time ago," Mr. Stanton says glumly. "It was a line item axed from the budget, which they published at the end of last school year."

"Like AcaDec," Brian mutters.

"And you didn't notice?" some Latin 1 asks accusingly.

"It's a big long document that no teacher reads," Mr. Stanton explains, turning a little green. "They don't send me a message saying, 'Hey, by the way, we cut the only funding we give your program all year.' I only found out because I tried to put in the paperwork for our trip yesterday and it came back this morning."

"Why would they do that?" Katie asks forlornly. Mr. Stanton shakes his head, his gaze a mile away.

"We can fight it, right?" Allie asks hopefully.

"There's not a lot I can do," Mr. Stanton says glumly. "I don't have a lot of pull. And even if I did manage to convince them, everything about the budget is a done deal for this year. The only thing we could change would be next year."

"Then we're on our own for State?" asks Cass. Mr. Stanton nods.

"I'll pay," a Latin 3 I don't know says immediately. I

see some uncomfortable looks as he does. A lot of people would pay right with him, but not everyone can afford that. I could, and Cass probably could too. I don't know about Brian or Jeff. Katie, definitely not. Especially not with Allie.

"We'll do fundraisers," I speak up. I'm the president, and I'm determined to show the leadership that our meaningless popularity contest of an election demanded of me. "We need ideas. How much does State cost per person?"

"Around $150," Mr. Stanton says.

"And how many people qualified?" I ask.

"Twenty-two," he answers.

Our treasurer, Ben, already has his calculator out. "$3,300," he says. Our secretary, a Latin 2 named Alice, pushes through the crowd to the board and writes the figure with a dry erase marker.

"The company my dad works for sponsors my little sister's softball team," Katie says. "I can ask if they'll give us some sponsorship."

"Good idea," I say. "Anybody else's parents have companies like that?"

We have a few more that say they do.

"Companies are usually good for a couple hundred a pop," Mr. Stanton nods, looking less ill than he did when I came in. "What else?"

With Alice writing as fast as we can talk, we come up with a board full of ideas. Some we have to dismiss because there isn't enough time. We can't get in the paperwork necessary to do something like selling candy at school. Some are just jokes to begin with, like selling organs, leasing ourselves as slaves, bank robbery, or prostitution. But there are some real ideas too. We divvy those up amongst the officers to research and put into action if possible.

"We've got two months," Mr. Stanton tells us, out of panic mode and into action mode now. "It'll take some serious work to raise over three thousand dollars."

"We're going to do it," I assure everybody. "We'll find ways."

"If we do a car wash, are we going to see Spencer in a bikini?" asks Allie.

"You'll see that no matter what we do," I answer.

I get a pretty good laugh, and adjourn the impromptu Latin Club meeting on a good note.

$3,300. I hope we can do it. I didn't actually become Latin Club president to deal with crises.

Chapter 16: March 11th   Brian Ganz

"I can't believe I'm doing this crap," Cass says, tugging at her floor-length Roman-style tunic dress, white with gold accents around the sleeves and neck.

"It's for a good cause," Spencer reminds her, adjusting his lyre on his hip and straightening his golden laurel crown.

"Honestly, standing around dressed like a Roman is something I thought I'd be doing more of when I joined the Latin Club, so I'm pretty okay with this," I say. My toga is voluminous. It's missing the purple stripe of senatorial authority, which I feel I deserve, and I have to hold my left arm up at a ninety-degree angle to keep it from falling down. I've got a stack of fliers in my left hand to make the position seem more natural.

The fliers are why we are here. We're standing around in Books & More Books, waiting to give them out. The store is going to donate to the Latin Club a percentage of every sale accompanied by a flier on this particular Saturday. The trick is, we're not allowed to just give people fliers inside the store and ask them to use them. The loophole is, we can tell them about the fundraiser if they're the ones who ask us.

Hence the costumes. The goal is for people walking by to ask us why we're dressed up, and then we're allowed to talk about our Latin program and tell them how they can support it.

The things we do when we desperately[35] need State money.

"I wish one of those sophomore[36] dinks would at least let me wear one of the helmets so I could be Athena the warrior goddess," Cass complains.

"Just because you have to dress like an actual woman for one afternoon..." Spencer teases.

"I dress like my kind of woman," Cass spits back.

She mostly wears pants and shorts, with tall, formidable boots. Dark colors and hard edges. It is strange to see her in such dainty clothes, her feet in sandals.

Still, I'm in a toga, so.

Mr. Stanton wanders up. He is not doing his part. He's in a t-shirt and jeans, because it's a Saturday.

"When are you putting on one of these togas, Magister?" Spencer asks.

"You know," he counters, "You guys are a lot worse advertisement when you're all bunched up in the Ancient Cultures section."

I've been browsing through the History books. Cass

---

[35] *sperare* is the Latin verb for "to hope," and the *de-* prefix here negates it: *desperare* means "to give up hope." We're not out of hope, I promise.
[36] Greek, "wise fool." If you've met sophomores, you know.

and Spencer have been standing idly next to me.

"You should get out there and mingle, like Jeff and the underclassmen," Mr. Stanton tells us, and walks back away. We stay where we are.

"How are things with Travis?" Spencer asks Cass.

"I broke up with him last week," she says with a look of disdain.[37]

"That was quick," I say. Immediately I feel like it might have sounded judgmental. But she just laughs a little.

"He was short-term boyfriend material," she says simply.

"Uh huh," Spencer slurps at the latte[38] he got from the store's built-in coffee shop. "Someone had a boy toy."

She shrugs. "We weren't very compatible.[39] He is way too obsessed with water polo."

"Like you're way too obsessed with Mythology?" Spencer prods.

"They're not obsessions that mesh well," I interject. "I mean, once you're done talking about how much the god Poseidon would have loved water polo, what else do you have to say to each other?"

"You know," Cass laughs, "That one never came up."

"Really?" I ask, mock-serious. "Missed opportunity. Your relationship could have lasted five minutes longer."

---

[37] "Disdain" is highly French-ified, but ultimately comes from the Latin *dignus*, "worthy," with the *dis-* prefix meaning "not." So, to look at something as if it is unworthy.

[38] Italian for "milk." In Italy they call it *caffè latte*, the *caffè* being the more important ingredient.

[39] "Compatible" has an unexpected literal meaning: "suffering together," from the Latin roots *com-* and *pati*. It's related to "compassion," as in feeling sympathy by feeling someone else's pain.

"Spencer, have you been keeping up with this?" Cass asks Spencer. "Because Brian is funny now, and it's breaking my brain."

"How did Travis take it?" Spencer asks her.

"Fine, I think," she shrugs.

"You think?"

"Hard to tell over text."

"Cass!" Spencer exclaims. I laugh.

"Please," Cass rolls her eyes. "It wasn't long enough or serious enough to merit an in-person breakup. Text was totally fine. Miss Manners would have approved."

"What did you say? Did he reply?"

"None of your damn business."

"I'll be the judge of that," Spencer says. "Let me just see the messages..."

"*Hell* no, I ain't letting you go through my texts with my ex."

Mr. Stanton comes up again.

"Do I have to move you myself?" he groans. He walks toward Cass brushing the air with his hands. "Shoo. Go. Move. You're being shown up by *freshmen*."

"Well of course," Spencer says on his way toward the front of the store. "They're little and cute. Who wants to talk to us? We're old and hideous."

I'm unhappy to split up from Cass and Spencer. They've definitely become my best friends in the last few weeks. It feels amazing, almost like it used to with Nora, except there are two of them.

But now it's time for bolder socialization. It's my job today to talk to strangers.

I walk around for a few minutes. No one is looking at me. I'm not allowed to start talking to them; they need to be the ones to ask me. Not that I would even have the guts to start talking to them if I could. What should I even be doing, other than walking? It feels bizarre, just putting one foot in front of another with no actual goal in mind.

I make a couple of loops on the same path: through Romance, then Sci-Fi, up to the front of the store through the New Release and Bestseller displays, back through toys, and across Mystery back to Romance. Through shoulder-height bookshelves made of dark wood and piled with more words than I could read in a lifetime. I like bookstores, even this hopelessly corporate[40] and character-free one, with its fluorescent light and its company-standardized tables of book recommendations. I skirt along the edge of the music section once per circuit, but I don't allow myself to go in. I'd definitely end up distracted in there.

On my third circuit, I see Spencer and Cass standing together at the end of an aisle.[41] I automatically start to wander toward them, but pause when I hear Cass whispering in a harsh tone.

"...Just what the hell you're trying to do to yourself."

"You're overreacting to nothing," Spencer hisses. The airy tone he usually adopts is gone. His brow is creased.

"You're telling me you're over him, and as soon as you're out of my sight, you're lurking on his Instagram

---

[40] Latin *corpus*, "body." Appropriate that "corporate" and "corpse" share a root.
[41] From the Latin *ala*, "wing." Like the wing of a bird, yes, but even better in this context, like a wing of the Roman army.

account."

"It doesn't hurt anyone for me to look," Spencer says glumly.

"It hurts you," Cass whispers, quieter than ever. "If you keep nursing this thing..."

She glances up and sees me standing a hundred yards away, watching them. Spencer looks a second later. Their stares feel like a physical force that jolts me backward. As if on a cue, all three of us turn and walk in different directions. I feel my face burning hot.

On my fifth aimless amble,[42] still with no fliers distributed, I catch sight of Jeff standing by the test prep books. I detour to see what he's up to.

He's standing with Mackenzie, his girlfriend. I know her separately, because I've been in various classes with her for all of high school. And I know that she and Jeff have been dating forever, in high school terms anyway. But this is one of only a handful of times I've ever seen them together. They come to Latin Banquet together, and dance like they're in church. But I never see them walking down the hallway, arms-around-waists, like most couples. They're a foot apart now. I can't even imagine them kissing.

"*Salve*, Jeff," I say to him. "*Bonjour, ma cherie*," I say to Mackenzie, because she takes French instead of a good language.

"*Bonjour*, Brian, *ça va?*" she replies cordially.

"You've got me there," I say. I don't speak French except for what I know from word roots and what I

---

[42] Latin, *ambulare*, "to walk."

learned from the Looney Tunes.

"*Ma cherie* is a bit forward," she grins.

"Yeah, don't make me use this thing," Jeff warns, brandishing his plastic trident. He's decked out like a gladiator, with trident,[43] net, and roly-poly segmented armor on one arm. Of course we can't have him dressed fully accurately, because Jeff can't walk through Books & More Books in nothing but tiny leather briefs. So the gladiator stuff is over his normal polo shirt and jeans.

Spencer passes to our right, sees us, then theatrically swings his whole body around to come toward us.

"Thank the gods, I was afraid we really were going to advertise instead of hang out," he sighs as he approaches. "Don't have all these memorized yet?" Spencer teases Mackenzie, who is flipping idly through an SAT guidebook.

Jeff shakes his head. "Just a few more opportunities to get the right score," he says forlornly.

"Lighten up," Mackenzie chides him, patting his arm.

Physical affection confirmed!

"Yeah," Spencer says, "How many spots are you below valedictorian?"[44]

"Six," Jeff says bitterly.

"Are you trying to kill him?" Mackenzie hisses at Spencer.

"She's only four," Jeff tells us.

"You can't obsess over stuff like that," she says quietly

---

[43] "Trident" is from the Latin words *tres* and *dentes*: "three teeth."

[44] "One who says goodbye:" Latin *dicere*, "to say," and *vale*, "farewell." Because of the speech they make at graduation. Because it would have been too on-the-nose to name them after the Latin for "Wow. I can't believe we're finally here."

to him. For a minute they look at each other like we're not here. Like they've had this talk before, and they'll have it again, and they're living every one of those instances at once.

"Well, don't let us interrupt your pillow talk," Spencer says.

"Mackenzie's going to get a study book with our flier," Jeff tells us.

"Way to support the cause!" I encourage her.

"I need one anyway," she shrugs.

"I am certain that you do not, but we appreciate the thought," Spencer says.

Allie buzzes by. She is lucky enough to be playing Hermes today. Someone years ago made winged sandals and a caduceus staff for a project, and she happens to have tiny enough feet to fit the shoes. She's like a Cinderella of nerdy ancient history cosplaying.

If she and Katie are here now, that probably means...

"Our shift is over," says Cass as she approaches. She's back in her street clothes. Today, ripped black shorts, striped purple and gray leggings, and a black t shirt with the cat bus from *My Neighbor Totoro* on it. "Go change in the bathroom so someone else can use your toga."

"No need," I say. I twist out of the toga, lay it down, and roll the legs of my jeans back down. *Et voilà,*[45] street clothes.

"See, this is why I hated my costume," Cass shakes her head. "Let's go. You coming Spencer?"

---

[45] More Looney Tunes French.

"I'm here all day," he says. "President and all."

"Have fun then," Cass laughs, and starts out. I hand off my toga happily to an incoming freshman and follow her.

Once we're in her car, she throws on an outsized pair of sunglasses and puts her key in the ignition.[46] The car shudders, and it takes Cass three tries to get it started. It's an old wreck that her mom let her have, a big boat of a full-sized sedan with plastic peeling off the dash. It's got a cassette deck, with one of those cassette-to-aux-cable adapters. I plug my iPod in to that. We've ridden together enough that it is now officially my job to pick music. I go with Dinosaur Jr.

After a minute or so of oscillating waves of distorted guitar attack, she starts to nod along.

"This is a good one," she says.

"Noted," I reply happily. (The Good: Dinosaur Jr, The Replacements, Mastodon, Ghost, late Nick Cave. The Bad: Meat Puppets, Scratch Acid, early Nick Cave. The Ugly: Rod Stewart. That was a joke anyway.)

"What is with him?" she sighs. I assume she means Spencer, even though she has given me no introduction to this new conversational topic.

"I don't know," I say, which seems like the right thing to say.

"It's been two months, and he's still obsessed with the guy. How does he expect the wounds to heal if he keeps picking them open?"

---

[46] "Ignition" is from the Latin *ignis*, "fire," same as "igneous."

"I am probably the single least qualified person to tell you," I joke. She laughs, but her face goes bitter again quickly.

"It's not like Danny is even worth it," she sighs. "He's better off without him."

"Yeah, I've never liked Danny much," I agree. He's in my year, and I have a lot of classes with him. "He seems... shallow."

"He is," Cass breathes. "And Spencer was too, when he was with him."

"I didn't know," I say. I barely talked to Spencer until a month ago.

"He acted just like Danny. He joined Danny's friend group, fawned over the lot of them. He's better off with us than with those dingbats."

"Does that happen a lot to people?" I ask, genuinely unsure. "In relationships?"

"What, losing your personality and glomming on to the other person completely?"

"Yeah."

"Unfortunately, yes," she says. "I haven't done it since the eighth grade..."

"I can't imagine you losing your personality."

She laughs. "I was a lot less sure of myself then. My boyfriend was really into *Star Wars* and Major League Baseball, and I abandoned my anime to follow him whole-hog into both."

"That can't be true."

"For two months. Left me completely disoriented when he dumped me for a girl who was willing to do second-base-over-the-shirt. Like I had lost a part of myself. I realized my mistake then. Swore I'd never do that again. But a lot of people, they haven't grown out of it. They get all wrapped up in their relationships and forget themselves."

We're in my driveway now. She throws the car in park and turns to me. "But you won't do that, okay? You'll remember this conversation and you'll hang on to yourself."

"That's a Bowie song," I say idly.

"But really," she says seriously. "When I finally find you your girlfriend. You're gonna still be the same Brian, and you're still gonna hang out with me and Spencer."

"Of course," I say, but I cringe a little when she talks about finding me a girlfriend. She's still all about that, and I haven't really loved her methods. She has shoved me into uncomfortable social situations with a couple of friends of hers in the past few weeks. I really just want to keep being her friend and have her forget the whole matchmaker thing.

But she's a woman on a mission, and I don't know how to tell her.

I get interrogated[47] by my mom when I come in. A few references to various friends send her to her happy place, allowing me to escape to my room.

Nora and I haggle for a bit over text, then settle on *Rocket League*. If only I could talk to every girl like I do to Cass and Nora. Is that how normal people feel?

---

[47] From Latin *rogare*, "to ask," a slightly more polite term.

CHAPTER 17: MARCH 16ᵀᴴ   KATIE NGUYEN

I hadn't been texting Monk—Jeremy—*that* much. There was even a whole day in the middle of last week when neither of us sent a single message.

But there were certainly a lot of messages gathering in our history. When I discovered that he had never seen a Harry Potter movie, we synched up our starting time and watched the first one together from our separate houses across town, live-texting the whole thing. I think he liked it. Or maybe it was just talking to *me* he liked.

I told him we were just going to be friends. I didn't think he believed me.

We talked a lot about State. We were going to find some time to meet up without our teams figuring it out. He had as much trouble with his friends as I did. After those Certamen finals, Our Lady of the Seven Sorrows was out for West Oak's blood. His Latin 3 class was already pledging sweet vengeance at Certamen next year. I told him to bring it on, because we'd be ready.

I hadn't told him anything about our difficulties

financing our State trip. I was determined that we were going to get there, and that he'd never need to know. Something about the guy at the rich-kid private school knowing that our public school had to scrape and save to pay $150 per student. It would have been embarrassing. I didn't want his pity.

We were making progress. We had around $1,000 raised out of the $3,300 we needed. Half of that was from two donations by businesses, and the rest were from the bookstore fundraiser and the car wash.

It wasn't great. We officers had been hoping that those two fundraisers would be more lucrative. But our situation wasn't hopeless yet.

On Monday the *Kleinsberg Herald* finally published the blurb about our Certamen team that I'd sent in two weeks earlier. That was part of my job as Historian—to try to get us mentioned in local papers anytime we did something good. I'd sent the same blurb to a whole list of nearby newsletters and papers. It was a tiny picture of us and two sentences about us making it to State. The *Herald* was the biggest paper to use it. They put in their "Kudos" section, buried in the middle of the paper somewhere no one would see it. But I was proud that something I'd written was published. Especially as Mr. Stanton excitedly put the clipping up on his wall.

On Thursday Jeff and I walked together to Certamen from the Physics room. We had both happened to be there doing extra questions to improve our test grades. Mine had been an 87, Jeff's a 96. He did four times as many as he needed to do, just to be safe.

We weren't in a hurry, because we knew that Cass and Spencer would be late from their meeting of the Gay-Straight Alliance. Cass was the president. She had taken over this year after the Alliance's founder had graduated—leaving, in Cass's words, "big Birkenstocks to fill."

When we arrived, it was just Brian and Allie. No Mr. Stanton even.

"He's at a meeting," Allie explained, "I'm in charge."

"In charge of Brian?" I asked. Brian was so far oblivious to all of us under his headphones.

"And you two, now," she said.

"Well, I'm mutinying," Jeff joked.

"You can't," Allie insisted.

"Look at me," Jeff motioned to his eyes. "I'm the captain now."

Cass and Spencer came in then, talking in hushed tones. Brian pulled off his headphones as soon as he saw them.

"Do you think he's going to do it tonight?" Spencer asked seriously.

"Who do what?" Allie butted in.

"A sophomore guy who will, for now, remain nameless," explained Cass, "Was asking everybody's advice about coming out to his parents. It was a very serious GSA today."

"Jeez," I said.

"Cass made him promise to call her afterward, in case it goes badly," Spencer said.

"He was afraid they might throw him out," Cass said. "I'm not gonna have him alone out there. I'll go pick him up myself if I need to."

"I don't envy him," Spencer said sadly. "My parents were cool when I told them. Said they'd known I was gay since I was in third grade."

"I knew you were gay before I knew what gay *was*," confirmed Jeff, who had gone to elementary school with Spencer. "Something about all those sequins at the talent show."

"Let me guess," Brian smiled, "Singing Liza Minelli?"

"What kind of gay stereotype do you take me for?" Spencer said.

"It was Elton John," Jeff said.

"'Bennie and the Jets,'" Spencer said fondly.

"Mine were a little wigged out when I told them," Cass said. "I only told them when I got my first girlfriend freshman year. They had a lot of questions. Looked like I'd told them I had a terminal disease, at first. But they came around."

"What was it like at school?" Brian asked, curious.

"Coming out? Fine, at first," Cass said. "I only told my friends, and my friends were cool with it. After that it was just some dirty looks from people in the hallway when I was holding hands with a girl. And who cares what randos think?"

"You came out in high school," Spencer said gravely. "It's a whole different game in middle school."

"What happened?" Brian asked.

Spencer shook his head. "Locker room jocks happened. Nothing that they weren't doing to me before, but with a new intensity and focus. Let's talk about somebody else."

"I don't think many people know I'm not straight," Allie said. "I don't think many people outside Latin Club even know my name. And, I mean, since I've never dated anyone."

"Which just leads to the dumbest question," Cass said.

"If you've never dated anybody, how do you know you're gay?" Spencer drawled in his ditziest voice. "And they all think they're the first person to have thought of it."

"Why don't you come to GSA?" Cass rounded on Allie. "I'm, like, the only bi girl there. I could use a sister in arms."

Allie shrugged, looking a little uncomfortable. "I'm just bi, I don't need to talk about it all the time."

"It's not just about you," Cass said. "It's about helping other people on the same journey. Mostly it's about being a part of a community."

"I'll think about it," Allie said.

"Next meeting's in two weeks," Cass told her.

Shortly afterward, Mr. Stanton came in with his mug of tea in his hand.

"Ah, you're all here," he said, "Sorry to keep you waiting. Take a seat and we'll get started."

Allie stood. "I move that we begin with the pledge of allegiance to Mr. Stanton's beard..."

It was a pretty brutal Certamen practice. Mr. Stanton had switched to using Nationals-level questions, to prepare us for the higher level of questions we'd see at State. It was a tough adjustment. I went from being able to get most of the Authors questions to getting under a quarter, and I even started missing some of the Life questions. Brian and Cass had similar experiences in History and Mythology. I didn't even recognize any of the names in their questions.

No one had as rough an afternoon as Jeff, though. He couldn't seem to get any of his Grammar or Vocabulary questions right. As the practice progressed, his problems became more mental than anything. Even questions he normally would have gotten, he started to flub just because he was second-guessing himself. He was especially hard on himself after those mistakes.

"I'm not trying to make you guys lose hope," Mr. Stanton told us as we were packing up and licking our wounds. "I just want you to go into this with open eyes. State is more challenging, and the teams there are playing at a really high level. Remember that it's an amazing achievement to make State at all. It doesn't matter what happens when we're there."

"We're going to surprise you," Jeff said with a kind of desperate certainty. "We're not going to State just to get creamed. We're going to work hard and take the whole thing. We're going to Nationals."

Mr. Stanton looked a little concerned at him. "Just don't hurt yourselves, okay?" he said to all of us.

***

After practice, everyone but Jeff (too much to do!) moved to a folding table in front of the small gym. We had gotten the coaches to let us sell concessions at basketball games. But their booster club already made big money doing that at the Varsity games, so we were only allowed to do the Junior Varsity and Freshman games.

Attendance was about what you'd expect for a JV basketball game.

The few people who did come buy from us were really happy that there were concessions. Usually JV gets ignored, they said. We tried to keep our desperation out of our eyes as we sold them candy and soaking wet cans of soda from our cooler.

"What are you guys fundraising for?" asked a girl as she bought some M&M's.

"Latin Club," I answered, handing her her change.

"There's a *Latin Club*?" she asked incredulously.

"Pig Latin, actually," Spencer said from behind me. "But ix-nay on that. The principal thinks we're working a *lot* harder."

We'd gotten that same question probably twenty times tonight. It was exhausting. But Spencer managed to think up a new snarky answer for every one of them. My favorites so far were: "Yeah, you should come to our next meeting on Tuesday. Bring your own sacrificial chicken." "Well, we used to be the Celtic Club, but we had a hostile takeover." And a completely straight-faced, "No."

We didn't need many volunteers for a job like this. Honestly, just one person could do it fine. But it was more fun with so many of us there. Cass and Spencer liked to whisper little made-up backstories for everyone we saw passing. Brian got involved, and soon everyone we saw was part of a massive conspiracy to assassinate the Emperor.

Not that I was always completely present with the group. I mean, we all spent a little time checking our phones. But toward the end, Allie caught me a few times texting you-know-who.

Jeremy had actually just gotten home from a basketball game himself. But he had been playing. I asked if he was JV or Varsity, but his school was too small to have JV at all. It was so small, in fact, that most of the athletes played on nearly every team.

I'm mostly focused on track and field, he explained. *But basketball needs guys, so I help out when there's no conflict.*

Jeez, I typed. *We have two to three teams per sport with almost no overlap.*

Must be nice to focus on one, he said. *But the cross-training is helpful sometimes. I hate when football decides they need me. I have to play my xylophone in cleats during halftime.*

"How's Jeremy?" Allie asked me on the drive home, with a devilish grin.

"Just fine, thank you," I said.

"Brave of you, texting him in front of everyone else."

I felt my face grow hot. Allie laughed.

"You should tell them about him," Allie said. "I swear they'd be cool with it." She watched me, but I kept my eyes on the road and let the music on my car stereo fill the silence. "I noticed your taste in jazz expanding."

I blushed again. "Just some Bill Evans and Oscar Peterson."

"It's all elevator music to me," she shrugged. "You must really like this guy."

"We're *friends*," I insisted.

"How foolish of me," Allie laughed. "If you liked him, you'd change your whole taste in music because it reminds you of him. Or check your phone every five seconds after you text him to see if he's replied. Or..."

"You've made your point."

"But I've got more!"

"I think I've got it, thanks," I put on the breaks at a stoplight. Allie propped up her feet on the dash and looked out the passenger side window.

"Such a silly thing, being ashamed of a crush. Or maybe you like it *better* that way..."

CHAPTER 18: MARCH 16ᵀᴴ BRIAN GANZ

When Spencer drops me off I'm still buzzing with energy. I can't get over how much I love hanging out with that group now.

I get online to play *Rocket League* with Nora. But I wind up talking to her a lot more than I play.

"I love that you've got friends like this now," Nora says into my headphones.

"Yeah, me too," I say. "I don't know how I'm going to survive next week now."

"Next week?"

"Spring Break. No school, so I probably won't see them."

Nora makes a noise somewhere between a laugh and a sigh. "Dude, people see their friends over Spring Break."

Now that she mentions it...

"But no one has said anything," I think out loud. "How do I..."

"Invite them to your house, you ding-dong," Nora almost yells, her voice distorting from her peaking mic.

"Right! Right. I think I can handle that."

"I can walk you through the steps if you're nervous," Nora says sarcastically.

"No, I've got that. But I do want to ask you about something else."

"I'm all ears."

"How do you know when you have a crush on someone?"

Nora laughs. If it were anyone else, them laughing at that question would make me feel about an inch tall. I'd never want to talk to that person again. But that's not how me and Nora are. I know I can tell her anything without her judging me. And I know that when she's laughing at me, she's not thinking any less of me.

"It's something I've been wondering, in the abstract," I explain. "I don't know that I've ever liked anybody."

"You still haven't had a crush?" she asks disbelievingly. "What about Cass?"

"I ran through a list of girls I knew in my head. She seemed like the best combination of friendly, funny, intelligent, and good-looking. So I decided she would make a good first crush."

"Is that how you explained it to her?" asks Nora with a laugh. "Because I think I can see why she turned you down."

"No, no, that's not what I said. But it's definitely how I decided."

"Well, that's number one. You don't decide on a crush. It happens without your permission."

"Okay, that makes sense," I say. "But how do you

know?"

"That's a hard question to answer. I guess you just feel different around them."

"Elevated heartrate, dilated[48] pupils," I list off from a Wikipedia article.

"Probably," she says, "But that's not what I notice. What I notice is, when we talk, I want to tell her everything about myself. When we're not together, I think about how I might want to share things I'm seeing with her. I start to explain everything to her in my head. Like she's with me all the time."

"Sounds exhausting," I say.

"Well, you start to think, if it's them, you wouldn't mind never being alone," she sighs. "So, you say you're just wondering in the abstract, but that's bullshit, right? You think you have a crush on someone."

I hesitate.

"That's all the answer I need," she laughs. "Who is it?"

"I don't, um," I start.

"Never mind. You tell me when you want to. I'll just be over here wildly speculating about every possibility until you do."

"I appreciate that," I say ironically.

She's right, of course. I think I might be feeling something. Something I might be a hair's breadth away from admitting. But I want to be sure first.

---

[48] "Dilated" is from the Latin *latus*, "wide." Which makes perfect sense, though it is arbitrary, because circular things also get taller as they get wider. They could just as easily have been called something like "disalted" pupils.

CHAPTER 19: MARCH 24ᵀᴴ   SPENCER OLSON

Jeff, I text on the Wednesday afternoon of Spring Break, *Certamen practice at Brian's house tonight at 7. You in?*

Is this an actual Certamen practice, or is that just what you're calling hanging out again? comes his reply a moment later.

What's the difference? I reply.

Practice questions, or studying of any sort.

Okay, you've got me there, we have none of that planned, I reply. *But Cass is bringing her WiiU.*

I've got too much to do. You know, State is only a month away, he types, and I can almost hear his patronizing tone. *It might be good to actually have some extra practices.*

Good point, I say. *But it's spring break, so...*

Let me know when you're ready to get serious.

Will do, buddy! I type, and add some kissy face emojis.

I like to bait Jeff a little. He's one of those straight guys who's a little uptight about the whole gay thing. Not in a "gay people don't deserve rights" way. He's just a little skittish. I figure, the only way to get over that is through exposure. And Exposure is my middle name.

(It's Dale, actually.)

***

Brian is a serious-type gamer, devotee of Xbox, PlayStation, PC. But he can let loose when less serious folk—in this case, Cass and I—bring in their WiiU for a little party. After a few rounds of Mario Kart, I decide that the room is sufficiently loosened up, and put in Just Dance.

It's me Cass, Brian, Katie, and Allie, who goes everywhere with Katie these days. Katie and Allie have just finished a dance together. They receive their pathetic score, laugh and high five anyway, and trot away.

I get up to take my turn next, evicting Brian's cat from my lap. Daisy shifts immediately to Katie, who squeals with delight. For my song, I choose "Uptown Funk."

To my surprise, Brian hops up next to me.

"I never thought of you as a dancer," I laugh.

"You thought right," he says, removing the iPod from his hoodie pocket. I guess so it won't fly out as he flails arhythmically about.

The song starts. I am, as always, flawless. Brian looks like a drunk person trying to flag down an airplane. I think even his avatar is laughing at him. But he's playing it for laughs, so we all have a good time with it. We get our scores, and I hold up my hand for a high five. He smacks it, genuinely out of breath.

"We'll do competitive mode next time," I joke.

"If you think you can take me," he replies with mock bravado.

I like it at Brian's house. It's clean without being too neat or fussed-over, and his room is a happy sensory overload of band posters, crammed bookshelves, stacks of CDs. His small gaming TV on one wall, his PC on another. It feels like I'm in his Fortress of Solitude.

When the pizza arrives, we settle in with Brian playing some music on a little portable speaker. It's angry and yelly, like usual.

"We've gotta do some DJ switching in a bit here," I tell him.

"Don't hate on Alice in Chains," Cass chides me. She's got pizza in her right hand and is stroking under Daisy's chin with her left. Brian was right about that cat being a slut.

"Sorry, I'm just not a fan of putting any women in *chains*," I reply. Cass rolls her eyes.

But Brian takes off the yelling and hands me the aux cable. "Be my guest."

I put my pizza to the side and scroll through my iPhone for a moment before making my first selection. The piano starts.

"No," Brian says.

"Oh yes," I reply.

"You are hurting me right now," Brian looks directly into my eyes. "Physical and emotional pain."

"You boys," Cass rolls her eyes again. "A little Journey never hurt anybody."

"Just a city boy," Allie sings along, "Born and raised in south Detroit."

"*Et tu*, Allie?" Brian moans.

By ten o'clock, we're all just talking. Brian, Cass, and Katie are strategizing and talking about their odds at State. I get them to help me think of more lucrative things we might sell at our basketball game concession stands. This is productive for a bit, but we end up joking about selling drugs and liquor, and of course steroids to the JV athletes, so they can make Varsity.

Brian bids Katie and Allie farewell at 1 am. Cass says something about a curfew and leaves at 1:30, clutching her WiiU under one arm. Then there were two.

I don't really want to leave yet, because I'm not quite exhausted enough to fall asleep without thinking. Brian doesn't seem to be in a hurry to kick me out either.

So I stay another hour. Brian teaches me to play one of his "I'm a real serious gamer y'all" games. I hang in there for a while, but then his friend Nora gets on from Michigan, and they really start to rake me over the coals.

"This is supposed to be payback for my kicking your ass at all those actually fun games, isn't it?" I ask as my avatar's brains fly out of the back of his skull yet again.

"I don't know what you mean," says Brian, making his avatar do something unspeakable over my corpse. "This seems pretty 'actually fun' to me."

I like talking to Nora on the dumb little headset. Who knew Brian was cool enough to have a trans best friend. Brian isn't bad company either, incidentally. He even found some punk music I like. While I humiliate myself at this game, we're listening to Against Me!, which is fronted by a trans woman named Laura Jane Grace. She writes a good chorus.

When I get to my car, I feel like I'll be able to sleep tonight. I wave goodnight out my window as Brian stands

186

on the porch. Before I pull out of the driveway, I put on Journey again so he can hear it through my open windows. He covers his ears and retreats dramatically back into his house.

CHAPTER 20: MARCH 30TH   JEFF MILLER

When I come into Certamen practice the week after spring break, Spencer is saying something to Brian that's making everyone else crack up. Some inside joke about dancing from their little party. I decide I don't need to know and take a seat near the door.

My essay for AP English could use another revision pass. I open up my laptop. About halfway through I notice it. A comma splice that the grammar checker overlooked. This is why the machines will never replace us.

I'm feeling a little sluggish, so I slip an Adderall out of my Aspirin bottle and palm it. When I'm sure no one is looking, I take it with a swig from my water bottle.

Mr. Stanton calls the practice to order. I brace myself for the storm.

Ablative of comparison? No, ablative of degree of difference. Jussive noun clause? No, optative subjunctive. Future passive infinitive? No, that one's just a supine with the *active* infinitive of "to go."

Mr. Stanton is very understanding. I don't want his

pity. I don't want him to point out the one question I got right, and single me out for praise. I want to get the answers.

I've read about these things in Wheelock's, why aren't they coming out right when I hear the questions?

As he adjourns the practice, Mr. Stanton gives us another Mister Rogers speech. He's very proud of us, he'll love us even if we suck, we're all very special, blah blah. I pack to go. My mind is buzzing with everything I want to do when I get home.

My first order of the night is going to be to do another round of moisturizing on my petri dishes. I've already made it past the District and Regional levels of the science fair, but one of the judges at Regional didn't seem all that impressed with my data set. I know that if I want to make it past State and on to National, I should do some more trials to fortify it.

Everyone on the team leaves at about the same time. I hear Brian, Cass and Spencer plotting a run for fries and shakes. They ask Katie and Allie if they want to come.

"Not this time, guys," Katie smiles. "I've got homework, and I just figured out that Allie is failing Algebra II..."

"The teacher hates me!" Allie protests.

"...So I'm going to help her sort that out."

"Jeff!" Spencer calls. I'm already moving in the opposite direction, toward my car. "You wanna come?"

"No thanks," I bark. "Too busy."

I keep walking to my car. I can hear, though they don't think I can, as Cass asks Spencer why he even bothers inviting me to things.

"He's our friend too," I hear Spencer begin, as I get into my car and shut the door.

My hands fidget on the steering wheel the whole way home. I need to get to work. Why do I have to waste all this time driving?

The house is completely dark when I pull up. My heart skips once, but I know I paid the bill.

My dad is asleep at his desk. He just fell asleep before dark, so he didn't turn on any lights. I close his laptop gently and tiptoe to the kitchen.

I make Grandma some oatmeal. While it cooks I go shopping in the freezer for myself. Just pizza, pizza, and pizza. I start the oven preheating. It always takes forever to get up to 450, so it'll probably be just finished by the time I get back downstairs.

In Grandma's room, I flip on the lamp next to the door. She starts and wakes in her bed, bewildered to see me.

"Frank," she says in a whisper. "What time is it?"

"It's only 6:30," I answer. "And I'm not Frank, I'm Jeff. Your grandson." Frank was her first husband, before my grandfather. He died in the Korean War.

"Oh, don't you get fresh with me, now," she laughs. "You know I'm no grandmother."

I sit on the chair next to her bed to feed her her dinner. On the end table is a packet of cigarettes and a lighter.

"Grandma!" I pick them up. "You know you can't be smoking!"

She shakes her head. She doesn't recognize them. The pack is mostly full; only two missing. One is unlit in her hand. I take it and tuck it in the pack. Shaking her cans of SlimFast, I hear the rattle of the butt of the other. Once the cigarettes are all accounted for, I slip the pack and lighter into my back pocket to dispose of outside her room. I need to talk to Dad about this again. He just gets her whatever she asks for when he puts in our order at the grocery store. He never thinks it through. I wish I could just do everything.

"It's really important," I say. "You're not well enough to smoke. Besides, smoking in bed is a huge fire hazard."

"I never knew you were so safety-conscious, William," she says as I spoon in her first bite of dinner. I'm not sure who William is.

I'm right about the oven. It dings just as I get downstairs with Grandma's empty bowl. I hastily slit the plastic and take out the tiny pizza, then find the least crud-encrusted cookie sheet to put it on.

My phone buzzes. It's Mom. She can Skype tonight. My mind reels, as all my plans reorganize themselves. I rush to pull my laptop out of my backpack before something else calls her away.

After she got divorced from my dad, my mom ran off with Doctors Without Borders. It was like she couldn't get far enough away from him unless she went to the other side of the world. Currently she's in Mali, Africa, or at least that's where she was the last time she checked in with me a few months ago.

I hit connect on Skype and it rings. I know that she

does important work, and I'm proud of that. I just wish that her running away from my dad hadn't meant her running away from me too.

She picks up. I'm always picturing that she's going to be wearing safari gear calling me from a hut made of reeds or something. I can't help it. But no, she's in scrubs, and she's sitting in a normal, drab-looking doctor's office. It's ten PM in Mali right now. She must not have wifi wherever she's living if she's Skyping from her office.

"Hi, honey," she says.

"Hi Mom," I say, my face feeling hot.

"I'm so sorry I haven't been able to call you before."

"No it's okay," I say quickly.

"No, it isn't," she says, "I want to do better."

"You do important work," I defend her to herself. "You're out helping people in other countries who would never have access to medical care without people like you."

"That's actually what I'm calling to tell you about," she says. "I'm coming back to America in a few months."

My heart leaps. I've always loved knowing she was out helping the less fortunate, of course, but there was always that part of me that just wanted her near me. That part has taken over, and I feel like dancing for joy.

"You're coming home?" I manage.

"Well, relatively speaking," she says. "I'll be relocating to Minneapolis."

"In Minnesota?" I say in a small voice. All that joy has just been sucked out as if through an open airlock, leaving a black void behind. "That's across the country."

"A quick flight," she disagrees.

"It might as well be Africa," I continue.

"Well, I've met someone over here..."

"Met someone?" I snap to attention. My vision is starting to blur on the edges. Is that the pill, or what?

"And we're going back to his hometown to set up a practice," she finishes.

"How many kids does *he* have in Minneapolis?" I spit. "Or is it just that you still can't stand to be within driving distance of your old family?"

"Honey..." she says.

My phone buzzes. I take it out.

A message from Mackenzie.

Can we talk? she asks simply.

I bang out a reply. *Not a good time.*

I'm in your driveway, she replies immediately.

I stare at my phone for a moment. What does she mean? Is this "We need to talk?"

The timer for my pizza starts to beep. My hands are shaking.

"Sweetie," my mom's voice comes out of my laptop speakers, sounding more distant and less real than it did a second ago.

"I have to go," I tell her hastily. "We'll talk more later."

I slam my laptop over her protestations. I don't even quit out of Skype first. I turn off the oven on my way to the door, not bothering to take out the pizza.

Mackenzie is, indeed, standing against her car in my driveway.

"I'm sorry for barging over, Jeff," she says, "But I

couldn't wait any longer."

"You want to break up with me?" I ask directly.

She looks at the ground. I had been hoping for an immediate denial.

"No," I say. The ground is spinning. "No, that can't be it."

"We can't keep going like this," she says, the tears starting in her eyes. She dabs at them with her fist. "I'm another item on your to-do list. Every time we're together, your mind is on the next thing you need to do. You haven't been present with me in months."

"I can stop," I say, not caring if I sound desperate. "I've been taking you for granted. I can see that. I'll be more in the moment. I'll make more time for you."

She's shaking her head. "It's too late for that. We're too far gone. I've been wanting to do this for a while. I was waiting for a time when you had less stress. But that time doesn't seem to exist."

"You can't," I plead. "Not now. Give me a chance to change."

"My mind is made up, Jeff," she says. She's still crying, but her voice sounds final.

"Please," I beg again, "Not now."

"I'm sorry, Jeff," she opens her car door.

"You can't," I'm sobbing now. My vision is fogging. "This isn't right."

I'm not blacking out. It's white instead. Do people white out?

I can hear her car pulling away. I don't see anything anymore.

I think I'm lying on my driveway. But wait, I feel grass, so it must be the side yard.

Petri dishes. Mackenzie. Mom met somebody. Certamen. Physics. Grandma. Dad. Calculus. College essays. Latin State. Volunteer hours. Mackenzie. Grandma.

I'm told that I was still lying there the next morning when Dad came out to go to work.

CHAPTER 21: APRIL 6TH   CASS WASHINGTON

We were trying out our third option for Jeff's stand-in for Certamen at State.

Our first attempt had, of course, been Spencer. But he was ill-equipped for Grammar questions at such a high level, and it was obvious that we needed to look elsewhere. So much for his consolation prize as Certamen alternate.

Next we had tried Anthony, who was the best at Grammar and Vocabulary in our AP Latin 4 class. But the Certamen format stymied him. He knew his stuff alright. He could get about three-quarters of the questions right, same as Jeff. But that was only if he had enough time to run through options in his head, possibly jot down a bunch of notes on paper, and make sure he was right. That wouldn't cut it in a rapid-fire Certamen round. We tried to teach him to go with his gut, to buzz in as soon as he even had an inkling of the answer, but he didn't seem to have that in him.

He was relieved when Mr. Stanton told him not to worry about it, that we'd find someone else.

Now we were trying out Shamil, the Language specialist for the Latin 2 team. She was a great Certamen competitor at her level. She was also one of about three girls in the entire school who wore hijab. Today it was a rich royal blue headscarf tucked into the collar of a very flattering long-sleeve dress.

Mr. Stanton warmed her up at the beginning of practice with some Level 2 questions, and she knocked them out of the air like a martial arts master breaking boards. After Anthony, Shamil was a breath of fresh air.

Then we tried out questions from the Advanced level.

"Present active infinitive."

"No, I'm sorry, that's the syncopated form of a third person plural perfect verb."

"What is that?"

"Well you see, sometimes, especially in poetry..."

"*Adispisciverunt?*"

"Sorry, but *adipiscor* is deponent, so it would be *adepti sunt*."

"Deponent?" Shamil asked, leaning in expectantly.

All the Latin 3's and 4's in the room shuddered.

"Nasty things," Spencer said.

"They look passive in all their forms, but have active meanings," Mr. Stanton explained.

"No, no, don't ruin her innocence," I groaned.

"Why do those exist?" Shamil asked with visible disgust.

"I don't know," Mr. Stanton sighed. "Life would be better without them."

We all nodded.

Shamil had been writing a list of things that she didn't know, and would need to learn to be competitive in Advanced Certamen. She held it up to us now.

"This doesn't seem doable," she said blankly.

"No, it doesn't," Mr. Stanton admitted.

"I'm a little worried for next year," she said.

"You'll get to most of it in class," Katie chimed in.

"It's not so bad when you build up to it," I said.

"But this year?" Shamil asked tentatively.

"I think we can spare you the stress," Mr. Stanton sighed, rubbing his eyes under his glasses.

"Thank you," she said, and started to pack.

"Thanks for trying," Mr. Stanton told her.

"You really are very good," I said.

"Thanks, Cass, you too," she said graciously. "Good luck to you all. Sorry I'm no Jeff."

After she left, the rest of the team stuck around to discuss our options.

"All three of you are strong all-around Latin students," Mr. Stanton said hopefully. "Between you, you can at least get some of the Language questions."

"Probably so," Katie said. She had taken a couple in these last few practices.

"But not enough to win," I said sadly. "Nowhere near as many as Jeff."

"Well, Jeff is out of the question," Mr. Stanton said gravely.

Rumor had it that Jeff had been checked into a psychiatric hospital following some kind of breakdown. The whole school was talking about it, even though no one had seen or heard from him personally.

The silence just fueled the rumors even more.

I thought of Rumor the goddess in the Aeneid, with her hundreds of eyes and wagging tongues. Treading the earth making humans confuse truth for falsehood. Spencer had liked those lines. Like they had been written just for him.

Spencer was being surprisingly good about this story, though. Normally he'd have been the first to spread whatever gossip he had heard, verified or not. But he was fiercely protective of Jeff. He had squashed many a damaging story in the hallways.

Poor Mackenzie was devastated. She blamed herself for the whole thing. She had missed three days of school when it happened, which I think is the most school she had missed total since Kindergarten.

Jeff wasn't taking visitors, but the team had sent him a card, and later written him some personal letters. Mr. Stanton had been explicit with us though: we weren't to talk about Certamen, or State, or any kind of schoolwork. Jeff had been under a lot of stress, and the last thing he needed was a reminder of everything he had been anxious about. So we had kept our letters confined to low-stress topics and well-wishes.

I wondered if Mr. Stanton had a guilty conscience. Jeff had disappeared after a pretty stressful Certamen practice.

"You guys are still studying your specialties, though?" Mr. Stanton asked the three of us still on the team.

We held up the books we were reading. Mine was the *Library* of Pseudo-Apollodorus (sent to me by Angela from

Huntsville along with a thing of Fruit by the Foot, some pencils that looked like sonic screwdrivers, and a Slytherin scarf she had crocheted herself with a pattern like green snake scales).

"Good," Mr. Stanton said, running a hand through his hair. "No good letting yourselves get rusty while we're trying to figure out this... thing."

We adjourned our practice with no better idea of what to do next than when we had started. Katie and Allie left pretty quickly, but Brian, Spencer and I lingered, in no particular hurry.

"What're you up to next?" Brian asked Spencer.

"We've got a freshman basketball game to vend at," Spencer said with a resigned tone. It was getting really old, but I was hanging in there with him.

"I'll join you, if you'll have me," Brian said happily.

"That'd be great," I told him.

"You guys are fighting the good fight," Mr. Stanton told us.

"How much have we raised so far?" Brian asked.

"Seventeen hundred," Spencer and Mr. Stanton said in unison.

Brian nodded, saying nothing. We were all thinking the same thing. The fundraising was looking pretty bleak, and we were running low on new options. Soon we would have to discuss priorities. Who would we pay for, and who would have their formerly-guaranteed spot at State taken away? It was a conversation that no one wanted to have, but it got more inevitable every day.

Spencer and I went to his car to get the cooler of

drinks. Brian took the folding table and sign down to our spot in front of the gym.

"I wonder if this is even worth it," I said sadly as we hoisted the cooler.

"Almost certainly not," Spencer laughed. "We make less than a hundred dollars per game."

"Not that," I said. "Going to State at all. Hobbled without one of our Certamen competitors. Why bother?"

"You sound like Jeff," Spencer said.

"Too soon."

"But really," he went on as we walked. "We've gone to State every year of high school so far and loved every second of it. And that was without making it to Certamen. But now you've had a taste of winning, and just because you don't think you can win again, you say it's not worth it? Now that you're doing better than you've ever done before, you want to give up?"

We reached the front doors. I hoisted one open and held it with my hip as we maneuvered the cooler in.

"You're a smart kid, Spencer," I told him.

"Please. I can't even hack it at Certamen."

***

I got home around nine that night. The lights were on in the kitchen when I pulled into the driveway, and I could see my mom and dad sitting at the table together. Not the best sign. I took as long as I plausibly could to get out of the car and walk to the back door, but they weren't going anywhere. I opened the door slowly.

"Where have you been?" Mom asked gravely as soon as I was inside.

"Nice to see you too," I said. "I was doing the concessions at that basketball game, for Latin State. I texted you." I had been taking out my phone while saying this, and I pulled up my conversation with the sent message to show her. I cringed when I saw it.

The message had one of those "failed to send" exclamation points on it. I hadn't seen.

"I'm sorry," I said, holding up the phone as explanation.

"We were waiting on you for dinner," Mom said. "We wanted to talk to you about your grounding."

"Is that still going on?" I asked. I had lost track.

"That's the problem," Mom sighed. "We think this isn't working."

Well, duh. What business does anyone have grounding a 17-year-old for grades anyway?

"We got your report card in the mail," my dad picked up. "You've got an F in Economics."

I inhaled sharply. I knew my Econ grade was pretty bad, but I thought I was at least passing. Our Certamen and State stuff had really been taking a lot of my focus. I didn't even realize there was a report card coming out.

"I'm sorry," I started. But my mom didn't let me get far.

"You're spending all your time on Latin and your friends, and you don't have any time left for anything that actually matters."

"Had that locked and loaded before I came in the door, huh?" I never could resist a little cheek when I knew I was screwed anyway. Graveyard snark.

Her lip curled, but she pushed forward instead of laying into me for that. "How many scholarships have you written lately?" she asked.

"A couple."

"Which ones?"

I sighed. I was sick of lying about it. "Okay, I haven't written any since Christmas break."

She stood to meet my eyes. "Do you even care about your future?" That wasn't really a question, more a statement of frustration. "You're whiling away your most valuable years on nothing."

"It isn't nothing," I started.

"You're supposed to join school clubs so you look good on your résumé," my mom barreled on. "What good are more hours with the Latin Club if you're failing your classes? What's it going to do for your future if you can't even get to college?"

"I'm sorry I'm such a bad kid," I spat back, "Out till nine PM at officially sanctioned, adult-supervised activities packed with high-achieving nerds. Would you prefer I be out getting drunk and pregnant like most 17-year-olds?"

"All we're asking for is balance, sweetie," said my dad, whom I had honestly forgotten was sitting there.

"Maybe we should call a pause," my mom barreled on. "Maybe no more Latin Club for a while until you can refocus on what's really important."

"This isn't just about me," I protested. "This is for the team. For *everyone* to get to State. This means something."

"And your future doesn't mean something?" she countered. "You have to get your attitude right about your own business, instead of wasting all your time on a—"

"Can we take a break to collect ourselves?" my dad interjected, standing up between my mom and me. I noticed then that we had been drifting closer to each other's faces the whole time we had been talking. I saw my mom's anger starting to boil over behind his shoulder.

"Cass," he said calmly, "Why don't you go get in a half hour or so of essay writing before bed, so your mother can sleep easier?"

I took the out and retreated to my room. On my way up the stairs I heard my mother say the phrase, "Why she wastes her time on that stupid club..."

Adults always talk out of both sides of their mouths. From the first time you can talk they tell you "Follow your dreams" and "Do what you love." But as soon as you're old enough to know that what you love is, say, Classical Mythology, all they can say is "You can't make any money off that."

I set my laptop on my desk and started drafting an angry Tumblr post. "Honest Slogans for the Signs in your Guidance Counselor's Office:"

Follow your dreams, as long as your dreams will guarantee a starting salary of at least $50k with opportunity for advancement.

Shoot for the moon, and by "the moon" we mean a degree in Mechanical Engineering or something else practical, Accounting maybe.

While I was trying to think up a third one (comedy comes in threes), my dad came in. He saw the blue Tumblr background on my laptop and laughed good-naturedly.

"Well, now you're gonna make a liar of me when I go

downstairs and tell her you were hard at work."

"Tell her what you want," I grunted.

"She's worried about you," he said, taking a seat on my bed a few feet away from my desk chair.

"And you?"

"I'm not *not* worried," he admitted. (Litotes.) "I want to see you happy. You're smart enough to do anything you want to."

"And you're worried I'm throwing it all away because I don't even know what I want."

"See? Smart, perceptive. Maybe you should be a psychologist."

I rolled my eyes at him.

"Listen," he said. "Of course I wish you knew exactly what you wanted in life and were raring to go get it. That's what a parent wants for his kid. I don't want you to have to spend years figuring yourself out, like I did. Ain't no father want to have his kid make the same mistakes he did."

"You're happy, though," I said tentatively. My dad had dropped out of college, worked as a mechanic for a while, met my college-graduate mother while he was waiting tables, and gone back to school to impress her. He worked in the City Planning office now, doing things with schematic drawings and computer programs that most mortals could not contemplate.

"I sure am," he said. "I always gotta remind myself how much dumber I was when I was your age. I was chasing skirts and souping up my friends' cars. I could never even have imagined all the amazing stuff you do with only your mind." He gestured to my computer, I guess to reference all the academic achievements I'd accomplished with its help. The greasy keys and meme stickers slightly undermined his point. "You're better than I ever was. You've got so much potential. I don't want to see you go through the stress I had to."

"Living up to my potential *is* stress. What Mom wants is stress."

"I'm working on your mother. She's a driven woman. All about results. She'll come around."

"Is she going to ground me from Latin?" I asked tentatively.

He sighed. I froze.

"I got her to agree to let you go to State," he said.

"But?"

"But you're grounded until then. Real grounded. No outs for school-sponsored events."

I sighed.

"And no electronics for anything but school."

My head whipped up. That was a new frontier. "That's bullshit!"

"Listen, Cass. I know your intentions are good, but you messed up this time. You've got some work to do to get your mother's trust back."

"I'm too old for this!"

"You're getting sloppy. And *I'm* worried you're self-sabotaging."

"Who died and made you my psychologist?"

My dad fixed me with a look that made me ashamed of myself. "Three weeks. Get your shit in order. Show us you can handle yourself." He tapped on my foot, which was curled up in my desk chair next to him. "I talked your mother into letting your grounding start tomorrow morning instead of now. Enjoy your computer for one more night."

He rose to leave. He looked older than he usually did to me. "I love you, Cass," he said on his way out the door. I didn't say it back.

I saved the guidance counselor post to my drafts and, thankfully, found PuellaStellarum online. I explained to her why I wouldn't be online as much for the next few weeks, and promised to flaunt the rules as much as possible to talk to her. Then I lost myself in conversation, talking about Mythology, bad AP classes, and my school's State woes. Her pity was mixed with the anxiety that she might not be able to see me there, as we had planned. I swore I would get there any way I could.

I wanted to meet this girl, bad.

CHAPTER 22: APRIL 10TH-14TH   BRIAN GANZ

Cass's grounding has terrible ramifications[49] for my social life. Not to make this all about me, but still.

The effect is that what used to be frequent hangouts with me, Spencer, and Cass turn into ones with just me and Spencer. This in and of itself would be perfectly alright with me. I like spending time with Spencer. But Cass also deputizes Spencer to take over her role as matchmaker, and keep hunting me a girlfriend. A role which Spencer feels himself ideally suited for, and into which he throws himself with great zeal.

In the next school week, I'm pulled along to group outings with Spencer on four out of five nights. At each one, he has some poor, unfortunate girl he makes sure to sit next to me. Then he tilts his eyebrows at me the entire time, as I try and fail to make good conversation with my ill-matched suitress.

---

[49] From the Latin *ramus*, "branch." The mostly-extinct English word "ramify" literally means "branch out," so "ramifications" are the result of something branching out.

Monday at froyo is a pretty Latin 3 girl I recognize from Spencer's Dramatic Interpretation team and my own Latin class. We have some good small talk about Area and State, but fail to find any more common ground. Her favorite musician is "Pandora Hits of the 90's."

Wednesday at the mini golf place is a senior straight-ally from the GSA who talks all night about Global Warming. Which I agree is a problem, but about which I just can't expend the amount of mental or emotional energy that this girl can.

Thursday at Dave & Buster's is a Theatre girl who couldn't possibly have cared less about me. And who could blame her?

Each night, Spencer splits his time between talking and laughing with the group of other people he has brought along to mask his attempts at fixing me up, and eying me to see how things are going. I try to telegraph "NOT WELL," with my facial expressions, but he never sees, or at least he never lets on that he does. Each night I try to invite him back to my place afterward for a movie or a video game or something, but he always has even more plans with different people to get to after he drops me off at home. How does this guy keep going? Other than the Red Bull, I mean.

I'm missing the part of being Spencer's friend that I actually enjoyed. Instead of one-on-one Spencer, who I was really enjoying spending time with, I'm getting manic crowd Spencer, who's all big gestures and jokes. Like he's on stage. I've spent almost every night with him, and I feel like I haven't even really talked to him.

On Friday night around 10:30, I'm at home gaming with Nora when my phone buzzes. I decide not to check it. A few minutes later I barely hear the doorbell ring over my game's soundtrack. Spencer comes charging up to my room.

"Come on, man! Didn't you get my text?" he shouts.

"Hi Spencer!" says Nora's voice in my headset. Spencer's voice was so loud she heard it through my mic.

"No, I didn't," I say, checking my phone as if I hadn't heard it before. Spencer's text reads, *IHOP run! Picking you up in 5.*

"I don't know if my mom would want me out this late," I lie.

"I just talked to her, she was fine with it!" Spencer says. "Come on. I know the last few girls I've tried haven't worked out, but I've got a *good feeling* about this one!"

I inwardly admit defeat. I explain quickly to Nora before I log off, and she tells me cheerily to have fun. I haven't told her how I've been feeling about Spencer's spree. She likes him, and loves that I have friends, so I don't want to disillusion her.

It feels like a bad idea the whole time I'm riding to IHOP in Spencer's car. I've picked Meat Loaf again for the music—I didn't have it in me to try anything original. My chest feels tight. I want to go home. I think about asking Spencer to turn around.

No, I tell myself. People with friends go out with their friends. They don't run home and hide.

We get to IHOP and find a big group waiting. A few familiar faces from classes or *Annie*, but mostly people I don't know. Before we even get our table, Spencer separates Jenny, a Theatre kid and a Latin 2, from the crowd. He introduces me. I'm pleasant with her, even though I'm starting to have some trouble breathing. When Jenny turns away to follow the hostess to our table, Spencer elbows me and wiggles his eyebrows.

"Yeah," I whisper, "She's pretty cute." I hadn't actually noticed. It's hot in here. Are my hands always this sweaty?

Everyone in the group of eight chooses places around the table. I sit next to Jenny, as I am expected to. On previous nights, I always wondered how much Spencer had told these girls. Some definitely did not know they were being set up, and some seemed to. I don't even have the capacity to wonder that tonight. I have to use most of my concentration on breathing.

Everybody orders big plates of breakfast food. I can't imagine eating. I say I'll just stick with orange juice.

Everybody is talking about school, about Theatre shows, about graduation, about other peoples' relationships. I'm only dimly following. My heartbeat feels like someone else is pounding on my chest with their fist. The restaurant's fluorescent lights are like police spotlights, putting an unnatural glow into everything. I keep my focus narrow. I command my hand to put my cup to my lips again. I have to focus through every movement.

My throat hurts. And do they just keep turning up the heat in here?

This is not normal.

I'm supposed to be a person with friends.

I can't believe how hot it is.

I realize that Jenny is talking to me.

"Are you okay?" she asks me again.

"I'm just tired," I tell her almost truthfully.

"Past your bedtime, Brian?" Spencer says teasingly.

I can't tell if that's mean or not. I can hardly think.

The night passes in this fashion. It's almost two in the morning when Spencer is driving me home. I haven't put on any music.

"Okay, so we haven't hit pay dirt yet," he is saying, about whatever he thinks is the reason I failed with Jenny tonight. "We'll keep trying. We'll find her."

"Uh huh," I say, watching the strip malls pass. Most of them have turned off their lights for the night. The street lights smear in Spencer's windows, making big blurry crosses of light. I focus on those.

Spencer wishes me a good night as I leave his car. I think I say something back, but I don't know what.

My mom is asleep when I get in. I wander into my room, crawl onto my bed, and put my headphones over my ears. On my iPod, I cue up Shellac's *1000 Hurts*. As I suspected, the chords sledgehammer my emotions right out of my head and replace them with Steve Albini's. I synchronize[50] my breathing and my heartbeat with the metronome[51]-like chords of "A Prayer to God." By the time the song ends, I'm feeling more myself.

I feel something on my face. My eyes have been seeping tears. That's new.

I try to pay attention to the rest of the album, one of

---

[50] Greek: *syn-,* "same" and *khronos,* "time."
[51] Greek: *metro,* "measure" and *nomos,* "regulating."

my favorites, but I drift to sleep after two more songs. I wake up a few hours later feeling disoriented, dark still outside my window, silent headphones over my ears. I take them off and get under my covers. My head feels like it's full of cotton.

When I wake Saturday morning, I don't feel any better.

I put my phone on "Do Not Disturb." Set so that the only texts or calls that will get through are my mother's. On second thought, I let through Nora's as well.

I end up leaving it that way for another week.

Chapter 23: April 14ᵀᴴ-17ᵀᴴ   Cass Washington

My next-level grounding was not going well for me. My mother seemed to be looking over my shoulder every minute of every day.

Before she had Phoebe, my mom had worked. Something in a law firm. But when she had Phoebe, she had decided to stay home with the baby. I could grumble about her obviously loving Phoebe more than me, since she hadn't opted to stay home with me, but it hadn't actually bothered me. What I resented was that now she didn't seem to have anything better to do than micromanage her children's lives.

No wonder she thought I should be writing all these essays. She had nothing but time. Maybe *she* should write the essays. (I knew better than to suggest it.)

I came home directly after school every day. My phone and laptop were imprisoned in the liquor cabinet, the one place in the house with a lock I didn't have a key to. I couldn't use my phone at all. I could use my laptop in her presence for homework and scholarship purposes only. So while I could still occasionally get away with drawing and inking in my room, I couldn't scan any of the drawings to color them. I ended up with a pile of drawings that looked half-finished on the corner of my desk, taunting me. I kept drawing, but after a while there was no joy in it for me.

But I was allowed to bring my laptop to school, and that was my one salvation. Mom knew that a lot of my classes required the use of my computer, so she had to let me bring it. She knew that the school Wi-Fi blocked Tumblr and other such social media sites, so she figured I couldn't do much harm with it there. What she didn't know was that every student (at least, every student who knew what was up) had patches on their computers that could bypass the school's filters.

So while my social life was certainly suffering, I could still talk to PuellaStellarum in school. That made a lot of difference. (Irony: My grounding led me to pay less attention in all of my classes.)

My communication with my face-to-face friends was limited to what I could get in during school as well. This must have been what life was like before the Internet. I had to actually *find* Spencer to swap stories with him. I didn't care for it.

I dreaded the thought of Mr. Stanton calling a Certamen practice, which I would have to admit to him I wasn't allowed to go to. I didn't want to be another burden on this dysfunctional team. But he never did.

He must have given up on us too.

In one of my hurried hallway chats with Spencer on Friday, I asked him how things were going trying to set up Brian with girls. I didn't share any classes with Brian, and hadn't managed to catch his attention under his headphones in the hallway.

"Swimmingly!" Spencer said with a huge smile. "I've gotten him out with all kinds of groups. I tell you, that boy is really coming out of his shell!"

"That's great," I sighed. "Any lucky ladies?"

"Haven't found the right one yet. Not for lack of trying. Don't you worry, he's in good hands."

I left with a pit in my stomach, wishing I wasn't missing out. Wishing I didn't have to sit at home while Spencer and Brian had fun without me. Wishing I could do more than go to school and go home to work.

Wishing I had a mother who cared about *me*, instead of *my potential*.

On Saturday night, all-work-and-no-play making me desperate, I was curled up on Phoebe's floor, playing Barbies with her. I had actually liked Barbies as a child, despite my current reservations against them as advertisements for bulimia. Most of mine had ended up bald, though, after had I cut off their hair in frustration because I couldn't make it look like mine. Phoebe's dolls were in better shape than mine ever were.

"Barbie wants to break up with Ken now," Phoebe said, wiggling the Black Barbie in her hand.

"Bout time," I chucked Ken over my shoulder. "Can Barbie date Nikki now?"

"*No*," Phoebe said emphatically. "Barbie is an

independent woman."

"That's good too." I rolled onto my back. "What does independent Barbie want to be when she grows up?"

"She already *is* grown up," Phoebe said with the voice of someone answering a stupidly obvious question. "She's a veterinarian."

"Is that what you want to be?" I asked her.

"Uh huh," she said simply.

"I wish it was that easy for me," I sighed.

"What's so hard?" Phoebe asked simply, running a massive light-blue brush idly through her Barbie's hair. "I wanna help animals, so I'm gonna be a vet."

"You'll understand when you get older," I replied.

Phoebe looked at the ceiling, exasperated. "Old people *always* say that! What's not to understand? I like animals. What do you like?"

I laughed. "Fairy tales from two thousand years ago."

"Then do that!" she said.

"Do what?" I asked.

Phoebe looked up from her doll, perplexed, then giggled a little.

"You weren't listening when I answered, huh?" I said.

"Mmmmmmmnnnnoooo," she gurgled.

"You were ready to say that no matter what I said, weren't you?"

She nodded, giggling. I laughed too.

"Does Barbie want to play fetch with her pet tiger again?" I asked her.

***

The weekend was an excruciating exercise in waiting.

Waiting, drawing, working, and more waiting. Monday was like an oasis. During classes I talked to PuellaStellarum and a couple of kids from my Mythology group. Between classes I talked to Spencer and Katie. Still couldn't get Brian to myself, though.

Then at the end of the day, I saw something that ruined the whole thing. Between sixth and seventh period I caught sight of Spencer at a distance, and I hurried toward him. But I stopped when I saw who he was talking to.

It was Beth Scalia.

I hadn't seen Spencer talk to Beth in months. She was one of Danny's group.

They were laughing like old friends. I didn't think he'd ever really known her independently of Danny.

I stopped to observe. He and Beth met up with Austin and Frances and a couple other Danny-friends that I didn't know by name. They all gathered into a knot and proceeded to make merry. ("Oh, do you think my undercut is trendy enough?" "Brah, it's on fleek." Or so I imagined.)

Keeping my distance, I swore under my breath. Spencer had been doing so well forgetting about Danny lately. But that had been when he wasn't part of Danny's circle of friends. Now here he was reintegrating himself into their shallow, shitty little scene. I didn't see Danny anywhere, but if Spencer kept hanging out with these people, he was bound to be around sometimes. And his proximity could be disastrous for Spencer's recovery.

Automatically, I reached for my phone. I didn't know what for—to text Spencer and tell him to step away from the zombie horde, to text Katie or Brian to see if they could help, or what. But, of course, my phone wasn't there. It was like a phantom limb.

I watched Spencer and his group of shallow Danny-friends walk off together, away from me. I felt like a shipwrecked sailor on an island, watching my right-hand man sail away with a cohort of the enemy.

CHAPTER 24: APRIL 15ᵀᴴ-19ᵀᴴ   SPENCER OLSON

As soon as Beth texted me, I could see the opening.

She was bored at a Dairy Queen Saturday afternoon. I was probably the fourth or fifth person she texted—desperation mode. But that didn't matter to me. She was a way back into the group I wanted back into.

She was a bridge back to Danny.

I met Beth at Dairy Queen. I was still with her that evening when she went to the mall to meet Rayna and Austin.

On Sunday it was Austin who invited me to hang out with Frances, Kurt, and other-Austin.

Before I knew it, I was back in.

I've spent every day since with some subset of the same group. It's a big group. Sooner or later, Danny has to show up at something. I'll wave nonchalantly. Ask him how he's been, as if I haven't thought about him in weeks.

I'll look like somebody who is over him. Which is not what I am, but is something I am becoming quite adept at pretending to be.

It's Monday before I remember. I'm supposed to be helping Brian find dates. I'd let the whole weekend fly by without texting him.

As soon as I know my plans for Monday night—coffee and shuffleboard (I told you it was catching on) at Dave & Buster's—I text Brian to invite him. I don't have a specific girl in mind for him, but this group is jam-packed with straight girls. I'll find him someone.

He never responds. I tried.

It's Tuesday when the hammer falls.

Trish, Beth, other-Austin, Mark, Rayna, Evan, and I are enjoying a nutritious dinner at a Whataburger. We're having so much fun that I've noticed some people shooting glares at us as they leave. Jealousy over our youth and *joie de vivre*.

While I'm dishing dirt with Trish over an imminent breakup between Travis Spierman and his post-Cass rebound, I hear Mark say Danny's name across the table. My ears tune to his conversation even as I pretend to be paying attention to Trish.

"Yeah, Danny says he's coming," other-Austin is saying.

"Oh," Mark says, somewhat downcast. I wonder about his tone.

Beth interrupts Trish to address me. "Hey Spencer," she says, delicately, like she's breaking it to an orphan that he won't be getting his portion of gruel today.

"Yeah?" I respond.

"Danny's gonna meet us at the movie," Beth says.

We were planning on heading to the theatre next, to

see the latest superhero movie featuring overly-muscled men in tights (not my type of attractive, in case you're wondering).

"Okay," I say.

"And he still doesn't want to see you," she continues.

"Oh," I say softly, my stomach sinking.

She starts to explain and apologize, but I don't hear what she's saying.

I'm supposed to leave so Danny doesn't have to see me.

I leave right then, even though the rest are staying a few more minutes. I haven't even finished my fries. They're all telling me it's okay, asking me to sit with them until they have to leave. But I don't want to hear it. I'm humiliated, ostracized, and worst of all, thwarted.

I drive home. I do not cry.

This is not the end.

✳✳✳

Cass finds me before lunch the next day.

"Spencer," she says seriously, looking me directly in the eye like she does when she's gearing up for something. I direct my own eyes to the ceiling. I know better than to match her intensity with my own. Hers is always greater.

"Yes, Cassidy?"

"I saw you with Beth."

"And?" I say as if I don't already know what she's driving at.

"You're trying to worm your way back in, aren't you?"

"I can't just be reconnecting with an old friend? This has to be about him?"

"You hated Beth," she spits back. "You said she was two-faced and could never be trusted."

"I was wrong. I've reevaluated."

"I don't believe you."

"Well, who am I supposed to hang out with?" I say, some genuine bitterness creeping into my voice. "With you under lock and key and all. Or am I supposed to wait around alone for you?"

"This isn't about me, and you know I know that," Cass says calmly. "You're deflecting."

"I don't know what you're talking about."

"Sometimes you really seemed to mean it," she sighs, talking softly now.

"What?"

"I really thought you were trying to get over Danny. I thought you were serious about it. But you've been lurking on his Instagram this whole time. You're hanging out with his friends hoping to see him. Most people would have moved on by now."

"Most people," I say defensively, "Didn't have true love."

Cass laughs humorlessly. "True love. You and Danny."

I meet her eyes then. "Just what do you mean?" I demand.

"Okay, I don't mean to imply that I know all of what goes on in anyone else's relationship," she says, her hands up. "Maybe you guys had a rich inner life that the rest of us didn't see."

"Cut the tolerant-side-of-Tumblr talk," I tell her. "Say what you mean."

"That from the outside," she says gently, "Your relationship seemed shallow. You were all hands and mouths, no substance. You talked about tiny things, fought about tiny issues, posted tiny moments to Instagram like they were momentous occasions..."

"You don't know what you're talking about," I tell her.

"Like when that traffic cone exactly matched his shirt, and you regrammed the picture like twenty times," she goes on.

"It was *funny*," I defend.

"And when he wouldn't talk to you for days because you said Selena Gomez was slipping," she continues.

"I was out of line," I say.

"Nothing about your relationship ever seemed sincere," Cass says. "You guys just fed off of each other's egos."

"You just hate Danny," I say.

"I don't *hate* Danny," Cass protests. "I just don't think you're right together."

"And what gives you the right?" I snap at her, much louder than I mean to. I catch myself, pull back. I don't want people to stare at us. When I speak next, it's softer, but still intense. She's cracked me. "You don't think Danny and I are right together, so I can't want him back. And if I dare to have my own feelings, ones that won't fit your hopes for me, I must be betraying you."

She pulls back as if I've struck her. I think I hit on something there. "You're my best friend," she says softly. "I care about you."

"Best friends support each other," I say. She doesn't

reply. "I'll see you," I say dismissively, and walk off toward lunch.

Cass stays where she is. I can't remember the last time I won an argument with her. I wonder for a moment if I might have been a little too rough on her. But there's no point in looking back. I've got too much on my mind.

CHAPTER 25: APRIL 15ᵀᴴ-19ᵀᴴ   BRIAN GANZ

I go to school. I listen to music between classes—noisy stuff, early Nick Cave and Steve Albini and anything on SST Records. I come home on the bus and read History or game with Nora. I feel good. Like myself.

That's right. Like myself. This is how I was always meant to be. Why was I ever fool enough to try to change it? I like to be alone. What's wrong with that? Some people like to be social, and some people are like me.

I don't tell Nora about any of this. I would have, until recently. I've always told her everything. But this is different. Nora loves being around people, and she wants me to be social too. She's one of *them*, so she wouldn't understand. For the first time, I start to see how good it is that she lives a thousand miles away. I can still be her friend, but on my own terms.

So it's all great. But every once in a while, some unwelcome thoughts visit.

Broken, they call me.

I have to be who I am. I have to do what makes me

happy.

You call this happiness? the thoughts ask.

I think I do. I'm not unhappy.

Not being unhappy is not the same thing as being happy.

Litotes, says Cass's voice in my head.

I am starting to miss the good parts. I look around my room. In my mind I see Katie and Allie sitting there sharing a soda. I see Cass, getting so competitive[52] at Super Smash Bros she can't stay seated. I see Spencer, whining about my music choices and singing his heart out when I let him pick. I start to miss them.

Then I remember how I felt that last night with Spencer. How my very body betrayed me. I slam the door on my thoughts. I put on Saccharine Trust's first album to drive them out good.

It isn't worth it, I tell myself. Stop missing them. They're not worth the cost.

---

[52] Latin, *petere*, "to seek or strive for or attack," and *com-*, "together." To strive toward the same goal, even at odds with each other.

CHAPTER 26: APRIL   JEFF MILLER

It's miserable here.

They try to make you comfortable enough. But the tedium is crushing. You can't do much of anything, except talk to lots of different therapists and go to group sessions. I hate the group sessions. They're starting to call me defiant, but I don't want to go. Those other people are crazy.

The therapist's favorite thing to tell me is that I've "externalized my self-esteem." That I only see value in myself because I'm good at things. Because I make good grades, win awards, etc. But I *should* see value in myself just as myself.

Just the kind of crap a therapist would say. I'm supposed to like myself no matter what, because I'm a special snowflake? How is anyone any good if they aren't good at things? Grades and awards are just the proof I need to show everyone else. To show myself, too. I need *evidence*. That's just science.

My dad has been here to visit a few times. Mackenzie

came once. When they told me she was on her way, I thought of all kinds of terrible things I wanted to say to her. But I lost my nerve as soon as I saw her. She looked so frail and worn out. I've never seen her like that. I told her I forgave her. It was a lie, but I'm sure I'll feel it someday. She didn't say much.

Mom called once. She wants to do a stopover in Texas next month before heading on to Minnesota. I wonder if I would have rated such treatment if I hadn't wound up in a looney bin.

They won't let me do my homework, or any of the work I'm missing in school right now. It's been weeks. I can't imagine how behind I'm getting. They tell me I can worry about it later. That right now my job is getting better. But how can I learn to stop stressing when I can't make progress on what's stressing me out? How can I get better when a mountain is looming up over me?

I can read the beat up books from the facility's library. None of them are on the AP reading list. Or, at least, none that I recognized. They laughed when I asked if I could look up the list. So I'm reading *The Girl with the Dragon Tattoo*. I was expecting some death and violence, but not much of it so far.

More than school, more than Latin Club or Science Fair, I'm worried about Grandma.

Dad insists that he's taking care of her. But he won't give me specifics when I ask him. Probably because the doctors told him not to. Don't give me anything that will keep me worrying about all the details I've been worrying about. So he just tells me she's fine, and he's taking care of everything. As if there were never a *reason* I was worried in the first place.

He was awful at taking care of her, when he was in charge. She would get food, but would go days without real human interaction. That was why I stepped in. You wouldn't even treat a dog that way.

So instead of getting to check in on details, I just get to worry about all the details instead. Can I still make the grades I need? Are all the bills paid? Does Grandma have enough to eat? Is Dad keeping that lighter away from her?

It would be enough to keep me up at night. But they give me pills for that.

CHAPTER 27: APRIL 20TH-21ST   KATIE NGUYEN

It was getting late, but I was working on the scrapbook for the contest at State. I wanted to finish it early, so I could focus on Certamen and my Roman Life test. I had been planning to devote a two-page spread in the scrapbook to our fundraisers for State, but when I mocked it up, it looked a little bleak. I decided to make it one page, and give a page to in-class activities on the other side. Freshmen in bedsheet togas look better in the scrapbook than more pictures of Cass at the vending table in front of the gym.

Jeremy was awake too, which was another reason for me to be up. He was telling me about some rocket competition he had gone to that weekend. Apparently West Oak had sent a couple of students too. When he heard my school's name, he got excited, because he thought I might be there.

I knew one person on that little rocket team. But, I explained, my school wasn't like his school. We didn't all do every activity.

I know, he said. *It was wishful thinking.*

This boy was getting too close. But I couldn't stop myself. I wanted him close. I just couldn't risk it getting serious, because the team could never know. I hadn't seen him in person since Area. He had asked, but I had pleaded *too busy*.

A lot of couples formed at State every year. People started dating within the Club, and between Clubs. That fact just kept popping back into my mind.

Jeremy switched the topic to Sherlock. He was watching it on my recommendation, and was, of course, hooked. We argued a little about Benedict Cumberbatch. He loved his acting, but didn't understand why everyone thought he was so hot. I told him that he was obviously blind. After that, we talked more seriously about the ethical ramifications of factory farming, and how our generation could make a difference.

We covered a lot of ground.

Allie was fast asleep. If she were awake she'd be giving me grief about still being so hung up on this boy. I was happy for the respite.

I had thought a lot about what she said in the car. About how maybe I'm the one who wants my crush to be forbidden and secret. I didn't think it was true at first, but I thought about what it would feel like to have my feelings out in the open, for it all to be no problem, and... well, it *did* seem like it would be less exciting that way. I had to admit, I loved that I was sneaking in all this texting with him while Allie was asleep.

It wound up being a bit of a late night for no good reason. But I still felt good arriving at school in the morning. It was a beautiful morning, with just the right amount of clouds to keep the rising sun out of my eyes on the drive to school. Allie was in a good mood too. She felt like she had a good handle on her Algebra II review from the last night, and was actually ready for her test today. I was glad that my tutoring was doing her some good.

We hit the halls about fifteen minutes before the first bell was set to ring. Something was off. I could tell as soon as I walked in. The people who hung out with me in the mornings—a bunch of juniors who tended to be in the same AP classes—were quiet and somber.

"What's going on?" Allie asked right away, being slightly blunter than I would have been.

"Jeff," said Rachelle, her voice full of pity. My chest tightened. What now? "His family's house burned down last night."

This was terrible news, but it wasn't nearly as bad as what I feared she might say.

Allie pushed forward again. "Was anyone hurt?"

"No," said Justin. "It was just his dad and grandmother inside, and they made it out fine. They think his grandmother started it, with a cigarette."

"He used to take care of her," added Rachelle. "Alzheimer's."

"I didn't know that," I said.

"No one did," Rachelle said sadly. "Except Mackenzie. She just told us. She says this never would have happened if Jeff had been at home."

"So she..." I began.

"Blames herself for all of this, yes," Rachelle said

darkly. "Selena dragged her off to the counselors' offices. She didn't want to go, but she's basically catatonic over this, so we're making her."

"It's not her fault," Allie said forcefully.

"We tried to tell her," Justin sighed.

We all let it hang in the air between us. All she did was break up with him. No one expects all this after a high school breakup. It was dreadful.

"His family will be alright, though, right?" Justin said after a tense moment. "They're doctors. They have the money."

"His mom works for charity," Rachelle sighed. "And his dad quit practicing a few years ago to be a professor. He works with my dad. And my dad can only afford to work for that little pay because of how much my mom makes."

"Jesus," Allie muttered.

"And long stays in mental facilities cost a lot of money..." Rachelle continued.

"We have to stop talking about this," Justin said, echoing my feelings perfectly.

We sat in an oppressive silence. I decided to head to class a few minutes early. Allie headed in the other direction with a tiny wave.

On my way I saw Spencer, sitting in a corner with his chin on his hands, looking miserable. I made a beeline.

"You heard about Jeff?" I asked.

"Jeff?" Spencer looked up at me, perplexed. "No, what about him?"

"What were you sad about, then?"

"Nothing. What is this about Jeff?"

I let fly with the whole thing. By the time I finished, I felt tears coming down my cheeks.

Spencer looked at me for a long moment. Then he took out his phone.

"Katie," he said, gesturing at me with the phone before unlocking it, "We are going to do something about this."

He turned and walked away with long, purposeful strides, texting as he walked. Spencer did have a flare for a dramatic gesture, but I wished he had stayed and explained himself instead. Maybe I could have helped.

Soon I got a mass text from Mr. Stanton about another emergency officer meeting after school. I went through the rest of the day just waiting for that meeting to come.

I hurried to the Latin room after school. It was exactly like the last emergency officer meeting. The whole Latin Club showed up. A bunch of them were asking Mr. Stanton what was up.

"Can't say I know," Mr. Stanton told them. "This one was called by your president."

"Are all the officers here?" Spencer asked, all business.

We stepped forward and were counted. Vice President, Secretary, Treasurer, Historian. Spencer called the meeting to order.

"I never expected," he began, addressing the crowd like Cicero on the rostra, "To have so many weighty issues come up during my tenure as president. Every other Latin Club president during my years here has had nothing more serious to decide than a few pizza or trophy vendors, maybe a fundraiser or two.

"But you don't get to choose what kind of year you're

president for. The latest news, which most of you have heard, is sad and distressing. Our teammate and friend Jeff, who is currently in the hospital after an emotional breakdown..."

"I don't know if we're supposed to be talking about—" Mr. Stanton started, but Spencer barreled on.

"Has just lost his house in a fire," Spencer continued. "We, your officers, have been working tirelessly to raise money to get us to State, which is in one week. Mister Treasurer, do you have a report?"

"Not officially, since this was not *planned* and isn't even actually a *Club* meeting," said Ben peevishly. "But I know that we have eighteen hundred something."

"Out of the over three thousand we need," Spencer said gravely. "Fellow citizens, we are not going to raise enough to bring everybody to State. It's too late. But we can do something worthwhile with that money." Spencer took a breath. "I will entertain a motion from the floor to repurpose the money originally raised for State to Jeff's family instead."

People started talking immediately. All the chatter was in favor of the idea. People started to ask Mr. Stanton if we could actually do it.

"The money was raised by the Club for the Club, so the officers have say over how it's used," Mr. Stanton said tentatively, "But I wouldn't want to do it without everybody who would have been going to State agreeing."

He produced the list of qualifiers and we took roll. In the thirty-something students packing the room were 21 of the 22 State qualifiers. The 22nd was Jeff.

We took a vote. It was unanimous.

The room erupted in applause. I saw Cass throw an arm around Spencer's shoulders. He laughed and hugged her. I ran up to give Spencer a hug too. What a president.

I got home feeling like the scales had fallen from my eyes. I threw my backpack on my bed and took out my phone right away.

Jeremy, I texted.

Hi, he replied immediately.

I like you, I sent, before my nerve could fail me.

I like you too, he said. *But I was saving that for when I could finally see you at State.*

I'm not going to State anymore, I typed. The tears started to sting in my eyes. What we had done for Jeff had been the right thing. I was as certain of that as anyone in the Club. But what I was giving up still hurt.

You're not? What happened? Can I call you? he asked in three quick messages.

I shot a glance over my shoulder. Allie was lounging on the ground, scrolling idly through her phone.

"Could I have some privacy?" I asked her.

Allie raised her eyebrows almost to her hairline. "Of course," she replied, "But I'd better hear all about it when you're done."

She closed the door on her way out, and I called Jeremy as soon as she did.

The whole story came out in one big burst. All the troubles that I'd tried to keep from him. I wished then that I had told him sooner. It felt good to unburden on him. He consoled me. Told me he wanted to see me again, and

237

soon. State or no State.

It felt good to hear his voice again.

We talked for half an hour. He was an even better conversationalist out loud than he was over text. I hoped I could see him face-to-face soon. But try as he did to set a concrete plan, I just couldn't think about it. I'd been thinking about nothing but State for so long. The future without it seemed unreal, almost pointless. I was still turning it over in my mind.

Right after we hung up, I had my idea. I spent the rest of the night on it, neglecting all my homework.

***

The next day, before first period Latin class, I waited at my desk for Brian to walk in. I was eager to tell him about what I'd done. Allie had said I was a genius. He came in with his headphones on and took the seat next to me, like usual. I waved to get his attention.

Brian moved aside one ear cup of his headphones. Was I imagining it, or did he look a little bewildered?

"Hey," I said.

"Hi," he replied in a low, non-committal voice. There was something different about him. Something wrong, maybe. My news fell right out of my head.

"How are you?" I asked him instead.

"Fine," he said distantly. He looked away, like he expected the conversation to be over.

I looked at him for a moment. He replaced his ear cup and lifted a book in front of his face until Mr. Stanton started class.

That was weird.

I texted Spencer. He didn't respond. Cass was grounded and didn't have her phone. So all day I kept an eye out for either of them in the hallway. I finally found Cass near the end of the day.

"Is there something going on with Brian?" I asked her.

"Brian? Not that I know of, why?"

"I tried to talk to him before class today, and he seemed really off. Like, *old*-Brian, but awkwarder."

Cass reached for her pocket, then cursed—no phone.

"I'm so out of touch," she groaned. "I need to ask Spencer about this."

"Let me know what you find out," I said weakly.

Cass hurried away. Too late, I realized I should also have told her what I did. Or anyone else in Latin.

Well, I reasoned, if it worked, she would find out soon enough. They all would.

CHAPTER 28: APRIL 21ˢᵀ   CASS WASHINGTON

"If I dare to have my own feelings, ones that won't fit your hopes for me, I must be betraying you."

That's what Spencer had said that made me come up short. Because it could easily have been me, talking to my mother.

I wished I'd asserted myself afterward. Chasing after someone who has already broken up with you was different. Exactly the sort of thing a best friend is supposed to try to talk you out of.

Problem was, that wasn't how he saw it. I didn't want to make him feel like my mother was making me feel. So I backed off. Maybe it wasn't the right thing to do, but maybe it was the least wrong thing I could do.

So when that officer meeting hit, and Spencer made exactly the right move and did something selfless and honorable and right, I gave him the props he deserved for it. I didn't think about Danny. I just thought about Spencer. And that made him a lot easier to love.

Then Friday, Katie asked me about Brian, and

everything went awry.

It was before my last period of the day, Speech, that she asked me. We were on the third day of a round of presentations, and I had given mine the previous day. I hunched over my laptop in the back of the room and pulled up iMessages, which I could use to send messages to Spencer's iPhone.

Have you seen Brian lately? I asked him. *Katie says he's acting weird.*

I got no response. I sent a few similar messages, just hoping one of them would catch his attention.

Then I tried to find Brian on iMessages, but he had an Android, so I couldn't text him without my phone. I buzzed his Tumblr and, a moment later, his Reddit account with the same message.

Are you okay? I haven't talked to you in forever.

I didn't get a reply. About halfway through class, Mr. Shipwright finally noticed me on my laptop and made me close it down.

I hadn't seen or heard from Brian in weeks. I didn't even remember him at the Latin Club meeting—he must have been there, but I hadn't talked to him. Had no one been talking to him?

On my way out of the building, I searched desperately for Brian, with Spencer my second choice. I caught a glimpse of Spencer getting in his car across the parking lot with Kurt Lundford, part of the Danny crowd. I tried to wave him down, but he didn't notice me. By the time I got to his car, he'd be gone. I cursed inwardly at him for being so absorbed with that crowd still, but I was still thinking more about Brian.

I sat on one of the benches outside to recheck Tumblr and Reddit, to see if I had any word from Brian. My pulse jumped when I saw that I had a reply on Reddit.

Sorry, he had said. *I won't be around, I don't think. I'll miss you, and it's not your fault.*

Someone had replaced my blood with ice.

It was vague, but it seemed pretty clear to me. The counselors talked to us at the beginning of every school year in gentle, soothing tones about recognizing the signs. But it didn't take a counselor to recognize these.

I was behind the wheel of my car before I knew it. I did twenty over the speed limit all the way to his house. I didn't care if I was grounded. A life was more important.

Moments later I was pounding on Brian's door. No answer, which I expected. His mom would be at work, and suicidal people don't allow themselves to be interrupted by a knock on the door. I tried the handle. It was locked.

I ran to the back. I had a suspicion, and it turned out to be right. Cat flap. I put my arm through it. To get my hand up to the doorknob inside, I had to put myself through all the way up to the shoulder. My face smashed against the side of the door. The cat flap was rubbery and coated with grime. (How did a cat flap get so dirty?)

I found the knob, turned it, and I was in.

"Brian!" I called as soon as I was in his kitchen. "Brian!"

CHAPTER 29: APRIL 21ST   BRIAN GANZ

I hope Cass isn't taking it personally.

She really was a good friend. They all were. It's just, friends aren't for me.

Cass tends to be pretty understanding, but she can also be pushy. I hope she can see that I'm better alone.

This is what I'm thinking the whole ride home. In between little reminiscences about her and Spencer, Katie and Allie. We did have some good times. I wish them all well.

All the way up my front steps, I'm rehearsing[53] what I'll tell her if she confronts me about it tomorrow. She'll try to convince[54] me that I need the group. But she doesn't know what I felt. I'll be calm, but firm. I'll make her understand.

---

[53] "Rehearse" comes from an old French verb, *rehercier*, meaning "to turn over again," which is ultimately from the Latin root *hirpex*, a sort of large rake for breaking up freshly-plowed soil. Meaning that "rehearse" and "hearse" (the car that carries dead people) are actually from the same root.

[54] "Convince" is rooted in the Latin verb *vincere*, "to conquer." It's a third of Caesar's famous *veni, vidi, vici*: "I came, I saw, I conquered."

243

I open the front door with my key. The first thing I see is Daisy in the armchair, which is not where she normally sleeps in the afternoons. The second thing I see is that she's in Cass's lap.

"You take the *bus*," Cass says, shaking her head, as if I've been a part of this conversation from the beginning. "Of *course* I beat you here in my *car* if you take the *bus*."

"Cass," I say shakily.

"Brian, we need to talk about what's going on with you."

"It's nothing personal," I begin.

"I don't care how personal or not personal it is," Cass cuts me off, moving Daisy to the side so she can stand. "I'm not going to lose you, Brian. I'm not."

I wasn't ready for this so soon. Why is she here? "It's not..." I start, and fall off. Talking to her about this doesn't feel anything like I thought it would. I try again. "I just can't hang out with you guys anymore. I can't be around people. And if you're really my friend, you have to understand that."

"So that means you have to end it all?" Cass replies. "You don't have to do it, Brian."

What?

End it all?

"I'm not suicidal," I say carefully. "I just want to be left alone."

"What?" Cass says blankly.

"You thought I wanted to kill myself?"

"'I won't be around anymore. It's not your fault. I'll *miss* you,'" she quotes.

Now that she says it out loud, I can see where she got that impression.

"I'm so sorry, I didn't mean..." I start.

"No no, it's okay, I've got you now. You just don't want to be our friend anymore?"

"It's not that," I'm shaking my head. "I, uh, I don't want to be *anyone's* friend anymore. I want to go back to how I was."

"Can we go back to how you started thinking like this?"

So I tell her about all those nights last week—it seems so much longer ago than just a week. I get to the disastrous Friday night, the sweaty palms, the pounding in my ears. I almost start to feel it while I'm describing it, but she cuts me off before I get too far.

"You had an anxiety attack?" Cass asks.

I hadn't tried to put words to it before. I was too busy trying not to think about it. But I guess that's exactly what I would call it. I nod dumbly.

"Shit, I can see why. Sounds like Spencer ran you ragged. I gotta talk to that boy. Not everyone is an extroverted social butterfly running on caffeine and power bars."

"I don't want to feel that way again," I tell her.

"I don't blame you," she says simply. "I used to have anxiety attacks. Wouldn't wish them on my worst enemy."

"You did?"

"Since seventh grade. Had my last big one sophomore year. Still have to be on the lookout for them, because meds ain't foolproof."

"Were they like mine?" I ask. I had no idea Cass had anything like this going on.

"They sound similar," Cass says. "Mine weren't triggered by social situations, per se. I had them more when I felt out of control, or when I wasn't living up to my own expectations."

"That sucks," I say.

"You learn to deal," Cass says pointedly. "Talking to professionals is best. But let me ask you: You didn't feel like that when it was just, like, me and Spencer, or us plus Katie and Allie, or whatever?"

I shake my head.

"So it sounds like Spencer just pushed you too hard. Again, Imma give that boy a talking to on your behalf, and don't try to stop me. But you don't have to pull away from us."

"I don't know," I say.

"You've missed us?" she asks.

"Yes," I say immediately. I curse myself, but it's the truth.

"I've missed you too. That's what's important. You want to be my friend, Allie's, Katie's, even Spencer's for some reason. We can figure out the rest. You can tell us when it's getting to be too much."

I'm not sure if I want to tell everyone about this. It feels like I've got some disease they'll all have to work around. I can't imagine burdening them all with that.

"You right, my bad," Cass says, seeing the panic in my eyes. "We'll keep it between you and me. But you can tell *me*. I can be your wingman. If you feel overwhelmed, we can have a code word and I'll get you out. Hippopotamus."

I laugh. "Hippopotamus means 'river horse' in Greek," I say.

"It might just be because I've missed your dumb factoids so much, but that is god-damned fascinating, Brian."

I laugh again.

"How do you feel?" she asks.

"Better," I say. "A little less broken."

"Good," she says.

"You wanna stay a few minutes?" I offer. I really have missed the company. "Play a game or two? I've got *Rocket League*."

"Might as well," Cass sighs. "I'll be grounded until college once I get home, so I might as well enjoy myself a little first."

"I'm sorry I made you panic," I say.

"That's alright. I'm glad I came. But while we're gaming, maybe I can go over the finer points of *not making your friends think you're going to kill yourself and giving them heart attacks, you rat bastard.*"

"I deserve that."

We start back toward my room.

"Oh, it's a little messy in there," Cass adds.

"I know, sorry," I say, a little embarrassed that she went back there.

"No, I mean before I realized you were just on the bus, I tore it the hell apart looking for clues about where you might have gone."

CHAPTER 30: APRIL 21ST   CASS WASHINGTON

It was 4:30 PM by the time I got home. An hour and a half after I was expected.

I could see my mom at the kitchen table when I pulled into the driveway. She stood as soon as she saw my car.

"I'm sorry," I said as I walked in the back door.

"You're damn right you're sorry," mom said. "Where were you?"

I sat down at the table, prepared for my lecture. "You don't need my excuses. I did wrong. I accept whatever the consequences are."

She sat down across from me. "Cass," she said. "I think you still misunderstand what we're doing here."

I squinted at her. This was not what I was expecting.

"You're seventeen," she said. "I'm not a prison warden, dealing out punishments for infractions. You're a good kid, and you've been good about this whole grounding thing. When you didn't come home, I was worried out of my mind. When I saw you drive up safely, I knew there had to be a reason you had stayed out. So I want to know what it is. I want to talk about it."

I was wary. This didn't sound like the mom I'd had for the past month. But I had already told myself I would go along with whatever demands my furious mother made, and I supposed that this counted.

"I was at Brian's," I began. "None of us had talked to him in a while. Then Katie told me she thought he was acting weird. So I..."

I hesitated here. Telling her I had contacted Brian with my computer was technically another infraction. If she was just pumping me for information to make sure my punishment fit the crime, then I would be further incriminating myself.

I examined my mother's face, and I decided to tell her the truth.

"So I messaged him on Reddit," I continued. "And he replied with this message. Here..." I pulled out my laptop. As soon as the screen came on from sleep mode, Brian's message was there. I had slammed it shut and gone directly to his house. Now I turned the computer around on the table and showed my mother. "You tell me what you think that means."

Mom read, then covered her mouth with one hand. "Oh, lord, is he okay?" she said, almost in a whisper.

"He's fine," I said. "Turns out he didn't mean that at all. He was having some social anxiety issues. And I leapt to the wrong conclusion and overreacted. Basically ended up staging a one-woman intervention for him."

Mom nodded. "I'm glad I asked." She shut my computer. "I'd have done the exact same thing."

"Yeah?"

"Well, maybe not exactly. Ever heard of telling an adult? Someone actually qualified to deal with all that?"

I cringed. "Fair point."

"But I love that you acted on your conscience," she continued.

This conversation had a distinctly pleasant tone that was keeping me off balance. The opposite of what I was expecting.

"What really had me worried," mom continued, "Was that you didn't have your phone. You could have been hurt, or in danger, and you'd have had no way to get help."

I didn't know what to say to that. (*Well, whose fault is that?* seemed like the wrong thing.) So I didn't say anything.

"I'm going back to work," mom said. I tilted my head at the *non sequitur.* "I've been unreasonable," she continued. "I've put too much pressure on you girls. Your dad thinks I'm projecting. I'm pushing you because I'm not satisfied with my own life. And that's psychobabble crap, but he has a point. It's not that I'm not happy being a mom. But with Phoebe in school and you about to move out..." she took a breath, like that was the scariest thing she could think of. "Your dad is right. I need other things to devote my energy to."

"He's annoying when he's right," I said. That made her laugh.

"Anyway. I know I've been unfair to you."

"You're not all wrong," I said. Ten minutes ago I could not have imagined a universe in which I would have said that to my mother. "I've been acting like a screw-up this year. Something about needing to move on without knowing to what."

"I know, sweetie," she said. "I want to help you with that. But you've got to find your own way. So do I. Can we do that together?"

And that's how I got ungrounded by breaking all the rules. Kids, do not try that one at home.

I thought that was going to be the most momentous thing to happen to me that weekend. Then, Sunday morning over breakfast, my dad showed me a tiny little article in our local paper that almost made me spit out my Lucky Charms.

Chapter 31: April 23RD

KLEINSBERG HERALD, PAGE 8

STUDENTS GIVE UP TRIP TO HELP FRIEND IN NEED

The West Oak High School Latin Club has studied. They have competed. They have raised funds. All to get themselves to the Texas State Junior Classical League competition in San Antonio next weekend.

"It's been a dream of ours to make State for a long time," junior Katie Nguyen writes. "We've put in countless hours of study time, and they all finally paid off. The Advanced Certamen [Latin Quiz Bowl] team made it for the first time in the school's history."

The students had raised thousands of dollars to cover the cost of the trip for all 22 qualifying competitors. But when one of their classmates, another junior on the "Certamen" team, experienced a devastating setback, these teenagers made a touching sacrifice.

"His house burned down, right out of the blue," Katie explains. "And we didn't want to sit idly by while his family struggled to get back on their feet."

And so the West Oak Latin Club donated all the funds

that they had raised for their State trip to the family.

"You'd think it would be a hard decision," Katie adds, "But it was instantaneous. As soon as Spencer [Olson], our president, suggested it, everybody wanted to do it."

The students of West Oak might not be traveling to San Antonio to compete next weekend. But to our community, they are already champions of another kind.

CHAPTER 32: APRIL 24ᵀᴴ-25ᵀᴴ   SPENCER OLSON

When I pull into the parking lot Monday morning, there are local news vans in front of the school.

My mind races with the possibilities. Did someone get hurt? Is someone dead? Did a teacher have a gross relationship with a student?

Whatever it is, it's probably the biggest story of the year. And I don't have any idea what it is. Has this been building? I feel like I have no context. What kind of gossip queen am I?

I rush into the building. I'm trying to load a local news site on my phone as I walk, but I get horrible data service near the school. I shoot a few texts off to reliable story sources around the school. Only Raul responds, saying that he heard it was *some Latin thing*.

What? What could this have to do with Latin? Did Mr. Stanton get gross with a student? I can't imagine that at all. Though they always say it's the ones you least suspect.

I think back to Mr. Jelliver my freshman year. Ew. Sometimes it's the ones you *most* suspect.

The websites still aren't loading. So I head upstairs to what I now suspect to be the source of the drama: Mr. Stanton's room.

When I come in, the antique TV mounted in the corner of Mr. Stanton's room, normally off and gathering dust, is tuned to a local news station. But they're just reporting on traffic. A Latin 3 is sitting in front of it with the remote, flipping it from channel to channel every few minutes.

Mr. Stanton isn't there. I see a newspaper on his desk and peer at the page it's open to. A small headline below the fold: *Students Give Up Trip to Help Friend in Need.*

Is that what this is about? It can't be.

Mr. Stanton breezes in. "Spencer!" he calls out, his grin a mile wide.

"Is the news seriously here because of us?" I ask, dumbfounded.

"Because of you, more specifically," he says jovially. "The reporters aren't allowed in the school. But I'm sure we can find some time to send you out to give a statement, Mister President."

"But why do they care?"

"Morning news shows have a lot of time to fill, and this makes a great human interest story," Magister says. "High schoolers giving up State to help a friend in need. It makes people feel good."

"That's not why we did it," I say.

"And that just makes it a better story," he beams.

Katie comes in for her first period Latin class, looking sheepish and excited.

"And here's the woman of the hour!" Mr. Stanton calls out. She blushes.

"Hey, a minute ago you said this was because of me," I object.

"Ah, but Katie's the one who got us on the news."

"I just sent out the story to my usual community newspaper contacts," Katie explains. "I didn't have any idea the TV news would pick it up."

"Technically, you are supposed to get sponsor approval before sending out any stories," Mr. Stanton chides, still beaming.

"I didn't want to wait," Katie says quietly.

"I'm not mad," Magister laughs. "The whole city's talking about how great our Latin program and its students are!"

"I think you're overstating this," I say. "Does anybody really watch morning local news?"

"We've got one!" calls the student from the corner.

Everybody in the room rushes toward the TV. A local CBS anchor is standing in front of our school. It feels surreal to see the building I'm in right now with a news byline under it. The window of Mr. Stanton's room is on camera—I wonder if I waved, could I see myself? The anchor runs through the broad strokes of the story we already know. No names, thankfully, so no one knows it's Jeff.

"Since this story was first reported in our last hour," the woman is saying, "A viewer has set up a GoFundMe page to help these kind students make their trip anyway. We've put a link on our..."

The room erupts in sound. Mr. Stanton is at his computer in seconds. I've never seen him move so quickly.

The GoFundMe has been live for just under thirty minutes, and it already has over a thousand dollars in it. It goes up in increments of tens while we're watching it.

Katie is gaping at the screen. I turn and hug her.

"I think there are some people who watch the morning local news," I say in shock.

"I would say so," Mr. Stanton chuckles.

***

I see Latin Club kids checking the GoFundMe progress on their phones all day. The person who created it didn't actually know how much State cost, so she had set the goal at $5,000, well over the $3,300 we actually needed.

By our Latin 4 class in 5th period, the donations stand at $3,400 or so. Cass is buzzing with energy. Mr. Stanton looks like he's in heaven. He does make us do some Aeneid lines, but mostly we make plans for State.

He hands over the list of participants to me. As president, one of my duties is to draw up the rooming lists for the hotel. Four students to a room, same-gender of course. One of those things the sponsor can't be bothered to think about, so he delegates it.

I've been planning on it.

***

After school, we're all too happy to think about homework. We have another "Certamen practice" at Brian's. I destroy at Mario Kart. Allie pays me back by kicking my pretty pink butt at Super Smash Bros. I'm always Peach. Cass plays Metroid. Katie, an inexperienced player, goes with Yoshi because he's cute. Brian analyzes who everybody else is picking and picks based on what he thinks will be strongest against them, which is galling. But Allie is a virtuoso on Pikachu. She's basically unstoppable. The afternoon slips into evening.

At one point in the night, Brian puts down his controller, tells Cass he's going to go "hippopotamus out," and disappears for about half an hour. We play without him, and he comes back like nothing's going on. I make a mental note to ask Cass what "hippopotamus out" means. I hope it isn't something gross.

We end the night with some karaoke of *Chicago*, the musical I have been most successful at getting Brian to like. He does a beautifully self-aware version of "Mr. Cellophane:" "You can look right through me, walk right by me, and never know I'm there..."

The rest mostly have to go home around ten or eleven, because it's a school night. But my parents don't mind. Something about raising two more boys before me have made them more *laissez faire* about my upbringing. And Brian's mom is chill. So I end up sticking around with just him until a lot later, playing *Dark Souls III* and talking Roman History. I forgot how much I used to like it, before I lost my spot on Certamen and threw myself mostly into Dramatic Interp. Brian knows every Emperor and palace intrigue in the book, I swear, but I've got a better handle on the military than he does. I manage to fill in some blanks for him about the sack of the city under Honorius. He lends me a Mary Beard book that I promise I'll read.

***

The next day, Mr. Stanton has two things to show us. The first is the GoFundMe, which has blown well past its $5,000 goal. Though we need to wait for a Latin Club meeting to ratify it officially, we decide that we will use as much as we need for State, and pass on all the rest to Jeff and his family.

The other is my rooming list, typed for students' perusal. I look at my own room. The floor drops from under me.

"Mr. Stanton," I say softly. "You changed my room."

"Ah," he replies awkwardly. "Well, I saw that you put yourself in with Danny. I thought it might be problematic, having you rooming with your ex-boyfriend. So I asked Danny if he was comfortable with it, and he told me that he wasn't. So I switched it. For him."

He looks at the ground, then hurries off as if he has just thought of something really important he needs to do.

I'm cursing a blue streak in my head. I was going to remind Danny how much he missed me at State. We would room together and it would be like old times. I had all sorts of things planned. Things to say, happy accidents. His favorite song popping up as my ring tone. His favorite movies in my luggage. He wouldn't even be able to help himself.

A lot of couples form at State every year. Why couldn't one reform?

I can see Cass glaring at me from across the room. But class is starting.

"You want to tell me what that was about?" Cass asks me, exasperated, in the hall after class.

"I'm just holding on to hope," I say. She's walking next to me even though our classes are in opposite directions. I'm looking straight ahead instead of at her.

"Every time," she spits back. "Every time you swear to me you're moving on, you keep doing this. Did you really think Danny would be happy to room with you for two nights at State?"

"I was willing to take the chance."

"You can't keep doing this," she sighs, deflating slightly from her puffed-up outrage.

"It was a Hail Mary pass," I defend. "I know it's probably over." I'm telling her what she wants to hear.

"This isn't want-to-get-better behavior," she says. "This is some stalker shit. Like, if it was me, I'd be taking out a restraining order on you."

"Your support is overwhelming." We're standing at the door of my next class now, and I'm waiting for her to leave so I can go in.

"I'm worried about you," she continues, "And not just about what you're doing to him. What you're doing to yourself. I feel like you're locked into this pattern and don't know how to get out. I feel like if a shot at happiness came your way now, you might ignore it just because it isn't Danny."

"I'm getting better," I promise.

"Are you?" Then she looks up at the wall clock near the classroom door. "Damn, I need to go before I'm late. We'll talk about this later."

I nod my goodbye and she walks away.

I'll make her believe me. Or maybe I won't. Doesn't

matter. I can't get dragged down by Cass's negativity right now. My plan may be on the ropes, but it's not over until it's over. I will still find my opportunity to talk to Danny at State. Even if now I am stuck rooming with two freshmen and Brian.

Chapter 33: April 28th   Cass Washington

The twenty-one State-bound students gathered in Mr. Stanton's room before school started. We all had our overnight bags, and we were dressed in comfy enough clothes to endure our four-hour bus ride to San Antonio. The volume level was high. We were excited. We had spent two months in limbo about State, then we had all adjusted to the idea we weren't going at all.

Now here we were.

In the end, the GoFundMe had raised just over six thousand dollars, with a few ostentatiously big donations but mostly small ones. I liked to picture old grandmas (who were, I thought, the main people watching any television news shows) seeing the story on TV or on Facebook (the social media site of grandparents and dying local media alike), being touched by our story, and kicking in ten dollars. And now we had *three thousand* extra dollars to give to Jeff and his dad and grandma.

Spencer had given a brief interview to one of the reporters outside the school, which had shown up on a couple of local news shows: the big-hearted student who had started the whole thing. The clips they showed mostly featured him deferring, saying it was the Club as a whole who had voted to donate the money. Spencer really had done well with this whole thing.

I hoped he wasn't still thinking about Danny.

This morning he was certainly busy enough to forget: counting students, ticking off the attendance, getting last minute shirt and food orders. Brian was following and helping.

Brian. Last year he would have been ducked down somewhere in the crowd under his headphones. Now there he was, his headphones around his neck, bobbing through the crowd with the president, chatting with all kinds of students. After his setback, he had bounced back admirably, and was more sociable than ever (with reasonable hippopotamus breaks, that is). He was getting to be almost popular among the Club. Maybe he'd even run for office next year. What a strange thought.

But I still hadn't managed to find him a girlfriend yet. It was a shame.

It would be a different Latin Club I would leave behind when I graduated in just over a month. Probably either Sandy the Vice President or Katie would become president next year. Allie wasn't just hovering around Mr. Stanton anymore, she was hanging with Katie and a knot of junior girls.

And Jeff. At this point, who knew if we'd even see him again.

I would be leaving this year. I'd watched senior friends

graduating before, and I was always so sure they were going on to great things. They were leaving us to change the world. What was I leaving for? A freshman year at a college I wasn't sure about, with no major and no plans.

"You okay Cass?" Brian asked. I hadn't even noticed him walk up.

"Yeah, I'm okay," I told him. "Just getting wistful."

"Because it's your last State?"

"Yeah," I nodded. I had watched seniors get weepy at State before. I guess I had never known what they were feeling before now. "How are you doing? Got a psychiatrist appointment yet?"

"In three weeks," he rolled his eyes. "Getting in as a new patient is crap."

"So we'll keep doing 'hippopotamus,'" I said. Brian nodded. State could be a pretty overwhelming place. A lot of people.

"I think I can use my headphones too," Brian said. "The right song can set me right if I'm a little out of whack. It can be a good band-aid. Get it? *Band*-aid?"

"I do get it, and I might have changed my mind about us being friends."

Brian leaned against the desk next to me and smiled dreamily. "It's gonna be a good year for State," he said, "I can feel it."

"Even after we get our asses handed to us in Certamen?" I asked with a grin.

He shrugged. "Inevitable things are inevitable. But there are better things to be excited about. You're meeting your crush there, aren't you?"

My genuine smile rushed forward at that. "Yeah," I said. "We promised to meet by the registration desks after Pentathlon." Pentath was the first big event at JCL State, a short test that every participant took. Before Pentath was always a chaotic mess, with everyone arriving, staking out spots for the weekend, figuring out nametags and meal tickets. After Pentath always felt like the eye of a hurricane. A strange pocket of calm and idleness, before dinner started and everyone had to get running to Costumes and Dramatic Interpretations and such. The perfect time to meet.

It was also the time for the first meetup for my Mythology group, but I had already told them that I'd be missing that one. (PuellaStellarum was in Roman Life, like Katie.) The Myth group was meeting again on the second day, Saturday, after academic testing, so I'd catch up with them then.

"I hope it goes well," Brian said. "Wish me luck with my crush?"

"What? Of course! But who?" I sputtered, my mind running through the possibilities. Katie? Sandy? Allie?

"Not telling," he said simply.

"No, Brian. No. You do not stick out a tantalizing detail like that and then not tell me."

"Tantalize, coming from Tantalus in the Underworld, who was cursed to be always hungry with a bunch of grapes over his head that he could almost reach but—"

"*I know who Tantalus is, Brian. Think of who you're talking to here.* Back to the topic at hand."

"I'll tell you if it goes well," Brian said, and turned to

leave.

"Brian Daniel Ganz!" I shouted.

"That's not my middle name," he said over his shoulder.

"I took a guess! But you have to tell me! Stop walking away from me! Brian! That's a *bad Brian*!"

Soon Mr. Stanton announced that the bus was ready for us to board. I sprung up before anyone else had time to move.

"Before we leave on this august occasion," I announced, "Will everyone please stand and join me in the pledge of allegiance to Mr. Stanton's beard."

Magister put his forehead into his palm while all twenty-one State attendees gleefully stood and recited:

"I pledge allegiance

To the beard

Of my Latin teacher Mr. Stanton

And to the majesty

Of its fluff and heft

Red and tangled

Full of crumbs

Perfect in the eyes of God and man."

We seniors would see this Club change a lot after we left, but I wanted to be certain that this bit of legacy would outlast us. (Unless Mr. Stanton shaved his beard. A thought too terrible to contemplate.)

After we finished, Mr. Stanton announced, "Well, if we're honoring anything today, let's get a round of applause for our officers, especially Spencer and Katie, for getting us here today."

We duly applauded. Katie blushed, and Spencer waved like the Queen.

"I am unspeakably proud of everybody here," Mr. Stanton continued. "We got handed a bum deal this year, and you guys never caved to the pressure. You've reminded me why I do this job."

"Let's get on the bus before Magister cries!" Spencer yelled out, to laughter and more applause.

We filed downstairs with our overnight bags in tow and found our beautiful yellow chariot awaiting. The Latin Club always took a standard school bus to State, no matter how long the drive—in this case, four hours. We threw our bags onto the first few rows and wedged ourselves into the tiny seats in the back. There were few enough of us that we could have each had a bus seat to ourselves, but we didn't do that. We used the extra seats for the bags, and we sat next to our friends. It was a rite of passage.

I boarded first and staked out the back row. The officers followed me in. Mr. Stanton always sat in the front row to direct the driver. So we always said that the teacher supervised the front, and the officers supervised the back.

We said that. The officers didn't do much supervising. And the luggage didn't need much supervision in the front.

Spencer joined me in the back row, though Brian claimed the seat right next to him. I ended up next to Vice President Sandy. Which was fine with me. She was a less fun but more considerate seatmate. I could do four hours in that arrangement.

Once we were on the road, Spencer broke out his battery powered speaker and engaged in another of our time-honored State traditions: bus karaoke. Latin kids belting the hits of yesterday and today at the tops of their nerdy little lungs. Caring less about tunefulness or talent, and more about volume. We drowned out Spencer's speaker so thoroughly that sometimes we ended the song at a different time from the official version.

Watching the back of Magister's head as he flinched was part of the fun.

Spencer started with Katy Perry, Michael Jackson, Lady Gaga—the underclassmen didn't know the words to that last one as well, but no one could resist attempting that "ra ra ah ah ah" part. Some of the less dedicated started to fade out during "Formation," so Spencer brought out the big guns next.

"Is this the real life? Is this just fantasy?"

I was afraid we'd break the windows. Spencer managed to conduct us well enough to get different halves of the bus on the different "Galileo" parts. The bus rocked noticeably up and down during the group-head-bang to the guitar solo, which we also sang.

It was magic. Only the State bus.

***

We didn't sustain that kind of energy for the full four hours, of course. We settled down around the one-hour mark. Some diligent folks did the homework they'd be neglecting for the rest of the weekend. Others looked over materials for their State tests, practiced Oratory speeches, ran lines for the Play—which an ambitious sophomore had written and which I had heard was hilarious. (Ironically, Dramatic Interpretation conflicted with the Play competition, so Spencer wasn't in it. An injustice we had all heard plenty about.)

Everybody cheered when we saw the road sign proclaiming "Now Entering San Antonio."

We reached the school twenty minutes after that and piled aimlessly out of the bus. No one ever actually knew where they were going at State. It was at an unfamiliar school in another city. So we watched Mr. Stanton dash in to get us registered officially, then we wandered into the building ourselves. We'd find where the crowds were, grab a table or two, and wait for him to come back with instructions.

At our table, last-minute studying was reaching a fever pitch. It was mostly among the underclassmen. The only test today was Pentathlon, and most of the juniors and seniors knew there was no real studying for that. At least, nothing you could reasonably expect to do last-minute.

Mr. Stanton came hurrying up with an overstuffed envelope. I noted the direction from which he had come, for my rendezvous with PuellaStellarum later. (Ugh, rendezvous. That's French, the dirty Gallic tongue. What would be the Latin for that?) He handed the envelope to Spencer and told him to start distributing name tags. Mr. Stanton himself distributed programs, and told us to pick our Pentath classrooms and get moving as soon as we had our nametags. We had about fifteen minutes.

We headed into the throng of students, and the crush of bodies promptly broke up the team. It was how I imagined the battlefield in the Iliad: a confusing churning in which you could just as easily kill your ally as your enemy.

State was so much bigger than Area. There must have been a thousand students in that hallway alone.

Before I knew it, I was completely separated from the group, and most of the crowd was turning bit by bit into different classrooms for Pentathlon. Since there was only one Pentathlon test and everybody took it, you could just pick any one of dozens of Pentath rooms. It didn't particularly matter which one you went into.

Except that you wanted one with your friends. Friends that I couldn't find anymore.

I texted Spencer, Brian, and Katie, trying to figure out what room they were in. Spencer and Brian were together in H109, and Katie didn't respond. The halls had mostly emptied now, with most people in Pentath rooms. Just a few stragglers like me left. I set about trying to find H109, but the numbering system made no kind of sense. I expected H109 to be near, say, H108 or H110. No such luck. By the time I found H109 between J144 and H216, it was completely full, and the test directions were underway. Spencer shrugged and made a face, his scantron already in front of him. I couldn't come in, and he couldn't just get up and leave. I'd have to go find any room with space for me. And quickly, before the test itself started.

I found one a few doors down. A French room filled with nothing but eighth graders. And the best-behaved middle schoolers are still way more squirrely than I want to deal with on a Friday evening. So I finished my test pretty quickly to get out of there.

Soon I was waiting in the school's front atrium by the registration tables for PuellaStellarum, feeling pretty alone.

Normally at State all I did was socialize, and here I was spending an hour without even making eye contact with anyone.

I perked up when I saw her walking up. I recognized her instantly from her selfies, and she recognized me from mine. She was gorgeous. Skin black like obsidian, lips covered by metallic green lipstick. Mine was a dark purple today. She wore her hair cropped close to the skull, while I kept up a pile of corkscrew coils. She was tall and willowy, while I was shorter and curvy. She had on a green flannel shirt on top, to match her lips, and black leggings on bottom, tapering into black ballet flats.

She was every bit as stunning in person as she was on her Tumblr. I felt weak.

"Puella Stellarum?" I asked as soon as she was close enough.

"Adie," she introduced herself with her real name at last. "And you're Black Athena?"

"Cass," I told her.

"Short for Cassandra?" she asked.

"I wish," I said. "Cassidy."

"Pity. For the reference."

"The prophetess who always tells the truth, but no one ever believes her," I said wistfully. "Just like me when I give relationship advice."

Adie laughed.

"What is Adie short for?" I asked. "Adele?"

"It's not short for anything," she answered.

"Oh," I said. "I don't think I've heard that one before."

Awkward. Banal. What was I even saying?

I could go on describing our conversation, but it didn't get much more interesting than that. The remarkable thing about it wasn't anything we said or did. It was the electricity moving through me. It was the magnetism drawing me toward her. She could have said anything at all. I would have said anything I needed to, as long as it kept her standing in front of me.

What I wanted was to kiss her, right there. I'd never felt such a strong urge so quickly with anyone else. In my head, the same movie kept playing over and over. Me grabbing her hips, pulling her toward me, feeling those green lips on mine. I had to exercise every iota of my self-control not to do it.

We kept up the small talk as the murmur of voices from the cafeteria down the hall grew to a roar. More and more kids were finishing their Pentathlons and joining their Latin Clubs. Soon we would be missed.

"Want to go meet my Club?" Adie suggested.

"That's a pretty big step," I joked.

"They're dying to meet you," she said. "I've already told them all about you."

That made my heart flutter.

But I had to consider the time.

"I need to go meet up with my Certamen team," I said. "First round starts pretty soon."

"Right, I almost forgot you were in Certamen tonight," she said. "That's so cool, that you get to compete here."

I shrugged. "We've got a snowball's chance in the river Phlegethon. We never found anybody to replace our

Grammar guy."

"Yeah that's a bummer," she agreed. "But you got here. You won your Area. It's amazing."

She was right, of course, just like Spencer and Allie and Mr. Stanton and everybody else who wasn't actually on the team. It was just hard to feel that way when you were about to compete.

We lingered there, leaning against the wall in front of the registration table, neither of us wanting to be the one to walk away. At least, I hoped that's what she was feeling too.

"How about I come with you, then?" Adie asked.

"No no no," I responded quickly. "We're going to go down in flames. I do not want you to witness that."

Adie chuckled, then took my hand and started to lead me toward the cafeteria. I felt my resistance melt away as soon as she touched me. I would do anything, let her witness even the most embarrassing moments of my life, just to hang on to that feeling.

"You're not, like, exclusively attracted to me because of my Certamen prowess, right?" I joked uneasily. As we entered the cafeteria, I steered her toward my team's table.

"Mm, it was the main factor, I must admit," she said. "But I'm sure I can find other things to like."

As we approached the West Oak table, I could see that a group was gathered around something. I couldn't see what.

"Cass!" Spencer called as he saw Adie and I approaching. "Where have you been? Come here!"

"What is it?" I asked, quickening my step, trailing Adie by the hand.

The crowd parted slightly and I saw.

"Jeff!" I yelped. "What are you doing here?"

"My dad agreed to bring me," Jeff explained with a smile, sitting casually in a cafeteria chair.

He looked different. No physical differences—same basic white boy haircut, same polo shirt and jeans. But his tense energy was gone. His movements were slower, more languid, like an underwater version of old-Jeff. Like someone had given him a pot brownie.

"He's going to compete with you guys!" Spencer said with excitement.

"Is that healthy?" I asked skeptically. I mean, the kid had just had a nervous breakdown because of all the pressure he was putting on himself. And State Certamen was the most nerve-wracking thing that had ever happened to me.

"It's not like that," he said. He leaned deliberately forward. "When you guys tried to give up State for me, it changed how I thought about things. I guess I had assumed that the only reason anyone in Latin Club liked me was because I won us awards. Because I thought the only reason *anyone* liked me was because I was good at things." He swallowed hard. "Y'all giving me the money you had raised for State was the glaring piece of evidence that didn't fit my worldview."

"That you mean something to us beyond being good at Grammar," Spencer chimed in. "That you're our friend."

Jeff nodded. He was getting a little emotional. Not, like, crying-style, but still.

"So, I'm not all the way better yet," Jeff continued with

a breath. "But I asked my psychiatrists' permission to come here and compete with you guys. Not because I want to win, but because I want to be with you. Support you like you supported me."

"That is ridiculously sweet, man," I said. "Gods above, you're talking like a self-help guru, and Brian is Mr. Personality now. If we can just get Katie to come out of her shell, we'll have a giant lovefest of a Certamen team."

Katie laughed uncomfortably nearby. She was snapping pictures dutifully, even though nothing could go in her scrapbook anymore. It was safely under lock and key in the library, ready to be evaluated by the judges the next morning.

"Speaking of lovefest," Spencer said aside to me, "Who is this?"

Adie smiled. She had been standing awkwardly just over my shoulder.

"Oh," I laughed. "Guys, this is Adie. She's from Dallas."

"You two look like clones," Spencer said.

"Spencer!" Allie censured. "Don't be racist!"

"Oh, no, I can't be racist, I'm gay."

"Spencer, I keep telling you, that is *not* a thing," I snapped. Adie was laughing.

It was then that Mr. Stanton hurried up, accompanied by an older, harried-looking man who had to be Jeff's father. "Father" was the only word I could think to use. Guys that dignified aren't called "Dad." The stress lining his face only served to make him look more formidable.

"Alright," Mr. Stanton announced to the crowd. "Mr.

Miller and I—"

"Dr. Miller," corrected Dr. Miller automatically. (He probably did that everywhere. He'd probably do it to a waiter at the Cracker Barrel.)

"Yes of course," Mr. Stanton said quickly. "Dr. Miller and I have discussed Jeff's situation. He has been told not to be put under any undue stress."

"So I will join Mr. Stanton in the room as Jeff plays, making sure that his reactions are healthy and nothing jeopardizes his recovery."

"Wait, Stanton's going to be in the room with us?" I said quietly. That was enough undue stress on its own.

"I know my exercises," Jeff assured them. "I can keep myself calm."

"If not, we'll pull you into the hall," Dr. Miller said. "Nothing is as important as your recovery."

"Don't worry," Jeff said. "I'm not here to prove anything or to win. I'm just here for my friends."

Neither of the adults looked like they believed him completely.

"Oh, hello," Mr. Stanton said, noticing Adie for the first time. "Who's this?"

"That's Adie," Spencer said. "She's from Dallas."

CHAPTER 34: APRIL 28ᵀᴴ   KATIE NGUYEN

Jeremy texted me half an hour before we arrived at State.

We're here, he said. *I'm staking out Pentathlon room J129 if you'd like to join me.*

Try and stop me, I replied. *Is anyone from your team with you?*

They're going to another room, he typed back. *I told them not to follow me.* Then he included two eye-roll emojis.

I knew I was driving him a little crazy with the secrecy.

Allie was on his side about that. She noticed me texting and grabbed for my phone. I kept it from her, just barely.

"Planning where to meet your boyfriend?" Allie asked teasingly.

"He's *not* my boyfriend," I replied, trying and failing to sound calm and factual.

"Yet," she replied.

"Yet," I allowed.

She settled back down. "I can't wait to meet him."

"You're not *going* to!" I protested.

"Come on," she groaned. "I have to see this guy. He's got to be quite a dreamboat to keep you this obsessed. And

277

to have you crossing enemy lines to see him."

"Keep your voice down," I hissed. "The 'enemy lines' are exactly the problem. I can't go introducing you, or the whole team might catch wind."

Allie laughed derisively. "I was *joking* about the enemy thing, but it is deadly serious to you, huh? I'm telling you, no one would care. You should introduce him to everybody. We're all Latin nerds here."

"No," I hissed.

"Okay. I guess forbidden Catholic fruit is sweeter."

"He isn't Catholic, he just goes to a Catholic *school*," I corrected her.

"You'd know," she laughed. "What is he?"

"He's a Buddhist," I said, and I guess I couldn't keep the dreamy sigh out of my voice, because she started laughing so hard she attracted the attention of other seats. I shushed her, but it took her a moment to stop.

"Well," she said finally, "You certainly can't stop me from following you around."

"Allie, don't!"

"It's a free country, I can go where I want," Allie said, crossing her arms theatrically.

"I'll just meet him when you're busy at Costumes," I countered.

"I'll skip it," she said nonchalantly.

"You will not!" I spat.

"It'll be worth it."

"Okay," I said. "If you're good and you keep quiet about it, I'll point him out to you. From a *distance*."

"You are too generous," Allie rolled her eyes. "But I've

got you negotiating. I'll get you to introduce me before the weekend is over."

"Keep dreaming," I said.

***

I met up with Jeremy in Pentathlon room J129. Allie, despite her threats, didn't follow me.

"Hey," I said casually, taking the seat next to him.

"Hey you," he said. "Pretty boring here waiting for you."

"I'll be enough entertainment to make up for it," I said coyly.

"Dance, monkey," he joked.

We talked about nothing for a while. He was amused that we had ridden four hours in a standard yellow school bus.

"What did you have?" I asked. "A fancy expensive charter bus?"

"No, just a van," he said.

"A white van? That you wrote 'free candy' on the outside of?"

He laughed. "The school owns it. I've been on it for all kinds of competitions. We usually paint spirit slogans on the windows. We put *VENI VIDI VICI* on them this morning. But I can't believe you spent four hours in a school bus. That has to be uncomfortable."

"Have you ever even ridden a school bus?" I asked back. "Have you ever gone to a public school?"

"Not really," he said. "I guess I just know by reputation."

"You've really been through private schools your

whole life?"

"My parents aren't snobs or anything," he said defensively. "They had me in the school's daycare before I was school age, and I was so happy there they just let me start in their Kindergarten. They always figured they'd transition me to my regular public school eventually, but they always found reasons not to. I had friends, and I was part of all these programs."

"I'm not trying to judge," I told him. "I'm sure I wouldn't want to leave either."

He played with one of his expensive-looking mechanical pencils. "It makes me feel self-conscious sometimes. A lot of the people I go to school with... I mean, they're good people, but they can't wait to tell everyone where they go to school. Rub people's faces in how snobby and prestigious it is. That's not me."

"Oh, I know," I said. "Because if it were, I wouldn't like you like I do."

He grinned.

The test started half an hour late, which was not bad for a Latin competition. Jeremy finished a few minutes before me, but stuck around while I finished so he could walk me out. He took out a History book and pretended to study, probably so I wouldn't feel self-conscious and rush through the end.

As if. Even if the *Pope* were waiting on me, I would be taking all the time I needed. And this was just a Monk.

As we left the testing room, he grabbed my hand, interlacing our fingers. I'd felt butterflies in my stomach before, but this was more like butterflies radiating from his hand, up my arm, and over my entire body.

We walked toward the cafeteria in no particular hurry and talked about the test. I asked him the History questions I wasn't sure about. I was right that it was Commodus who had threatened a group of senators with the head of a dead Ostrich. I was wrong about the Battle of Lake Trasimene, because I got my First and Second Punic Wars mixed up. Then we talked Life questions, my specialty.

"I can't believe they asked what the Romans' favorite meat was *again*," I groaned. "I swear they ask that every State."

"I hadn't noticed," he laughed. "Why do you care? You have to know the answer if they always ask it."

"Because it's a dumb question," I said. "And because all the Latin 1's always pick peacock instead of pork."

Jeremy chortled. We had been circling some less populated hallways, putting off the time that we'd need to enter the cafeteria and not be seen together for a while. Finally, we felt we could put it off no longer.

"You're sure you don't want to come by my table?" he asked me. "My friends want to meet the girl that has me all turned around."

"You haven't *told* them—"

"I haven't told them who you are or what school you're from," he completed patiently. "I'm keeping my promise."

"Thank you," I said, unsure what else to say. "I'm going to get back to my own table. But still meet me at the Play competition later tonight?"

"Wouldn't miss it," he answered. "After your

Certamen rounds are over. You're *sure* I'm not allowed to come watch?"

I shook my head forcefully. "And that's not just because of my Club. You'd make me too nervous."

"I guess I'll take that as a compliment," he said. "At least I'll be able to watch you in finals tomorrow."

"Not likely," I laughed.

"See you at the plays, Chopin," he told me.

I felt myself blush a little. "See you there, Monk."

I had admitted to him quite recently that I had been calling him "Monk" in my head before I knew his name, and he thought it was hilarious. In return, he insisted on giving me a musical nickname of my own. Hence Chopin, a Romantic piano composer I liked. I said I didn't know if I'd call him my favorite, but Jeremy pointed out that Monk wasn't his favorite jazz musician either. He said that Monk was just his recommendation for pretty girls who like piano.

Inside the cafeteria, I got a windfall in the form of Jeff. See, I had already been plotting the follow-up piece that I would send to every paper that printed our story. But I hadn't been able to think of anything more interesting than a recitation of our awards and the fun we'd had. Now that the sick boy we'd helped had actually shown up, I knew I could get published again.

CHAPTER 35: APRIL 28TH CASS WASHINGTON

We arrived early to our first Certamen round. I had been picturing an auditorium, like finals at Area, but instead we were in a dingy old regular classroom. A math room, judging by the faded cartoony posters on the walls. An entirely inappropriate setting for the crowning achievement of my four-year Certamen career.

As soon as we walked in, my heart began to pound. There was already a small crowd. No one ever showed up for the preliminary rounds at Area. Did people come to watch at State?

Then one of the crowd turned and I realized. It was Angela, from my Mythology group. She smiled at me and nudged Warren, who was sitting next to her. Soon they were all waving and hooting and hollering at me. There were about fifteen of them there. Fifteen extra spectators for the hardest Certamen round of my life. I felt the blood burning in my face. I wanted to pass out.

I waved quickly and headed with the rest of the team to take our seats. We took our lucky places at the B buzzers. Jeff didn't take B1 like usual. The plan before Jeff's return had been for me to be team captain. It wasn't a plan I loved, but we stuck to it because it put less spotlight on Jeff.

That put me in the hot seat. B1, team captain for the Area E Certamen champs.

The inside of my mouth felt sticky. When you imagine the big moment, the inside of your mouth is never sticky.

I turned toward Adie, who was sitting close to Mr. Stanton in the spectator's desks. (It was weird to see them together. I had even seen them exchange a few words, which just seemed wrong.)

"Adie," I whispered. Then I realized it was ridiculous to whisper, because our team and our hangers-on (Mr. Stanton, Dr. Miller, Adie, Allie, Spencer, most of the Latin 2 Certamen team, and my entire Mythology group) were the only ones in the room. "You got a water or something?"

"I got you, boss!" Allie said instead, and dashed out the door.

"No, you really don't need to..." I started to say, but she was already gone.

"Relax, dude," Adie laughed. "It's an experience. It's not about how you do."

"Smart girl," said Mr. Stanton.

When the other two teams filed in, I wasn't as scared of them as I thought I would be. They acted just like teams from our Area. One was super rigid and uptight in matching blue argyle sweaters, like another Our Lady of the Seven Sorrows. The other was more laid back, laughing and joking. The way we normally were. When we weren't

CERTAMEN

terrified about facing the hardest Certamen round we'd ever been in. And sitting next to our friend on furlough from a mental hospital.

I listened to the other teams talk. Both had played in State Certamen before. They knew what they were doing.

The proctor came in shortly afterward, an angry looking white dude in a private school blazer. He had a bald head and a voluminous, walrus-like mustache that completely overshadowed his mouth. He set his binder— The Binder—on the podium at front and made sure everybody was here. He cracked a few jokes about the rules before reading the Aurelia passage.

I guess he wasn't an angry person. Probably I was just nervous.

The round was brutal. It wasn't that we didn't know any of the questions. We knew plenty. The problem was the next-level buzzing abilities of the other teams. I swear, sometimes they answered correctly before the proctor had gotten past the "Which."

We got zero. I couldn't remember the last time I'd actually gotten zero in a round of twenty Certamen questions. Brian had managed to buzz in first one time, but he'd said the wrong Emperor Constantine.

It was a shameful round.

Adie rested a hand on my shoulder as we stood looking forlornly at the big board. The Our Lady of the Seven Sorrows stand-ins had swept up a hundred and eighty points, and the others had gotten fifty. Seeing the proctor write in the big "0" for Area E was heartbreaking.

"You've got this, Cass," said Hazel from my

Mythology group.

"You guys don't have to stay for all of this," I said nervously.

A couple of them peeled away to hit the Play competition, but most of them stayed put, being aggravatingly supportive.

"I've got to go get ready for Costume," Allie said apologetically. "Sorry, guys, better luck next round."

We all wished her luck as well. She had greatly improved her costume between Area and State. She looked like a Trojan king in his robes now. No more man in a dress.

"Do we really have to play two more rounds of that?" I groaned. "Can't we just forfeit?"

"Don't kick yourselves," Adie said kindly. "Those were really good teams."

"It's not about winning," Jeff said earnestly. "It's enough for me to be here with you."

"You're really into this whole being cured thing," I chuckled. It was like he and I had switched places.

"No way in hell I'm slinking away with my tail between my legs," Katie said with fire. "We're getting some points in next round."

"I'm with her," Brian chimed in. "It's our school's first ever State Certamen. We're laying a foundation for many teams to come after us. I want to let these super-players know who we are."

"Hey, is it inspirational speech time?" Spencer said, wandering back with a Coke in his hand. "Because, go team, okay?"

"Thank you, Spencer," I rolled my eyes.

We fared better in the next two rounds. In round two both Brian and Katie scored a few points. Katie was especially fierce, buzzing in so quickly I saw looks of envy cross the faces of the other teams.

You could never catch a proctor off guard, though. They stopped their questions on a dime as soon as they heard the beep.

Jeff and I didn't get any questions right in the second round, but he got one in the third. I would have to be content with never answering a question in a State Certamen round. I knew plenty of the answers. It was the nerves that got me.

After the third round, I stared at the buzzer in my hand. Gray plastic with little white stripes, the blue button on top no bigger than the eraser on a pencil. Four years of my life staring at these, and now I'd probably never hold one again. Jeff and Katie and Brian were already gathering up their papers and standing, but I was frozen in place. Stuck. I couldn't believe that was it. My last Certamen round.

"Are you BlackAthena17?" a voice asked me. I looked up to see a square-headed dude in black rectangular glasses.

"Yeah," I said, a little dazed.

"I follow you," he said. "I love your fan art."

"Thanks," I grinned.

"It *is* her?" asked another voice from behind him. A skinny blond kid in a shirt two sizes too big joined the first one. "I thought you were just racist."

"Not this time," I said.

"This is Sean," the first guy said. "I'm Riley."

"Cass," I said. "Nice to meet you. Where are you guys from?"

"Amarillo," Sean said. They were two of the guys from the team that had just come in first in the round. They always introduced the teams by Area letters, and I could never remember which one was which.

"Your art is really cool," Sean said.

"Thanks," I said again. "Would I recognize your usernames?"

"Nah, neither of us really post," Riley said.

"Man, I'd love to have someone like *you* on our team," said Sean, cutting his eyes to their own Mythology expert standing across the room talking to some adult. I thought I knew what he meant. Their Mythology guy had been the weak link on their team. He had flop sweat so bad he looked ready to pass out. He'd barely said a word all round. Not that I was in any position to judge, of course.

That wasn't why his friend wanted to talk to me, though. "What are you doing after this?" Riley asked me, with obvious intentions. "You wanna hang out?"

"I've got plans," I said politely. "Do you guys follow PuellaStellarum?"

***

In the final reckoning, our team was several hundred points out of the range for finals. First place going into finals was San Antonio, followed closely by Austin. In a more distant third was Amarillo, the guys I had just talked to.

Honestly, I was relieved we weren't moving on. Finals

were the next day. I couldn't live with that kind of pressure.

The important thing was that we ended up in fifth place out of the six teams there. That giggly team we met in the first round had had less luck in the other two, and had ended up beneath us in points.

"The gods have smiled on us!" I called out. "We are not in last place!"

The team laughed and swapped self-effacing high fives.

"There were only six teams here," Jeff pointed out. "Six teams from the entire state. We don't need to call ourselves second-to-last. We were the fifth best Certamen team in the state of Texas this year. I'm proud of you guys."

"Wait for it," I murmured.

"This will look amazing on our college résumés," Jeff continued.

"*There* he is!" I said.

And that, I figured, was the end of my Certamen career. Not with a bang, but with a whimper.

Sic transit gloria.

***

The next thing I wanted to go to was the dance. It was where most of West Oak and my whole Mythology group was going. But Adie wanted to go to the SCL recruitment meeting, and she really wanted me to go with her.

SCL was the Senior Classical League. Junior Classical League was for high school, Senior for college. Every year at JCL State, SCL members pitched their organization to the graduating JCL seniors. Which included me all of a sudden.

"I thought there were only, like, three people in the

whole SCL," I protested on our way. Adie laughed.

"I think there's a little more than that," she said. "Anyway, why not look into it?"

"My more pressing concern is, 'How do I avoid letting you out of my sight?'"

The recruitment was less of an organized presentation and more of a loose hangout. It was in an English classroom, with a couple of desks pushed together as a makeshift buffet table for some sodas and store-bought baked goods. Adie and I were two of about five high school seniors there, along with four SCL college students. Which gave me some evidence for my "No one joins SCL" assertion.

But I took a Coke and a cookie and talked to some people.

In particular there was this girl, Lea, with giant glasses, gauges in her ears, and bright green hair. I talked a bunch of Mythology with her while Adie was grilling a History major.

"Are you a Classics major?" I asked Lea after a bit.

"No, I'm in Biotechnical Engineering," she said. "Classics is just a passion of mine. I take at least one class per semester in it. Except for last semester, when I really wanted to take this Jewish American Lit course in the English department."

I liked Lea's version of college. My parents had made college sound like a job training pipeline. Lea made it sound more like a buffet, where you could try tastes of whatever you might be interested in.

"Did you ever get to take that class on the Biology of Dinosaurs?" one of the other college guys asked her, having heard our conversation.

"No, it was always full," Lea replied. "Cass, if you're interested in Classics majors, Matt is one." She motioned to the interlocutor, a heavyset Latino guy with a tall, unruly bush of hair and a black hoodie.

"Oh, are you thinking of taking the plunge?" Matt asked me with an easy grin.

"Not really," I confessed. "I don't know what I want."

"No biggie," he said. "Where are you going?"

"UTSA."

"Oh, I started there," Matt said. "If you like Mythology, you've got to take the Folklore survey course they offer. You compare Greek Mythology to Norse, Old German, Native American, Sub-Saharan African. It's fascinating."

It did sound good. But I brought him back to an earlier point. "You *started* at UTSA. Where are you now?"

"UT Austin. I loved it at UTSA, but I moved over to the main campus when I decided on Classics. UTSA doesn't have a major."

"I could never make it in to UT Austin," I grumbled.

"Well, neither could I out of high school," he chuckled. "I was a C-student in AcaDec. I was in the bottom half of the class because I used to sit on my ass playing video games and I didn't do any homework. But college is different. I love college like I never loved high school, so I work for it. And UT only cares about your college transcript when you're transferring."

I raised an eyebrow. Everyone in high school was throwing everything they had into getting in to the right college. We all thought we only had one shot.

"I decided on Classics after a couple of Greek Philosophy courses at UTSA," Matt continued. "Before that I was doing Literature, but my first major was Early Education." He chuckled again. "What was I thinking?"

"What are you going to do with your Classics degree?" I asked, trying hard to ask casually, not with the kind of judgmental tone my parents would have used for the question.

"Probably some kind of teaching or writing," he said. "I want to go to grad school, but I'll have to get good scholarships and TA stipends to afford it. I might spend a few years doing something else before I go."

"A friend of mine graduated with a Philosophy degree last year," Lea jumped back in. "She's working for Random House right now. Copy editor, but she's working on moving into the actual publishing side."

"Yeah a lot of people go that kind of route," Matt said. "Guy I know with a History degree is working his way up in the *New Yorker*. But really, you never know what you'll end up doing. My brother's fiancée, whose degree is in Psychology, is the CFO of a non-profit that gets grocery stores opened in food deserts."

My mind was racing. Moving colleges. Changing majors. Chasing interests. Landing in careers that had nothing to do with your major. None of it made any sense with the world as I had understood it.

I'll be damned if these twenty-year-olds weren't the most inspiring people I'd met in a long time.

When I had a moment alone, I texted my dad.

Start working on Mom for me.

Oh my, he replied. *What?*

I've decided to start out as a History major, because UTSA doesn't have Classics. But I might want to transfer somewhere so I can get a Classics major. I have no idea if that's what I want long-term, or what I want to do with it. But it's what feels right at the moment.

And, I didn't add, I wasn't looking forward to testing the boundaries of my mother's newfound supportiveness.

There was a pause on his end.

I'll start laying the groundwork now, he said finally.

Thanks.

Have fun up there. I'm proud of you.

I love you, Dad.

"So," Adie asked me as we left to go to the dance, "What did you think?"

"I think I'm finally excited about college," I said in a distracted haze.

"I meant about the SCL."

"The what now?"

CHAPTER 36: APRIL 28TH   KATIE NGUYEN

After our slaughter in Certamen, I slipped away from the team as they were walking to the cafeteria. I think they were going to drop their stuff in there and go to the dance, which was an event with lots of neon lights, thudding bass, and kids who can't actually dance. So, usually pretty fun. But I was meeting Jeremy at the plays, where we could be more inconspicuous.

The play contest was in the spirit of the drama competitions of ancient Athens, but much abbreviated. Since it was pretty hard to accomplish anything serious in the seven-minute time limit, most students resorted to ridiculous humor and farce. Most of the plays were pretty cringy, so not many people stayed through all of them.

The contest wasn't in the full auditorium. It was in a smaller teaching theatre. The stands would only hold about fifty people, and they were half empty. The stage wasn't lit with stage lights. The regular classroom lights were on in the whole room.

When the four actors of the most recent play were

taking their bows to tepid applause, I slipped in and found Jeremy. He was saving the seat next to him with his State program, even though there were five open seats on either side of him.

"Katie!" he beamed. "How'd it go? Are you playing in finals tomorrow?"

I laughed. "Nope. Fifth place out of six teams."

"Bummer."

"Actually it's quite a relief," I said. "How have the plays been?"

"A couple of good one-liners," he said, "But seldom more than one per play, so it's been pretty slow. Honestly the best part was when an actor lost his contact lens in the middle of a play about Romulus and Remus, and the rest of the cast ran out the clock helping him find it."

"Do you think that was really just part of the show?"

"That would be quite the postmodern theatre experience," Jeremy said.

"Well, don't keep me in suspense," I said. "Did they find the contact?"

"Remus found it eventually," he said. "It was quite a relief. The god Mars said his mom would have killed him if he lost another one."

"Are we ready for the next play?" the judge called out from up front. An actor came out on stage to give him a thumbs up. The audience applauded. Have you ever heard sarcastic applause? It was my first time. The same actor came back out to give the prologue.

Jeremy offered me a pack of Twizzlers, and I took one silently. It was like going to see a movie together, except that instead of big-budget explosions on a screen, it was a bunch of nerdy high schoolers trying to be funny about Latin stuff.

He took my hand again, and we sat with our arms intertwined on the plastic armrest. A few moments later I leaned over and let my head rest against his shoulder. I felt him sigh contentedly, and I melted a little further in.

Then I noticed King Priam sitting two rows in front of us. *Allie*, with her masculinized costume and fake beard. She wasn't watching the play. She was goggling at Jeremy and me. I tensed. Jeremy noticed.

Allie gave me a big wave and mouthed, "He's cute."

I groaned. Allie would come up after this play was over. I couldn't get away with not introducing her then.

"Somebody from your Club?" Jeremy whispered in my ear.

I nodded. He didn't need to look so amused. Jerk.

CHAPTER 37: APRIL 28TH   SPENCER OLSON

On State Friday, I hardly see Danny at all. As soon as we're off the bus, he's out of the picture. He's in a different Pentathlon room. I don't see him at dinner. After dinner, I'm with our team for the first two Certamen rounds, then I have to go do my Dramatic Interpretation speech.

The wait in the holding room is interminable. I'm in there alone with a thirty or so other guys of all levels, practicing lines for a bunch of different characters.

My mind starts to circle on Danny. In all my visualizations of this weekend, I'd pictured being around him a lot. I assumed that he'd be forced to acknowledge my existence.

I'd forgotten how big State is. You can avoid someone pretty easily, if you want to.

Running the lines for my speech gives me comfort, though. It's from the Aeneid, which means it's metered. I mutter it under my breath again and again, letting the syncopated rhythms of the dactylic hexameter block out everything else. It was the closest I'd ever get to meditation.

I don't love the Aeneid while translating it in class, but reciting the meter will always be a joy. No English poetry has ever matched it. Anybody who thinks Shakespeare wrote beautiful meter needs to spend some time with Vergil.

> *at non ille, satum quo te mentiris, Achilles*
> *talis in hoste fuit Priamo; sed iura fidemque*
> *supplicis erubuit corpusqu-exsangue sepulcro*
> *reddidit Hectoreum mequ-in mea regna remisit...*

I finally get to recite for the judge after about an hour. Just me and a squat older lady with a little too much lipstick on, in an empty classroom. State really does know how to make a Theatre kid feel at home.

I do pretty well. The speech is the death of Priam, requiring me to dredge pain and sadness from the depths of my soul. No problem. There's plenty in there. When I curse Pyrrhus for his wickedness I pretend to spit at his feet, which I think my judge enjoys.

Once my speech is done, I hurry to the dance. It's still half an hour to eleven, when they'll be shutting the whole thing down.

As soon as I'm through the gym doors, I grab a couple of glow bracelets from a table laid with them and head for the floor, moving to the pulse of an outdated "Call Me Maybe." I find Brian, Cass, and Adie-from-Dallas pretty quickly. They yell my name happily over the music. It's good to see them.

"How'd Certamen go?" I ask in a barely audible yell.

"Awful!" Brian shouts back.

"You'll get 'em next year!" I respond. "Where's

Katie?"

They both shrug. Strange. Most of the Latin 3's are here. I look for Allie, and I can't find her either. What are they up to?

We dance in a group for a few songs. Adie has some pretty good moves, almost as good as mine. Cass holds her own. Brian is a disaster.

The last song is a slow song, so the couples all pair up. I see Cass and Adie holding each other, swaying like they're at an eighth grade dance. They look so good together, it makes me sick. I can't deal with beautiful displays of same-sex love tonight, not with Danny on my mind. I turn the other direction.

At 11:15 the music shuts off and the lights come up. We all slink away toward the cafeteria. Adie-from-Dallas tells Cass she needs to go the other direction and says goodnight with these heavy bedroom eyes. Cass looks totally smitten. It's adorable and it hurts.

Mr. Stanton is waiting for us, looking tired. He adds us to his headcount.

"Twenty-one," he announces. "Let's get on the bus and get to bed, we've got another big day tomorrow."

"Where's Jeff?" I ask him as we file out.

"His dad got them their own hotel," he answers. "They left right after Certamen to get some decent sleep."

"Unlike what we'll be getting," I say, smiling. Almost everyone has a cache of junk food, soda and video games for their hotel room.

"That's right," he says with a chuckle. "You know, some of us are old and actually *need* that sleep..."

I sit next to Cass, watching as Katie gets into her seat next to Allie. I'm wondering what they were up to when we were at the dance.

"Cass," I whisper, "Tell me if I'm crazy…"

"You're crazy," she says without hesitation.

"Ha ha," I say drily. "Tell me if I'm crazy, but do you think Katie and Allie have a thing?"

Cass looks over at them for a moment. As if scrutinizing them at this very moment will give her the answer.

"No," she says finally. "Katie's straight."

"We've been wrong before," I point out.

"I'm rarely wrong about girls," Cass replies. "Plus, would Allie be capable of keeping the secret?"

"Maybe she has unplumbed depths," I speculate.

"I think they're just close friends," Cass says.

"Yeah, me too honestly," I sigh. "It's just, I know there's something going on with both of them, and I have no idea what it is."

"You hate not knowing."

"I am what I am," I say.

It's 11:45 by the time we're settled in the hotel. In my room, everything is quiet. My two freshmen roommates are not very talkative, and Brian is Brian. After so many hours of noise at State, the quiet is like a noise of its own. It presses against the sides of my head.

We take turns with the shower. The freshmen lay out blankets to sleep on the floor while Brian and I take the two beds. Straight boys never want to share beds, even with other straight boys. Like they'll somehow catch gay that way.

My thoughts circle around Danny again. I try reciting my Dramatic Interp speech, but it has lost its urgency. The dactylic hexameter is just a collection of artful syllables, not a mystic chant anymore.

Danny is in the room with me, in my head. Like he was supposed to be. We're talking through the last few months. We're healing. We're finding our way forward. Like we were supposed to be doing. Like what was supposed to happen.

"You all right?" Brian asks me quietly, breaking me out of my head.

"Yeah," I answer untruthfully. "Yeah, just tired."

Chapter 38: April 29th   Katie Nguyen

Allie and I emerged into the hotel lobby at 6:30 am to find it full of Latin students from a bunch of different schools. The West Oak team was wearing this year's Club shirt, which was blue. I saw another group in purple, one in orange, one in lime green, and a prep school in button-ups and sweater vests. Various groups were sitting in circles all over the floor, running declension tables or sequences of emperors. I saw textbooks and SparkCharts and laptops. A lot of people had visited the continental breakfast bar and had tiny plastic plates piled with rock-hard bagels or scrambled eggs with the texture of upholstery foam. Latin students covered chairs, sofas, benches, and most of the floor along the walls.

There was one unaffiliated Midwestern family over at one of the breakfast tables, gaping at us all.

I was wearing my favorite skirt and a nice pair of flats. Allie had laughed at me. Everyone else was in leggings or shorts, tennis shoes or flip flops. This was our long competition day, from 7 am to 7 pm, and most people dressed for comfort. They didn't have anyone to *impress* today.

We spotted Cass by the registration desk and walked over. She was gazing out at the crowd, lost in thought. She snapped out of it when I greeted her.

"Hey," she smiled at me. "What's up?"

"Not much," I said, a little guiltily. I hadn't spent nearly as much time with her and the rest of my friends as I normally would have at State. Not that I had any immediate plans to *change* that, mind you. "You looked like you had something on your mind."

"Yeah," she said, and gave a quick glance around. "You two can keep a secret, right?"

Allie and I leaned in.

"Brian," Cass said quietly, "Has a crush on somebody here. He told me. But he wouldn't tell me who."

I gasped. Allie laughed.

"So I'm watching him," Cass continued, motioning with her head to where Brian was across the room, standing near Spencer in a crowd of History kids, "Trying to see if I can spot any signs."

"Anything yet?" Allie asked.

"Kid's got a great poker face," Cass said gravely.

"Any *theories*?" Allie probed. She looked just like she did when she was talking to me about Jeremy: amused, engaged, a wicked spark in her eye, like a shark circling a wounded swimmer. She was as bad as Spencer.

"I've been thinking maybe Sandy," Cass said. "Or you," she said casually, motioning to me. Allie laughed when I blushed.

"But you haven't seen anything?" Allie asked.

"Nah, he's normal around everyone. Which is to say, abnormal, but in the usual ways."

Allie looked at Brian too. "Did he tell you it was someone from our school?"

"No," Cass muttered. "All he told me was she'd be at State."

"He could have the hots for someone from another school," Allie said, staring directly at me. "Could have met her at Area, or even the invitational meet. A lot of potential for romance there."

I could have hit her.

But Cass didn't have any inkling that Allie was talking about anyone except Brian. "Clever," she muttered. "But that'd be a tougher one to figure out."

"You'd be surprised," Allie responded.

"What?" Cass asked.

"*Nothing*," I said, too forcefully.

"I don't think that's it, though," Allie said. "I think it's Spencer."

"*Spencer?*" I gasped.

"That does make a little bit of sense," Cass murmured.

"But Brian isn't gay," I argued.

"That we know of," Cass countered. "Who knows what kind of secrets he has up in that mind palace of his?"

"That'd be my bet," Allie said firmly. "I think he likes Spencer."

Cass smiled at Allie. "Stakes?"

We all started to go through our bags. There was a lot to choose from—anyone with any sense packed a lot of snacks for State. I came up with Sour Patch Kids. Cass had a big carton of Whoppers. Allie brought out chocolate Hello Pandas.

"Katie can hold on to the pot until we find out," Cass said, mock-officially. "As she is clearly the most trustworthy of the three of us."

"Agreed," Allie said.

"Okay," Cass said. "I think the three options on the table are someone from *our* school, someone from *another* school, or Spencer. Allie has Spencer. I'm torn. Katie, which do you want?"

"Oh, *she* wants someone from another school," Allie said immediately.

Then I did hit her.

***

There weren't many chances for me to hang out with Jeremy in the morning. The team went almost directly from buses to testing rooms. The rooms were done by subject, so I was in a Life room while Jeremy was in History. He texted me good luck before the test started. I texted back the same, and hid my big dumb grin from the West Oak underclassmen who were in the room with me.

The test went well enough. I took both the Roman Life and the Latin Literature tests in the same sitting, so I felt lightheaded as I left. I was right to take my stronger subject, Life, first. The Lit test had started to feel like nonsense toward the end.

Back in the cafeteria for lunch, I waited until I was pretty sure no one was looking at me before I texted Jeremy.

We started our afternoon with a lecture by a college

professor of Archaeology. It was less exciting than it had sounded in the program, but he did have some real Roman coins that he let us touch. Then Jeremy needed to report to play basketball in Ludi. I headed for the stands to witness his athleticism. A bunch of West Oak people were there to watch our team, so I sat with them, secure in knowing that they wouldn't realize why I was there.

Ludi basketball was exactly what you might picture when I say "dozens of Latin students playing basketball." Uncoordinated running, clumsy shooting, yard after yard of pasty white calves sticking out of gym shorts. There were the occasional extremely athletic outliers, who easily led their teams to victory. The teams that happened to have *two* good athletes had the run of the court. Most of the best players were actually girls, shooting perfect baskets over the heads of guys a foot taller than them.

Jeremy was somewhere between Latin nerd and athlete. He was alright, but not one of those players wiping the court with his opponents. His team had one really good player though, so they went pretty far in the bracket. I liked to watch him run. I started to get paranoid that my teammates next to me could tell. Like they could read my mind or something.

After his team was eliminated, I told my teammates that I was going to go check out the Art exhibits in the library and left. I met up with a slightly sweatier Jeremy outside the gym. He had changed his clothes, but it was obvious that he had been running. From the stands I had been imagining a rugged musk, like in a bad romance novel. That was not what I got. He stank.

And apparently, it showed on my face. "I think one of the other guys had some deodorant," he said quickly, "I'll be right back."

He returned smelling acceptable. Not great, but I could walk with him to the library in comfort. Once there, we walked up and down the aisles, which were set up like a museum gallery. There were some amazing pieces, and a few that looked like my eight-year-old brother did them. I pointed out the ones that I knew were made by members of my team. He didn't know of any art submitted by his. He was actually pretty surprised that all of it was there. He had never seen the Art exhibition at State before.

We both spent a while flipping through the scrapbooks. Rather than appreciating them, we were appraising the competition against mine.

"I don't think you have much to worry about," he said as we left the library. "None of those were better than yours."

"Thank you," I said with appropriate humility.

"I mean, the news clippings about your Grammar guy have got to help too. Sympathy points. Plus, you come off really well spoken in them."

I thanked him again. We dallied for a while outside at the catapult competition next, before separating again for dinner with our teams. We had held hands for about half an hour through the Art, and he had put his arm around me for the Catapult. But I think he got a little frustrated with how often I looked around to make sure no one saw.

Throughout dinner I was thinking about Jeremy. I had been in a few short-lived I-like-you sorts of relationships in seventh and eighth grade, before anyone knew what they were doing. But I hadn't been in any since high school started. This felt so different. So *real*.

I looked around the table at my friends, digging into the pasta piled on their styrofoam plates. I wanted to tell Cass, Brian, Spencer, Sandy. Even Adie-from-Dallas, who was eating at Cass's elbow instead of with her own team. I wanted everyone to know. I wanted Allie to look happy for me, instead of frustrated with my stubbornness.

But he was from Our Lady of the Seven Sorrows. He was untouchable. I couldn't tell them what I'd done. The betrayal I'd been perpetrating since Area. I *couldn't*.

CHAPTER 39: APRIL 29ᵀᴴ   SPENCER OLSON

I'm wearing Danny's favorite shirt of mine. I'm the only one in the Club not wearing our t-shirt, and everyone's been asking me why. Everyone except Danny, of course.

I catch glimpses of him a few times, sitting with other juniors in the cafeteria or walking with someone down a hallway. He's never alone. I need him to be alone.

I stick with my crowd as I look for my opportunity. Now we're in the auditorium for Certamen finals. It doesn't matter that no one we know is in it—all the Certamen kids go watch finals. At least, we all have in the past.

"Where *has* Katie been all day?" I wonder aloud.

"None of us have gained any new information since the last time you asked that," Cass responds saltily. Adie chuckles. Cass is just acting up for company.

The Intermediate round just ended. At least the robots who won that one looked like they'd all been through puberty.

They're just starting to reset the stage for the Advanced teams when a guy I don't recognize stops at our row.

"Cass!" he says too loudly, and she jumps.

"Hey," she says warily. "Sean, right?"

"Right," he says, a little out of breath. I can smell the cream he uses for his acne as he leans over me to talk to her. "You wanna play some Certamen?"

"What?" she says blankly.

"Peter, our Mythology guy, has food poisoning," Sean explains. "We think from when we got lunch on the way up yesterday. He's out. You wanna play with us?"

"That's gotta be against the rules," I smirk.

"It certainly is," Jeff confirms.

"We don't care," Sean laughs. "We hardly had a chance against Austin and San Antonio before, and we'll never win now. We just want to play with someone who can make the round fun."

"You don't have an alternate?" Cass asks.

"Our alternate is just a Life guy," Sean replies. "Didn't make the cut and our sponsor felt sorry for him."

"I know how that goes," I say.

"So, what do you think?" Sean asks.

We all look at Cass, giddy smiles on our faces. Her brow is furrowed.

"Do it, dude," Brian says.

"Yeah, get up there," Jeff laughs.

"It's your last year," Adie says.

Cass blinks at her. "Okay," she says.

We applaud her as she climbs over our legs and follows Sean toward the stage. The rest of his team is already up there. They smile and shake Cass's hand as she joins them.

"I cannot believe Katie is missing this," I shake my head. "Everyone text her now."

"On it," Adie says.

I barely realize she's kidding before the players are introducing themselves on the stage. We hoot and holler for Cass when she says her name into the mic, which nicely covers up the fact that she almost says the wrong school name.

The moderator starts the first question, something about a wife of Jason. A beep cuts him off before he gets too far, of course. A4. It's Cass. She answers something I couldn't even begin to spell, and gets it right. Her "team" laughs and claps her on the back. Her grin is a mile wide.

The first Certamen question she ever got right at State, and it was in the finals. No matter if she was playing for a school she doesn't go to in Amarillo.

Cass gets both bonuses correct. Her team is elated. It seems to embolden them. The other teams do well, but Amarillo stays ahead the whole time. Cass even gets two more questions for them.

At the last toss-up, they're up by 25 points. It doesn't even matter that Austin takes the last question. Amarillo still wins.

The moderator announces that the Area D team will represent Texas at the National convention. The rest of the team high five, cackling, and give Cass a group hug. The West Oak team is on their feet applauding. I see a very pissed-off-looking adult striding self-importantly up to the moderator.

"Oh, guys, the jig is up," I point him out to our group.

Cass and the Amarillo team's smiles don't fade as the moderator walks calmly up to confer with them. We see the guys on the team nodding and scratching the backs of their heads, as Cass shrugs. The moderator goes back to the mic.

"It has come to our attention," says the moderator evenly, "That there is an anomaly with the Area D team. Therefore, the winners of the round, and our representatives at Nationals, will instead be the team from Area B..."

We meet Cass at the foot of the stage steps.

"You guys could have *won*, though," she was saying to the Amarillo team. "I wouldn't have gone up there if I knew you actually had a shot! If you hadn't broken the rules, you could have gone to *Nationals*."

"We wouldn't have traded it for anything," one of the Amarillo guys was saying.

"You were amazing," Adie breaks in.

"We're so proud of our little round-ruiner," I say.

"Did you see how red that sponsor guy's face was?" Brian laughs.

"Better than any win," Sean agrees.

"And now you can put it on your résumé," I tease. "First place in the State final round, whether they liked it or not."

"My résumé can jump off a cliff," Cass laughs. "That one was all for me."

***

An hour later, we're all eating our pasta dinner in the cafeteria. Cass has just left to go buy another soda when I see it. Danny's sitting on his own, eating his dinner with two empty chairs on either side, scrolling through his phone while he chews. It's the only time I've seen him alone all weekend.

Casting a quick glance over my shoulder to make sure Cass isn't watching, I rush over and take a seat beside him.

"Danny," I say, "Listen..."

Danny looks up at me. I freeze. All the words have left me. The arguments, the pleas I've been spinning in my head for weeks. They've all just fled. I feel like I'm in a spotlight on an empty stage, and I never memorized my lines.

"I..." I stumble. He's still looking.

"Never mind," I say. Then I'm up and walking, letting the crowd in the cafeteria swallow me.

I don't stop when I get to the cafeteria doors. The people thin out as the cafeteria recedes behind me and the halls fill with lockers and classroom doors. I pass small groups hanging out against walls without looking at any of them. Finally, the halls around me grow empty. I keep walking for another few minutes without seeing a soul, then duck behind an outcropping of lockers. Squatting on the floor, I put my arms over my head and stare at my shoes.

Danny's look—the one that had stopped me—was something I hadn't prepared for. I had run through all kinds of scenarios. I had prepared for him to look annoyed, angry, fed up. I had prepared for him to get up and walk away. I had prepared, in my less realistic fantasies, for him to look relieved, welcoming. But instead, he had looked terrified.

He was afraid of me. Frightened of what I might say or do. In hindsight, I can't believe I'd never considered it. Cass's words come back to me. Stalker. Restraining order.

I've been terrorizing Danny.

I have to stop. He doesn't feel safe anymore. I've been thinking about this from my own perspective for so long. How I need closure. How I need another chance. But I'm only half of the equation. It doesn't matter how I feel.

It's like stopping a book in the middle of a chapter. The middle of a sentence, even. But I have to. Because finishing this sentence might be worse for everyone.

The tears have just started when my phone buzzes. Cass texting, asking where I am. I wait a few minutes before I stand and head back toward the cafeteria.

CHAPTER 40: APRIL 29ᵀᴴ   KATIE NGUYEN

"Watching paint dry" doesn't really capture it. Neither does "watching the grass grow." It was more like we were watching a snail slithering forward on the world's slowest treadmill. And our eyes were being held open by that wire contraption from *A Clockwork Orange*.

That was sitting through the awards ceremony at every State. It was the most fun weekend of the year, and it culminated with the most mind-numbing two hours of the year. Yeah, sometimes your school got called for an award, and that was nice. But there were so incredibly many awards that, even if your school had a huge team and won a lot of them, they were still few and far between. And Mr. Stanton didn't want to see us on our phones while it was going on. It was disrespectful, he said, and he wanted his Club to project the right image. So we sat and watched the awards be presented, and we all went slowly and silently mad as we watched.

Brian said the awards at AcaDec were worse. But I wasn't *in* AcaDec.

We were on the bleachers in the same gym where Jeremy and his friends had played basketball earlier that day. He and the Our Lady of the Seven Sorrows team were across the gym floor from us. Jeremy waved, and I gave a tiny, imperceptible wave back. He held up his phone, a silent cue to text him. I shook my head sadly.

They called Ludi and Olympika—all the sports—first. A couple of our West Oak kids got awards. When I looked across the gym, I noticed that Jeremy was cheering and applauding for us. Every time our school name got called, he was clapping above his head. Some of the members of his Club were starting to give him strange looks. I saw him saying something to them with a shrug. I wondered what it was, and my cheeks burned.

The Creative Arts came next. Our Club tended to do well in these. Scrapbook was one of the categories. But there were about a thousand categories. Most of the room became absorbed in their phones or their DS's. The West Oak students' eyes began to glaze over.

But every time our school won an award, we snapped out of our torpor to yell and clap. Mosaic, third place. Acrylic painting, fourth place. Pottery, second place. Jeremy applauded them all along with us. Especially when Allie and Maddy took fifth in Couples Costume for their much improved Priam and Hecuba. His Our Lady of the Seven Sorrows friends were starting to laugh at him, though some of them had started to join him.

It emboldened me. I started clapping every time an Our Lady of the Seven Sorrows name was called. Which wasn't that often in the Art categories, but it got my message across. Jeremy beamed at me. Allie smiled knowingly next to me, her hard-fought fifth place ribbon hanging off her wrist, and clapped too. It was oddly contagious. Soon, everyone in our immediate vicinity was clapping for every OLotSS victory, just as Our Lady was applauding West Oak. I don't even think they thought about why—it was something to do.

After what seemed like an eternity, the announcers came to the Scrapbooks. I tried to bite back my nerves. My legs were bouncing. I had put a lot of work into mine. It was my duty as Historian. More than any other Art contest, the whole team wanted this award. Everybody had been part of the activities inside. It was *our* contest, not just mine. I wanted to bring it home for them.

Fifth place wasn't me. Fourth wasn't either. That was alright, I wanted higher.

Third wasn't me. That made me nervous. We were getting into risky territory. Was I good enough for the top two?

Second wasn't me. Most of the students in the gym couldn't have cared less, but my fingernails were white as I gripped my knees. I was either first, or I wasn't anything. Could I really have won?

I really could have, and I really did. The Club around me erupted with cheers. We seldom got first place in anything at State, and we made a big deal out of it when we did. Allie, Spencer, Brian and Cass were so excited they followed me down the steps, but they hung back as I strode onto the gym floor to accept my first place. It was just a cheapo ribbon, but it might as well have been made of solid gold. It was a symbol.

I collected my symbol and shook the hand of the student officer handing them out. Before I turned to go back to my Club, I noticed Jeremy on the floor on the other side. He had hurried down, just like my West Oak friends had. He waved, beaming.

So I headed toward him. He grinned, pleasantly surprised, and opened up his arms. He meant to give me a hug.

I decided to do one better.

CHAPTER 41: APRIL 29ᵀᴴ   SPENCER OLSON

"*Who* is that, and why is Katie kissing him?" I scream.

Cass and Brian are roaring with shocked laughter. Allie is Snapchatting it. Mr. Stanton doesn't notice the phone. If being on a phone during awards is disrespectful, making out on the awards floor is a *disgrace*.

"Isn't he from Our Lady of the Seven Sorrows?" Brian asks.

"Oh yeah," Allie says, looking up from her phone. "That's Jeremy." She points her malicious eyes straight at me. "Didn't you know that Katie had a crush on a guy from Our Lady of the Seven Sorrows?"

A fire is burning behind my forehead. Obviously I did not. You think you're the gossip queen now, Allie? Just because you have the unfair advantage of living with the subject?

It does sting though. I feel like I've been oblivious to everything lately. Katie is kissing a stranger. Cass has a girlfriend, whom I hate for how fantastic she is. Brian had something going on that I don't fully understand. I still don't know what happened with Allie and Katie. Danny is nothing but a mystery anymore.

Mr. Stanton is shouting Katie's name with increasing urgency. Katie unlinks herself from "Jeremy" and heads back to our side. Magister collapses back into his seat as she passes, his ears bright red and his expression resigned.

"Hey," Katie says nonchalantly, re-entering our ranks.

We all start to make fun of her at once. It comes out a garbled mess. A Tower of Babel of friendly mockery.

"Guys, guys," Allie quiets us down. "Katie's playing it cool right now, but she was really nervous about one thing. She was worried that you'd be down on her for liking a guy from Our Lady of the Seven Sorrows. So what do you think?"

Everyone laughs.

"Why do we care if he goes to some snooty Catholic school?" I tease. "He seems perfect for you already."

"You don't think I'm fraternizing with the enemy?" she asks sheepishly.

We laugh again at the seriousness of the phrase.

"Ain't nobody taking that rivalry seriously," Cass says.

Katie colors slightly as she sits back down with us, looking like her worldview has shifted.

Moments later they call me for Dramatic Interpretation. My Priam speech got me third. I'm elated. It's the same place I got last year, and I didn't really dare hope for better.

Then they get into the academic awards—the longest slog. We win a few here and there, but mostly it's just white noise and waiting. Brian gets second in History, a personal best for State. I don't medal in History. Jeff manages fourth in Reading Comprehension. Where the old Jeff would have been foaming at the mouth for not getting higher, this Jeff looks pleasantly surprised and runs to collect his ribbon. Our Club cheers him especially loudly.

When they start calling Mythology, Cass gets so nervous she grabs my hand. We have to sit through Latin levels one-half through three. But when the Latin 4's come, she gets fifth. It's only her second time medaling at State. She did it freshman year, then it was a rude awakening to miss it for the next two years. So she is really jazzed.

Katie gets fifth in Level 3 Roman Life. Adie-from-Dallas gets called shortly afterward, fourth in Level 4 Roman Life. We all cheer for her too. Cass runs down to embrace her after she collects her ribbon. Mr. Stanton looks nervous, but they part after a quick hug. Cass winks up at our Magister, and I hear him sigh.

It's past ten at night when we head back toward the buses. Some years we head straight home from State, but this year we opted for a second night in the hotel. I'm glad. It's way better than sitting on the bus for four hours after a long day at State and getting home at 3 am.

I stand next to Mr. Stanton as we watch the students pile on to the bus, the windows blindingly bright in the dark parking lot.

"I didn't think I was gonna survive this one, Spencer," he says softly, his eyes still fixed on the bus.

"Crazy year," I agree.

"I've never had one like it," Mr. Stanton says. "Not for highs, or for lows." He turns to me now. "I couldn't have done it without you. You've done an amazing job as president. You had no way of knowing what was coming, and you've handled it all so well."

"Any of them would have done the same," I say modestly, gesturing to the two-dozen students crowding onto the bus.

"They might have tried," Mr. Stanton says, "But you did it. I'm really proud of you."

Normally I'd make a joke here, but I don't have one in me. "Thanks," I say instead.

"Spencer!" I hear another voice call over my shoulder. I turn.

It's Jeff. He's walking briskly up. As soon as he gets to me, he grabs me by the shoulder with his left hand and shakes my hand with his right. Like a politician. Except sincere.

"Thank you for everything," he says, looking straight into my eyes.

"You deserved it," I reply.

"I didn't," he laughs, and lets go of me. "But I'm not talking about the money. Thanks for the invites to every party you guys threw. The cards in the hospital. The proof that I'm worth something to someone." He wipes at his cheek. Do Jeffs cry? I had no idea.

"I hope you're getting better," I say, lamely.

"I'm going to," he says. "I'm working on it. What's the next Latin Club party? I want to be there."

I laugh. "I'll send a text."

"I believe you." He pauses, hugs his elbows a little, looks like he's going to cry again. I don't know how to handle this from him. "If I'm not back before school is out..." he begins.

"You will be," I say.

"Then good luck in college," he continues. "Tell Cass I said same to her. You guys are both going to do so great."

"You are too," I say.

"Thanks," he smiles. "Right now I'll settle for 'okay.' We'll see about 'great' later. I'll see you." He turns.

"You're not coming to the hotel?"

"My dad and I are driving back tonight," Jeff says. "I'm checking back in tomorrow morning."

I wince, unsure what to say about that. What do you say to the boy on his way back into a psychiatric hospital? "Good luck," I manage.

"I'll need it," he says, disappearing back into the parking lot.

When I board the bus, everyone else is already ready. Brian has saved me a seat next to him in the back. The doors close and the bus lurches away while I'm still making my way back there, meaning my last few steps are a stumble and I almost elbow Brian in the face on my way in.

This has been a hell of a State. I see weary smiles on the faces of the Club members as they hang limply over the seats, talking contentedly to each other. We pulled it off after all.

The one wrinkle I can't iron out is Danny. I've avoided eye contact ever since our awkward encounter. I've made him a promise in my head that I won't be his problem anymore. I'll only be my own.

I settle on top of the covers of my hotel bed while I

wait my turn for the shower. The maids came through while we were at competition, so everything is clean and antiseptic again. There are vacuum marks on the carpet.

One of the two freshmen is showering first. The other is lying on the ground, playing a DS with earbuds in. Brian is on the other bed scrutinizing his iPod, his headphones not on yet. I had planned on sharing this room with Danny. Now I'm glad Mr. Stanton caught me and stopped that from happening. Probably better that it's just Brian in here. And me sitting with my last chapter ending with a fragment...

"Spencer?" Brian says, looking up from his iPod.

"What's up?"

"I need to tell you something," he says. He looks serious.

"Yeah?"

Brian darts his eyes over to the solitary freshman on the floor, who is in his own world, unaware of us. Like Brian always used to be, before this semester.

"I found my first crush," he admits.

I smile. Love certainly has been in the air this State. Which, granted, is not unusual. A lot of couples get together at State. What happens at State certainly does not stay at State.

I scoot closer to the edge of my bed. "Is that right?" I ask. "Who?" I'm excited to be in on some real gossip for once this weekend.

He swallows hard, looking at the fugly pattern of the comforter on his bed. "You," he says, almost in a whisper.

"What?" I gape.

Brian looks up, grinning shyly. "I've learned a lot about myself, lately."

My mind is galloping through our recent history together. He did seem to like hanging out with me best, what with the musicals and the late-night movie marathons. I look at his face, which is twisted with nerves. I can read all the uncertainty. I see the fear of rejection, the same kind I felt back when I was trying to start my first boy-boy relationship. I see the mixture of doubt and relief that is part of coming out to someone you care about. I see the hope he has invested in me. That's when sadness rips through me.

"You don't want me," I say. "You deserve a lot better."

"Don't sell yourself short."

"I'm a self-absorbed ass."

"Among other things," he says with an impish grin.

"You've seen how I am with a breakup," I go on. "I'm damaged goods."

He crosses the three feet of floor between our beds and sits next to me on mine. He leaves two inches between us. Keeps his hands stiffly on his own legs.

"I don't know anything about breakups," he says, "But I know something about feeling like damaged goods. And I know the best way to help that feeling."

"Yeah?"

"A friend," he grins again.

I laugh a little at how pithy that is. "And you're a good friend, Brian. I like having you as one. But beyond that... I don't know."

"Don't know what?"

How do I feel about him? His awkwardness had my gaydar all jammed, so I've never even thought of him as a possibility. I've been thinking of him as another straight boy in the crowd. I do like hanging out with him. And he is cute, in an "I don't know what I'm doing yet and need a boyfriend to teach me how to dress and do my hair" way.

But I've usually thought out every turn in a relationship before it even starts. I usually know how I feel, and how I'm going to feel every step of the way. Like how I've plotted a hundred ways of getting back together with Danny. This isn't like that. This is a blank.

"I don't know if we'd work together," I say finally. The tiny gap he's left between us feels like a canyon.

Brian looks puzzled, like a dog tilting its head. "I'm new at this. How do you know if you work together with someone?"

That's a good question. Because I've always played out every turn in my relationships, and I've never been right. Not even close. Maybe it's me who has been doing this all wrong.

"Well," I say after a moment. "I guess you just try."

I put my hand across those infinite two inches between us. I pull his face toward mine and gently give him what I assume is his first kiss. I feel the tension relax out of him. The kiss extends a little longer than I mean it to.

He's got no technique yet, but I guess he'll be trainable.

I definitely feel something.

Part of that something is relief. I feel relieved of

Danny. I feel like even if the last sentence in our relationship is still a fragment, I can close the book anyway.

But part of the something is definitely about Brian. He's an enigma who has been opening himself to me, and the rest of the world, for only a few months now. But every new level I've seen, I've liked. I'm looking forward to discovering more.

I don't know if it will work out. But I guess you never do. You just try.

I pull away. Brian looks lost as he stares into my eyes. Like he's not even aware that he's doing it. And I'll admit it, I'm a little lost too.

A lot of couples form at State.

"Whoa," says the freshman on the floor. Then, "Dibs on the other bed."

Brian and I do share my bed, but all we do for the rest of the night is hold hands. Fully clothed, fully chaste. There are the freshmen to consider, after all. I might be a depraved queen, but I do not corrupt young innocents.

Chapter 42: April 30th, technically   Jeff Miller

My dad and I get "home" around 1 am. I'm still feeling ebullient from the evening. It was a pleasant surprise, both getting that Reading Comp award and having my dad see me get it. He's never been there when I've won something before.

By "home," I mean my aunt's house where my dad and grandma have been staying, across town from our house that burned. Aunt Jean, my dad's sister, has done a lot to let her little one-story house accommodate the two of them. Her two sons are sleeping with her in sleeping bags on her bedroom floor, while Grandma has their room. Dad is on the couch in the living room. It's tight, but luckily for them I won't be staying here after tonight. I'll check back into the facility first thing tomorrow.

My dad piles some blankets on the floor so I can take the couch. It's thoughtful of him. I don't need that kind of consideration, per se. But it's something the old Dad would never have thought of doing. Since the fire, he's been promising to be less in his own head, more present. Little things like this give me hope.

He says he's looking for a good apartment or condo for us. Something affordable with two bedrooms. Just two, one for him and one for me: my aunt is taking Grandma for now. Apparently Adult Protective Services got involved after the incident. They didn't like what they heard from my dad. He won't tell me much, but I think he's been to court about it. And I heard Aunt Jean say something about him taking classes.

If that's true, those classes have a lot of work to do before he's ready to be in charge. After two years, I know how to run our lives a lot better than he does. But he brushes me off when I ask him about our bills or the money in our accounts. He says he'll promise to be the adult if I can promise to be the teenager. Jury's still out.

I've been getting better at being at the facility. They've been easing me off most of the meds they had me on, now that I'm cooperating with my cognitive behavioral therapy. They say my cessation of self-medicating with Adderall is helping a lot too. I've even been to some of the group sessions. Some of the people in them are okay.

As I drift to sleep on the couch, I think about all of this getting better. And I think about Mackenzie. I don't want to, but I do. I'm telling myself that I'll leave her alone, even after I'm back at school. It will be another hard thing I will have to control about myself. But she deserves the break.

I have subjected her to enough of my personality for one lifetime.

CHAPTER 43: APRIL 30TH CASS WASHINGTON

As Allie, Katie and I were loading up our bags in the morning, Spencer came buzzing up behind us.

"You think you're taking my gossip crown," Spencer crowed at Allie. "But I've got the scoop on you this time. Brian is gay."

"Yeah, I know," she said with a grin.

"What?" Spencer spat.

"Oh yeah, we figured that out," I said, rolling with it.

"It was so obvious," said Allie.

Spencer gaped. Brian came walking up too.

"How did you," Spencer sputtered, then turned to Brian. "Did you tell them about us?"

"No," Brian said, taken aback.

"Then how did they already know?"

Brian looked at us, perplexed.

"We're kidding," I said, taking pity on Brian's expression. "We didn't know, we just needed to take the air out of Spencer's sails."

Spencer huffed and started to walk away, but Brian

grabbed his hand with a grin and pulled him back. It was weird, but somehow right, to see him holding Spencer's hand.

"Congratulations, you two," Katie said, taking the spoils of war out of her bag and handing them to Allie, winner of our wager.

"Yeah, seriously," I smiled. "You're cute together."

"Spencer's beauty counterbalances my gargoyle-like face nicely," Brian joked.

"If you don't mind me asking," I said to Brian, "Do you think you're bi or gay?"

Brian shrugged. "Dunno. My first relationship is with a guy. Maybe I could feel this way about a girl too. I feel like I could. But I don't care to find out right now."

"You might want to work on that answer before your first GSA meeting," Spencer said.

"I think it's a perfect answer," I countered. "Have you told anyone else?"

"Nora," he said. "She was all honored that I came out to her first. It had never even occurred to me that I was coming out. So I told my mom too. I thought she was going to throw me a party. She called my grandmother. It was weird."

Mr. Stanton passed by, and stopped short at the sight of Brian and Spencer holding hands.

"Brian too?" he asked.

"I flipped him, Stanton!" Spencer joked. "No one is safe from my masculine wiles!"

"Good for you," Mr. Stanton said to Brian.

"I have great, supportive friends," Brian beamed.

"So what's with you and Adie-from-Dallas?" Spencer asked me as our teacher walked back away through the crowd. "Did you get the girl, or what?"

"Oh I got her, but we're keeping it casual right now," I said, twirling one of my curls and trying to look nonchalant.

"Right now?" Katie asked. "Where is she going to college?"

"Trinity," I answered.

"That's here in San Antonio, right?" asked Brian.

"And you're going to UT San Antonio?" Spencer added excitedly.

I let my joy bubble over in one short smile, then pulled myself back. "Right, and right," I said.

"Katie's got her man on lock, right?" Spencer continued. Katie nodded. "He's cute, too," Spencer added. Katie looked self-satisfied.

"Don't go keeping secrets like that from us again, you hear," I told her.

"Are you still staying at Katie's?" Spencer asked Allie slyly. Trying to get some clues about why she was there.

"For good," Katie said. "My parents went to city hall and registered as foster parents so no one could take her away."

"And I'm paying rent," Allie said, "So I don't have to feel bad about using her family."

"You *don't* have to feel bad," Katie started, but Allie kept going.

"I've got a job at Whataburger starting next week, and a bike to get there."

Katie smiled and shook her head. I learned the deal

from her later: her parents stashed away all the "rent" Allie paid them as a secret college fund.

"Can you believe it?" Brian said. "Jeff is the only Certamen member not in a couple."

"It's weird," Katie's eyes bulged. "He and Mackenzie were a thing for so long."

"Do you think he's going to try to get her back, now that he's all fixed up?" Spencer asked.

"I really don't think he's all fixed up, Spence," I said. "It's a process." Spencer gave me the look that I knew meant, *"I'm Cass, I read Tumblr so I understand everything."*

But it's true, so.

"I give them a month before they're back together," Spencer said.

"I don't know," Allie muttered.

"Care to bet on it?" Katie asked.

Spencer eventually did win that bet, but by then everyone had eaten their prizes already.

I was getting wistful. My anxiety about college had been replaced with drive and excitement. I felt better about my new temporary major, and about Spencer running off to California or DC or wherever. We still had time to figure it out. Our lives, that is.

"This is it," Spencer sighed to me while the juniors were putting their luggage on the bus, leaving us alone together for a moment. "Our last State is over."

"It's been a great four years," I said. "I wouldn't have wanted to spend it with anyone but you."

"I'm going to miss all this."

"Me too," I agreed. "But there are better things waiting

for us out there."

"You sure about that?"

"Not really," I laughed. "But I'm excited to find out."

"Yeah," he said. "I think that's right. I think we've just got to go try."

EPILOGUE: MAY 23RD

"Teaching anything of real value to high school students is difficult. This is not their fault. Children are born curious. But by the time they're teenagers, our culture has drilled passion out of them. The high achievers have learned to chase grades and résumé items, while all the students who feel disconnected with or disqualified from that particular arms race are concerned with maintaining facades of apathy, lest they begin to feel like failures.

"This is why our school needs institutions like this Latin Club. A Latin Club is more than an academic achievement, more than a competition, more than a résumé item. It encourages students to chase passions, to create spaces for themselves, to find new niches in a tradition that has been going for two thousand years. In a culture obsessed with short-term results and tiny, targeted goals, a Latin Club is an organization that grants slow, subtle, and immense benefits to the whole student. A Latin Club is a community.

"No year has better illustrated that idea than this one.

The students of the West Oak High Latin Club have, indeed, achieved outstanding honors by succeeding academically and bringing home trophies. But they have learned even more about what is truly important. About each other. About mutual support. About acceptance. About loving themselves while still pushing themselves. About reaching out when they're in trouble, and reaching back when another needs their help.

"The function of an education is not to get a grade, or a degree, or a job. The function of an education is to understand yourself, the world, and your place in it. Certainly I believe that the words of the ancients are one important way to do that. But this year in Latin Club, as you have seen from the articles in our local papers, the most important lessons for the members did not come from the Romans, nor were they about ancient history. They came from, and were about, life itself.

"That is why I am here to plead with you, august members of the school board, to reinstate the former funding for our Latin Club. I entreat you on behalf of my students, their parents, and the world at large. What may appear to be nothing but a small line item on a budget has far-reaching ramifications, and this particular line item has the opportunity to make our community a better place. Thank you."

"Thank you, Mr. Stanton. Board will now move to item 16..."

ACKNOWLEDGEMENTS

I have a lot of people to thank for their support and inspiration. No writer is an island, and I couldn't have written a single word alone.

Thank you to all of my family, friends, and students who read drafts of this book and gave me suggestions and reactions, including in no particular order: Maya, Kayla, Lacey, Carrie, Andy, Anne, Lauren, Abby, Mila, Kimberly, Kim, Christy, Tess, Karlie, Eric, Ansleigh, Lindsay, Ava, Sabrina, Braden, Celeste, Hannah, Gloria, Auburn, Chloe, Brian, Adair, Katherine, Amy, Mom, Dad, and anyone I have inexcusably left off this list. This book would be much worse without you.

Thank you to my husband, Elliott, who was my best cheerleader and my most exacting critic, and always knew which he needed to be at any given moment. And thank you to my two-year-old, Irvin, who together with Elliott makes my life worth living.

Thank you to the Junior Classical League (both Texas State and National), an organization that collects the best educators and students into one place. You all inspire me on so many levels. I wouldn't want to teach any other subject.

Thank you to my school and my district, an extended family that makes the teaching and inspiration of students possible. I am fortunate to have the professional support of a great team.

Thank you to the Tumblr classics community, who have obviously inspired much of this book. Keep being you. And to anyone reading this who doesn't already: go follow the tagamemnon tag.

And finally, thank you to my 2017 Advanced Certamen team, who, AFTER the first two drafts of this novel were already complete, did indeed win our Area and become the first team in our school's history to make it to State. I couldn't have scripted it any better myself.